EVERYWHERE WE'VE NEVER BEEN

MIRANDA VALENTINE

AUTHOR'S NOTE

Dear Reader,

Thank you so much for picking up Everywhere We've Never Been. It's always important to me that the content of my books doesn't take you by surprise in a negative way, so please note that this book does contain adult content, discussions of absent parents and child abandonment, and portrayals of anxiety and depression.

Take care of yourselves.

Love,
    Miranda

This book is dedicated to anyone who has ever let fear control any aspect of their life.

Keep fighting. You're strong and deserving of the world.

November 4, 2019 1:35 PM
TO: thatkat451@tmail.com
FROM: e.amos@topsecrettravel.com
SUBJECT: Your Biggest Adventure is Here

Dear Kathryn and Ben,

Guten Tag, and Hallo! (This is the first clue for your mystery tour, 100% customized to you!)

Today is the day you've been waiting for. Attached, you will find the itinerary that will finally reveal the surprise destination for your January honeymoon. I have paid the most careful attention to your requests, and believe you will be quite pleased with your decision to be so spontaneous.

A cool climate, bountiful history, rich food, and breathtaking architecture await you! What are you waiting for? Click the link below to view your digital travel planner!

I'm here for any questions or concerns you may have. And don't forget, you still have one month to make any changes you see fit. Although, we recommend that you embrace being outside of your comfort zone. That's half the fun of traveling!

All the best,
Ellie Amos
Secret Travel Agent
Top Secret Travel

CHAPTER 1

ELLIE

I believe it's safe to say no child dreams of working an office job when they grow up.

Or, maybe I'm being presumptuous. Perhaps there are kids out there sitting at their doodle-covered desks, daydreaming of files and spreadsheets and business casual office wear while their teachers stand at the front of the room explaining the long division that they're never going to use again. Maybe these kids are itching for the day that they trade playground shenanigans for water cooler gossip.

This is a stream of consciousness that runs through my mind often, as I spin in my ergonomically-friendly chair and attempt to word an email in the most precise way. Over the past three years, I've become far more dedicated to working in an office than I ever thought I would be. For my first 25 years of life, I, like most, dreamed of a career filled with passion—a life of adventure greater than my daily commute.

That is, until my fear of exploration outgrew my desire to have meaningful experiences, anyway. Now I just work in an office that makes exploration possible for others.

"Hey, El." Sherry, Top Secret Travel's most seasoned agent, pops her blonde head around our shared cubicle wall. Startled, I plant a foot on the ground to bring my rotating chair to a halt. "I'm so sorry, I didn't mean to scare ya!" She brings a hand to her mouth to suppress a giggle.

"No worries." I stand up to retrieve my pen that went skittering into the empty cubicle behind me and smile at her. "What's up?"

"Well, apparently Iceland is cold. Did you know that?" Her amusement fades as she removes her headset and throws it onto her desk.

"Is...this a trick question?" I squint at her.

"I just assume that *anyone* who requests adventure travel in a cold climate is prepared for, you know, *cold*. Especially after they receive their itineraries and preparation guidelines."

"Uh-huh..." I say, still not following.

"So tell me *why*," Sherry continues, practically shouting now, "Elizabeth VanBeek just left us a two star Google review because the weather in Iceland was 'too frigid.'"

Sadly, it isn't the first time we've received negative feedback because a client wasn't happy with the weather—the weather that they had been advised of numerous times, or in Elizabeth's case, had specifically requested. That's the nature of human beings though; sometimes the thing you think you want is actually not what you want at all. This applies to both travel and life. It's also why Top Secret Travel now allows clients to see their itineraries two months early. Everyone isn't as spontaneous as they wish to be...myself included.

"Didn't you know?" Rick appears from the cubicle on my other side, grinning and rolling his chair up next to mine. "We can control the weather now."

He smells like Abercrombie & Fitch. The scent produces a familiar pit of high-school dread in my stomach, but his green

2

eyes give me the opposite sensation of butterflies. They flutter around said pit, bumping into each other and making it impossible to hold his gaze for more than a second. By the time I've regained composure, Sherry has disappeared back into her cubicle with a huff. I can hear her long, pointy nails clacking angrily on her keyboard.

"How's your day going, Ellie?" Rick asks, peeking around me to glance nosily at my monitor. "Working on anything exciting?"

Rick Williamson possesses that unique combination of male qualities that makes me want to simultaneously avoid him in the hallways and fall into deep, sense-destroying love with him. As our newest sales agent, he's been at TST for less than a year, but has quickly risen in the ranks, sitting just behind me in the top earner position, and right next to me in the shared cubicle office.

He's the office charmer and sneaky sales snake all at once. A couple of weeks after his arrival, I overheard him flirting with Jade, the receptionist, coyly requesting that she route more prospect calls to him since he "needed the practice." Sherry got wind of that rumor pretty damn quickly. She can be scary when she wants to be, so all it took was one conversation with Jade to get the sales call routing order back to its normal rotation.

Rick has been an intimidating presence ever since. None of us agents are ever quite sure if he's being genuinely friendly or if he's just searching for a leg up. That still doesn't stop the majority of us from being enamored with his perfectly coiffed brown hair and expertly fitted trousers though. Sometimes I get angry when I think about how much easier it is to be a good looking man in this world.

Then I quickly forget about that as I fantasize about Rick's blindingly white teeth and replay all of our daily conversations in my mind on my walk home at the end of the day. Fuck it...I'll just say it. I have a convoluted crush on the man.

"Oh, the usual." I scoot my chair away from him, backing up to block his view of my computer screen. "I just sent that Germany honeymoon itinerary off."

"Nice, nice," he replies with a smirk. "Let me know if they come back with any requests you need help tweaking. I've been to Germany a couple of times."

"S-s-so have I," I stammer, mentally kicking myself over my faltering confidence. "I'm sure it will be fine, but I'll let you know."

I spin to my desktop and begin clicking around on my homescreen, hoping he'll take the hint of dismissal. The sound of his chair wheels scooting away finally comes and I release a breath as quietly as possible. Normal sounds of typing and phone calls resume as the sales staff gets back to work, the room free of conversations to eavesdrop on.

My inbox pings with the arrival of a new email and I freeze. I can't tell you how many trips I have planned over the past three years or how many itineraries I have sent off. The anxiety of not meeting a client's expectations never gets any easier though. I've never received anything more than a simple activity swap request. Every traveler has always been thrilled with the chosen destination. The element of surprise is what makes it so difficult, regardless of the questionnaire we have prospects fill out up front.

Maybe I'm just waiting for someone to question my credibility—to call out the lack of experience that I secretly have. Part of me is consistently confident. When you're a perfectionist who's addicted to research, it's easy to pretend you know everything about everything. But the other part of me knows I'm a liar, and that portion of my brain screams the same message at me all day long.

Fraud. Fraud! FRAUD!

The email is just a reminder of Friday's meeting. I should have known from all of the other incoming message chimes around the room. Clicking sounds intensify as everyone deletes, files, and sets reminders. I set a second reminder, just to be safe, and turn my attention back to my task list. Every call I've made today has been met by a voicemail greeting, and I have two other travel planners to finalize before they go out tomorrow.

"Does anyone have a sample itinerary for Buenos Aires they can send me?" Lucia's voice floats over the cubicle across from Sherry, interrupting my train of thought once again.

"I do," Rick yells back before anyone else can open their mouth, standing to look in Lucia's direction. "I'll email it to you."

"Oh, you're just the best." Lucia's doe eyes come into view as she stands to thank him. Her shiny black ponytail gleams, even underneath the overhead fluorescent lighting. Their disembodied heads bob above the barriers as they continue their conversation across my desk. It's virtually impossible, but I try to ignore them.

I love my work, but god, do I hate cubicles.

After an eternity, Lucia sits down and I make the mistake of looking up at Rick. He winks at me before dropping back into his chair. *Curse him*, I think dramatically as I fight to suppress a Chesire cat-level grin.

"Lucia, I have one I can send you if Rick's isn't enough," I call to her. The energy in the room shifts and I envision Rick erupting into a ball of flames just a few feet away from me. Sherry snorts on my other side. She's the only one in the office that seems to be immune to his allure.

"Thanks El, I'll let you know," Lucia replies, her voice void of the sweetness it had held for Rick. The atmosphere lightens again as his frustration is replaced with an heir of smugness.

Oh well, it was worth the shot.

"There are donuts in the breakroom!" Lamar, the fifth and final sales agent, comes shuffling in from his late lunch with two crullers in hand. "Petra in accounting got them from that new place down the street."

"You don't have to say 'Petra in accounting,' Lamar. We know who she is," Sherry grumbles as she stands and stretches. "It's a small office."

"Who spit in her coffee?" Lamar asks as she exits to the hallway with Rick and Lucia in tow. Laughing, I give him a "you know how she is" look. He shoves half of a cruller in his mouth and offers the other to me. I decline it and he shrugs, using his free hand to gather his dreads to one side before he sits down.

Another email whooshes into my inbox and I hurriedly click over to read it. This time, it is a response from Kathryn about the Germany itinerary:

Hi, Ellie!
Holy moly, this looks so great! Germany...Ben will be thrilled! I'll have a closer look at everything this evening and let you know if we want to tweak anything, but I doubt we will. The proposed air schedule also looks perfect. Can you go ahead and have your air department reserve those flights? You can use the card I have on file.
Talk to you soon,
Kathryn

My heart rate slows only when I finish reading the email, my lips forming into a proud smile. I believe everyone should feel some type of satisfaction when they do a good job at work. My previous sales position made me feel fulfilled to some extent, but nothing like this job does. There's something about planning these trips for people and knowing that I'm helping give them a once in a lifetime experience. It makes me happy. It also helps me live through them vicariously, since I can't travel myself.

Or I guess it's more fair to say, I won't travel myself.

I open our inner office messaging system and find Eren's name at the top of my most popular contacts.

Ellie Amos:
Hey there pal!

Eren Polat:
Hey stranger, I feel like we've barely spoken all day!

Ellie Amos:
Monday and stuff, ya know? Do you still have that schedule for Kathryn Miller and Ben Styles saved?

Eren Polat:
We haven't spoken in hours and you have the gall to message me about WORK?

Laughing to myself, I ignore his bait and begin typing another work-related response.

Ellie: They're ready to book. You can use the card in their file. Just send me the final cost please!

The system intermittently shows that he's typing before he stops all together. Several minutes go by before I prod him again.

Ellie: I always knew you'd start ignoring me some day!

7

Still no reply.

Ellie: Our friendship was nice while it lasted. I guess I'll see you around the office.

Deciding to busy myself with a new itinerary while I wait, I open Microsoft Word. The document finally loads and I immediately notice that the opening photo of Chichen Itza is blurry and will need to be replaced with something of a higher resolution. Sighing, I open my Mexico gallery and begin searching.

"Have time for a coffee break?" A baseball glove-sized hand lands on top of my head, playfully ruffling my pixie cut and startling me half to death. It's the second scare I've received in less than an hour, and I nearly topple out of my chair as I spin around to come face to face with Eren in the flesh. His six-foot-five frame is stooped to my level, and he's grinning so big his cheeks nearly cover his brown eyes.

"Thanks for that." Embarrassment creeps over my neck and face. I reach up and attempt to smooth my hair back into some semblance of a style.

"When was the last time you left your desk?" he asks, crossing his arms and leaning against the wall connected to Rick's currently empty cubicle.

"Lunch time?" I try to remember.

"I figured as much. You're overdue." He reaches around me and locks my computer screen. "Let's go see if there are any donuts left."

Only partially willingly, I stand up to smooth my skirt and follow Eren down the aisle to the doorway. His button-up shirt is covered in a sunflower pattern, and the rhythm of his gait gives them the effect of swaying in the breeze along his back. His thick, dark hair is pulled into a low ponytail. He pauses briefly at Lamar's cube to give him a high five before we leave.

"I swear, El, would you ever take breaks if I didn't force you to?" He looks down at me, the joke dancing in his eyes as we maneuver around people in the hallway.

"Probably not." I appease him. "But I would get a lot more work done."

CHAPTER 2

EREN

D onut days are the one unexpected surprise that get me through the work week sometimes.

And that's pretty sad, seeing as it's only Monday. I look over my shoulder to make sure Ellie hasn't discretely scampered off back to her cube. She does that every now and then —pretends to take a break with me so I'll leave her alone, then disappears somewhere along the walk down the office's main hallway. She knows I won't go back for her a second time.

This afternoon though, she's still there, raising her eyebrows at me as if to say, "You win, Eren. There better be a plain glazed left."

Her dress is periwinkle today. Something about the color makes her eyes look insanely green. I would give her a compliment, but I know she won't accept it. Instead she'll change the subject and tell me I have to say stuff like that because I'm her best work friend.

More than once, I've attempted to make her a friend outside of work too. I've invited her to happy hour several times, tried to get her to meet Kristen and I for brunch on Saturdays, hinted at setting her up with one of my brothers...you name it, I've tried it. Alas, the answer is always no. Ellie is witty and interesting and kind. Add dedicated (and also super fucking private) to that list, and you have her in a nutshell.

Kristen says I need to stop being so pushy. I can't help that I'm a social person who likes to make friends. Especially when there seems to be something special about a person.

I run my hand along the vintage maps that line the hall as I lead the way. It's an act of habit at this point—five years in the same space is bound to generate random routines as familiar as the ones curated in your own home. Even in my sleep, I could navigate this place. I know the exact amount of steps it takes to get from the front door to my desk, to the break room, and to the back patio picnic tables.

The monotony is a lot for me to handle sometimes. I enjoy a little change, a little surprise to break up the pattern, just as our clients do. But like the majority of people employed by TST, I'm happy with my job and my career path. Plus, you can't beat the perks of working in air travel.

Rick is exiting the break room just as I'm about to turn in. "Eren, what's up man? Haven't seen you all day." He claps me on the shoulder before backing away to make room for Ellie and I to enter.

"I blame you," I joke, holding us up outside the doorway. "I've been tucked away working on your flights for the Sorrenson group."

His gaze flicks over to Ellie before he continues our conversation. It's a brief action, but I still catch the smallest sparkle of admiration in his eyes. "Thanks again for that. Sorry for the last minute change."

"Hey, it's what I'm here for." I hold my hands up in mock surrender and back into the kitchen with the rest of the afternoon donut crowd.

Rick sweeps an arm out in an "after you" motion to invite

Ellie into the room. Her facial expression gives off "annoyed," but her pink cheeks tell an entirely different story. "Good job getting this one to step away from her keyboard," he teases over her head before departing back to his desk.

"I'm telling you…" I lean down to whisper in Ellie's ear. "That dude cannot keep his eyes off you."

She elbows me and stalks toward the family-sized table, which I'm pleased to see, still holds two full boxes of donuts. "Yeah, me and every other woman on the planet," she hisses over her shoulder.

"But especially you." I lift a lid from one of the boxes and eye the selection. One day, I'll get her to admit that she's into Rick.

"Come off it, Eren Polat." She stabs a plain glazed pastry with a fork and dumps it onto a paper plate before retreating to find an empty space to stand.

I follow her, internally telling myself to drop the subject, but outwardly preparing my final statement. "At least admit that you think he's good looking. I think he's good looking. They all think he's good looking." I motion to our coworkers around the room.

"You think everyone is attractive, to be fair." She bites into her donut.

"That's not fair," I argue, even though she is right. Like I said…I'm a people person.

I take a quick survey of the room. Most of the office still seems to be hanging out, eating their donuts as slowly as possible and checking their watches to ensure they'll have as little actual working time left in the day as possible. Petra from accounting flits around nervously, looking to confirm that we were all able to partake in the snack she so graciously provided. She holds a couple of spare mugs in one hand; a half-filled coffee pot dangles from the other. Her glasses always look like they're dangerously close to slipping off the end of her nose.

12

"Hey Ellie, Eren. The two E's!" Reaching us, she offers the cups and raises the pot. "A little something to wash it all down?"

Ellie declines. ("It's too late in the day for caffeine.") I graciously accept, because caffeine or no caffeine, you only live once. Petra can hardly stand still long enough to fill my mug for me, eventually sloshing coffee down the side of it and onto the old wooden floor that I assume was the original in the historic Tudor-style home that serves as TST's headquarters. Ellie grabs a napkin to mop it up just as Yuke, the company's owner, walks into the room.

"Hi, Yuke. Come have a Monday trea—" Petra's voice fades as she rushes away to bombard her new target.

"I know you think I have a hard time relaxing," Ellie says, polishing off her donut. "But Petra always makes me feel like the epitome of calm and collected."

"She's like twenty-five years older than you," I point out. "Don't worry, you still have time to get there."

Ellie stares at me coolly, probably imagining shoving the chocolate cake donut I'm holding up my nose. She has a combination of facial features that makes even her most scathing expressions somewhat endearing. Maybe it's the crinkle of her nose. Or the dimple in her chin. I'm not really sure.

She stops frowning only to snatch my paper plate from me and toss it into the trash can with hers. The break room has been rapidly emptying since Yuke's arrival. She's extremely laid back, and makes it openly known that she trusts her employees, but she's still the boss. And the boss can always bring an heir of "you should probably be doing something" to a crowd. A quick glance at my watch shows it's just after 3:30.

"Sadly, I believe it's time to go see how much work I can finish in the next hour and a half." I swirl the final dregs of my mediocre coffee around the mug and gulp it down.

"Is a certain Germany schedule included in that work?" Ellie asks with a quirked eyebrow.

"If you insist."

"Only if you have time, of course. It can always be done tomorrow."

"You'll have it in an hour or so," I assure her with a grin, moving to the sink to wash my mug.

She leaves, stopping to say a quick hello to Yuke before disappearing into the hallway. After paying my own respects, I'm on the way back to my desk, running my fingers along the familiar map—some of places I've been, and some of places I haven't yet. Just past the room of sales cubes is an oak staircase, which I use to ascend to the second floor.

Being one of only two air agents, I'm lucky enough to have my own office. Walt, the second, has been at TST for nearly twenty years, and therefore, has earned his own space. Mine is technically more of a closet than anything, but I'll certainly take it over the downstairs cubicle situation.

Top Secret Travel's HQ is a bit of a hodgepodge, to be honest. I don't think Yuke ever anticipated the company would grow any larger than the three employees she originally started with, working out of her own home. When it did, she had to find new spaces to house everyone with each expansion. And now we're here with twenty-five employees, in this beautiful house that has to be well over 100 years old and is in a constant state of reorganization and remodeling in an attempt to make our workflow as seamless as possible.

Hence, some of us have giant, antique desks that are so heavy they're impossible to move, and others are stuck in beige three-sided stalls with padded walls. It's a mixture of old-school and modern around here. Just like with any office, you learn to take the good with the bad.

I flop into my chair, shaking my mouse to wake the monitor. A framed photo of Kristen and I sits just to the left, and I stare at it for at least the fiftieth time today. It was taken at last year's office Christmas party, just after we had started dating. Her hair was purple back then. It had been a fun night.

We haven't talked much today. She's been ignoring me for the most part. We had a small disagreement last night over how to spend Thanksgiving and she went back to her apartment to sleep. Sometimes I wish her hair was still purple. Maybe then we wouldn't be consistently more unhappy with each passing day.

I know that's not how things work. It would be nice if it was though, huh?

Once everything has properly loaded, I sign back into the global distribution system we use to book flights. The tickets for Rick's group are finished, so I generate the information into a PDF and email it over to him. Then I'm free to work on Ellie's request, which I do with a slight smile on my face, because helping her always seems less like my job and more like volunteering for some reason.

November 4, 2019 4:37 PM
FROM: e.polat@topsecrettravel.com
TO: e.amos@topsecrettravel.com
SUBJECT: Miller/Styles Flights

Hey El,

As promised, the flights for Miller and Styles are officially ticketed. A PDF is attached with details on seat and ticket numbers, connections, etc. I've sent everything to them directly as well.

Have a good evening! I'm planning to stop at Verve for coffee in the morning. Want me to pick up your usual for you?

Eren

Happy travels,
Eren Polat
Flight Investigator
Top Secret Travel

CHAPTER 3

ELLIE

When you think of cities you'd like to visit in Florida, I'm willing to bet Jacksonville isn't the first one that comes to mind.

Sure, it's the most populated in the state. And, actually, one of the top ten largest cities in the United States by landmass. But we're not really known for anything special, other than a professional football team and the annual PGA golf tour that takes place just outside city limits. We do have the close proximity to beaches going for us, but almost every other major Florida city can claim the same.

Regardless, it's home for me. I've learned to love it. I've had the opportunity to sniff out what I like, and what I don't like. It's always been my preference to stick close to my own stomping grounds anyway. Which isn't a difficult thing to do when (and maybe I'm just biased) I live and work in the most idyllic part of the city.

Avondale is a historic district that lies just near the St. Johns River. The streets are lined with adorable homes of all styles; many of them are new, but most have been carefully preserved for decades. The majority of the restaurants and shops are locally owned, and it's always a quick, enjoyable walk from my house to the office, or to grab dinner or a quick coffee. Add museums, the nearby Saturday arts market, shade-providing oak trees, and a slight, steady breeze from the river, and it's quite picturesque. Especially in November and December.

I often think it's similar to living in Seattle, or Portland, or maybe even certain European cities, minus the differences in climate. At least, the vibes are the same as what I imagine those places are like. I've never actually been to any of them.

Or much of anywhere else, as a matter of fact.

The iron gate squeaks its familiar tune when I push it open, making sure to close it behind me. A brick walkway leads directly to the front door of a two-story, Spanish-style home. Through the front windows, I can see that all of the lights are still off inside: an indicator that neither of my uncles have made it home yet. The path splits and I take a right to continue around to the backyard, where I live in the guest house above the garage.

Clambering up the stairs, I fumble through my bag for my keys. Once inside, I can't kick my heels off fast enough. I always tell myself that the walk to the office isn't far enough to cause pain, and I'm always wrong. Pedaling my feet, I slowly readjust to the feeling of my arches meeting the floor, then head to the dresser for leggings and a t-shirt, taking extra care to hang my new Phillip Lim dress up properly after I peel it off. I got it for a steal off of EBay, which is practically unheard of for a size twelve, so I intend to treat it like my first-born child.

The smell of the scrambled eggs I made for breakfast still permeates in the studio-sized apartment space. Scrunching my nose in distaste, I make a mental note to light a candle when I get back from my walk. I drop onto my blue velvet couch long enough to pull some socks on, then walk back to the front door to slip into my sneakers, placing the haphazardly discarded heels on the shoe rack while I'm there.

Now I'm ready for the actual best part of my day.

I lock back up and head down to the main house. My spare key hasn't even entered the lock before Brat's head pops up into the window of the back door. He scratches at the glass, tongue lolling out of the side of his giant, toothy grin.

"Hold on, bud, I'm coming." I finish unlocking the door and open it just wide enough to slip in.

Brat bombards me. His meaty paws catch the backs of my thighs and I lower myself to his level before he can completely knock me over. After licking me on the face a few million times, he begins rooting his giant head into my armpits. Laughing, I pull his 75-pound body into a hug against my chest, where he relaxes and looks up at me lovingly.

"Are you ready for our walk?" I ask him, planting a kiss behind one of his black velvet ears. At the sound of the "w" word, he catapults off of me and begins to run zoomies around the butcher block-topped kitchen island.

"Bratwurst, do you ever run out of gas?" Uncle Sai's voice comes from the entrance to the adjoining dining room.

"Oh, hey," I say, standing up and brushing black and white dog hair from my shirt. "I didn't realize anyone was home yet."

"Yeah, I actually took a mental health day." He walks to the refrigerator and opens it to retrieve a can of Diet Dr. Pepper. I shake my head when he offers me one. "I've been napping for most of the afternoon."

"Good for you. Is everything okay?" I note his silk pajama pants and unkempt salt-and-pepper hair. He's also wearing glasses instead of his usual contacts.

"Everything is fine. Sometimes you just need time for yourself though, ya know? A bit of a 'long weekend' if you will."

I nod, understanding. Brat comes to a halt in front of Uncle Sai, dropping to sit on top of his bare feet. Sai plants a hand on the counter to keep his balance.

"You know," he recalls. "The lady at the shelter did tell us that pittie mixes have never ending energy supplies. I guess she wasn't lying."

Brat's attention snaps back to me when I laugh, a surprised look overtaking his face. He barrels back to me at top speed, full of so much excitement it's like he's forgotten I was here. I bend down to squish his face between my palms. "You better be glad you're really fucking cute," I tell him.

Uncle Sai walks to the back door, retrieving Brat's leash from the hook beside it and passes it to me. I clip it to his collar and give him a final peck on the nose before standing up. He may not technically be my dog, but he brings me the same amount of joy as if he were. Uncle Rob adopted him from the humane society just after he and Sai were married three years ago. He had wanted a golden retriever, but Sai insisted they adopt instead, and who can say no to a snuggly black and white meatball puppy?

"It's getting dark earlier now. I know you're a grown woman and the area is safe, but please be careful and call if you need anything," Uncle Sai says as Brat and I step out of the door. He says or texts some version of the same thing to me every evening, but I know it's from a place of love. He's only been my uncle by marriage for three years now, but he and Uncle Rob have been together since I was a teenager, well over ten years at this point. The two of them have been more like parents to me than my actual parents ever have been.

"I will. Plus, this guy always has my back," I yell over my shoulder as Brat pulls me down the steps and in the direction of the front gate.

Like myself, Brat has become a creature of habit. Even without my assistance, he would be able to lead us along the same route we've been walking since I started working at TST and moved into the guest house. Take a right out of the gate and go until you hit the second stop sign, then turn right again. Stop in front of Mrs. Warner's house, where she'll be waiting on her porch swing to come down and give Brat pets and a treat covered in peanut butter. Then it's on down to the river, where we continue along the paved path until we hit Edgewood Avenue and circle back home.

Most of the year, we brave the heat and push our way through the humidity just like every other person out and about for walks or runs. Now that we're in November though, the sixty-degree temperatures provide an extra pep to my step. Even Brat is appreciative, sniffing the new fall smells and looking back to smile at me every few minutes.

The cool wind flushes my cheeks. Several people are out in their front yards, taking down Halloween decorations and getting an early start on putting up their Christmas lights. Most wave at us as we pass. It's truly the most peaceful part of my day.

A time where I don't have to worry about deadlines, or meeting sales goals, or my confusion over Rick. A time where my constant need for everything to be perfect doesn't exist and where the lie I'm living at work doesn't gnaw at the back of my brain.

It's just Brat and I, out in the world.

CHAPTER 4

EREN

We're having takeout for dinner again.

I can't recall the last time Kristen or I cooked—together or individually. For weeks, it's been a mixture of Thai, pizza, burritos, and when we start feeling too guilty, we add a side salad. For balance, of course. Tonight, it's burgers from our favorite hole in the wall down the street.

If our schedules lined up at all these days, it could be different. If one of us isn't out of town, she's working late. I only stay past 5:00 if I have something to sort out, like an emergency cancellation or schedule change. I think she secretly enjoys not walking in the door until 8 p.m. or later.

"How was your Monday?" I ask from my spot on the couch, trying my best to convey genuine interest in my tone.

She drops the paper bag of burgers onto the coffee table and the smells of grilled onions and tater tots waft through the open top. I'm starving and it takes everything in me not to immediately dig in.

"It was fine," she answers, disappearing into the bedroom. I can hear the thud of her shoes hitting the floor as they're kicked off. Then the bathroom door opens and closes, and the sound of the TV once again fills the space around me.

"Mine was fine too, thanks for asking," I mutter to myself quietly.

I settle deeper into my squishy couch that desperately needs to be replaced. The hope I had for a normal, relaxing evening with my girlfriend wedges itself into the cushions beside me and disappears. Maybe my brothers are right... maybe I am cursed when it comes to relationships.

There are downsides to being a people person—an extrovert, social, a mixer, outgoing. Meeting people is fun for me. I like to ask questions. I like to make them laugh. I like to make them feel comfortable. I like finding that thing about them that sets them apart from every other person I've crossed paths with in life.

This also means that I have a higher probability of eventually falling romantically for a larger percentage of the people that I come into contact with. Don't get it twisted, I'm not what the kids these days call a "fuck boy." I actually crave monogamy; I love being in a relationship. But I've been thinking lately, maybe I just enter every relationship too quickly?

What if I'm meant to be waiting for a specific person that I haven't even met yet?

My brothers say I'm cursed because things always go south with my partners around the one year mark. I'm thirty-years-old, and I've had twelve different year-long relationships. When the shoe fits, the shoe fits.

It all started with Mara in high school. Then in college, there was Sidney, Dana, Penny, and Aanya. Through my 20's, there was Amelia, Danielle, Bella, Stephanie, Ingrid, Monica, and of course, Kristen.

All of that being said, I've never had an overly dramatic breakup. My partners simply seem to drift apart from me, and one year appears to be just the right amount of time to learn that you're actually not compatible with someone. Kristen and I have been together for eleven months, so I'll let you do the math. I love her...I know I do. I've loved everyone I've ever been with. At least, I think I did. But just like all of them, I can feel Kristen pulling away. I can no longer feel the heat of the flame that she once carried for me. I'm just here, waiting to be alone again.

Should I start planning my next trip to "find myself?" I'm thinking Morocco.

Kristen emerges from the bathroom in one of my T-shirts and flops down next to me. She's piled her blonde hair into a bun on top of her head. Her makeup has been washed off but the smell of her work perfume still lingers. I lean over for a kiss and she pecks me on the lips before grabbing the bag of burgers from the coffee table.

"What are we watching?" she asks, passing over my mushroom and Swiss.

"Whatever you want. I mainly had it on for background noise."

"Okay."

She makes no move to grab the remote. We sit in silence, eating our dinner and staring at whatever sitcom rerun is on the screen. I steal glances at her out of the corner of my eye, trying to gauge her mood. Is she still mad about Thanksgiving? Is it something else I've done? Is she just tired?

Deciding I refuse to sit in silence all evening, I muster up the courage to speak again. "How's your food?"

"It's good."

"They got it right this time?"

"Yep."

Her eyes never leave the TV. The concern that has been sitting in my chest over the past few weeks sprouts horns and transforms rapidly into frustration. Wrapping my half-eaten sandwich back in its wrapper, I toss it onto the coffee table and push myself up from the couch. I'm not sure where I'm heading. All I know is I have the sudden desire to not be sitting next to her.

"What's your problem, Eren?" she sighs after me.

Her question makes me want to laugh and cry at the same time. I've only made it a few paces from the couch. My back is to her, but I can't bring myself to turn back around. Another argument may be escalating, but I'll take it over the silent treatment.

"My problem," I say calmly, staring through the patio door in front of me. "Is that last night's fight was the only semi-passionate moment we've shared in a solid month and a half."

"What are you talking about? Don't be dramatic."

"That's unfair, Kris." I turn to find her standing now, arms crossed over her chest. "I feel like we barely speak anymore. We rarely go out. We come home and sit in silence most evenings. I try to talk to you and you give me nothing half the time. Not to mention, when was the last time we had sex?"

"Sorry, but some of us work fourteen hours a day. Maybe I'm tired." She throws her arms up and moves further away from me. The coffee table separates us; a physical barrier to complement our emotional one.

"I hate when you act like I don't understand what it's like to live through the stresses of everyday life."

"I'm not saying that. I just think that you love your job, and I hate mine. And that definitely makes things a little easier for you."

I stare at her, eyes so wide I can actively feel them drying out. "Kristen, I didn't force you to become a lawyer. When we met, you had just passed the bar and were thrilled to be getting started. I know it's not everything you thought it would be, and god knows I'm not perfect, but I have always tried to encourage you."

Her arms fall to her side. Her mouth opens and closes a couple of times as an expression of vulnerability slowly settles on her face. It's a breath of fresh air compared to the stony demeanor she has possessed lately. For a moment, I think maybe we've had a breakthrough. I think maybe we're going to fix this.

"I'm going home to sleep again."

She snaps out of her daze, hurrying back into the bedroom. I don't follow, pacing in circles around the couch instead. When she comes out a couple of minutes later, she's back in her work clothes, her arms overflowing with her purse and other belongings.

"Please just stay and talk to me," I beg, following her to the door. Socks and other items fall from her arms to the floor. I try to help, but she quickly snatches them up before I can get too close. I think she's going to leave without saying anything at all, but when she steps onto the front porch she faces me one last time.

"You're too damn much sometimes, Eren. You don't know how to just let things work themselves out."

And then she's gone. All I can do is stare after her as she rushes down the steps and struggles to unlock her car. This disagreement may have contained different subject matter, but everything else is a carbon copy of the night before. A sense of deja vu overwhelms me as I watch her white BMW back out of its usual parking space.

The chilly night air is the only thing that forces me back inside, leaving me locked in an apartment, drowning in memories of failed relationships.

CHAPTER 5

ELLIE

I t's not unusual for me to get to the office thirty minutes
early most days.

I honestly don't aim to do it. But every morning while I'm
getting ready, I play the same game: *Well it takes ten minutes to
walk there. If I stop for coffee that's another ten, then what if my
usual route is blocked off for some reason? I'll have to take an
alternate one, so maybe I should give myself a bit of extra time
just to be safe.* It's how my brain functions, and I've accepted it.
I was closing my uncle's front gate behind me before I remembered a coffee stop wouldn't be needed since Eren is bringing
me one.

That is all just a long way of saying, it's 7:20a.m. when I
make it to work. No one else will arrive for another half-hour
or more, but it's okay because I have a key. A few days after I
was hired, Yuke had shown up to find me sitting on the front
steps, waiting for someone else to get there. Later that same
day she came by my cube to drop off a spare key. "Use it
anytime you need to," she'd said.

I don't know why that pleased me so much, but it did.

The front door is one of the few parts of the old house

28

that has been updated, so the key turns easily in the lock. After hanging my jacket on one of the hooks in the entryway, I head straight to the break room to put my lunch—some of Uncle Rob's leftover stir fry from last night—in the refrigerator, flipping lights on as I go. The wooden floorboards creak rhythmically underneath my footsteps, finding cadence with the tapping of my heeled boots.

Being alone here is one of my favorite things. Sure, it's kind of creepy. Just like any old building, the office makes constant noises as it attempts to wake up. Other than that though, it's peaceful. For the first part of my day, I can work as I please. There's no one here to interrupt me with a question or favor and no one around to start a frustrated argument in the background over the consistently-jammed copy machine. There's no one in the neighboring cubes to clear their throat more than any human should have to; there's no one to make me breathe in the scent of their overpowering yet enticing cologne.

A random photo of Big Ben is secured to the front of the fridge with a magnet. Like every other day, I stare at it for a few moments, wondering what it would be like to see it in person. Is it actually that large? What would it feel like to stand next to it? Do Londoners find it as exciting as tourists, or do they just pass it by each day with their heads down? If I lived there, I don't think I'd ever get bored of it. I'd probably bump into people constantly because I'd be so tied up in staring at the spot where the clock's face meets the sky.

Sadness overcomes me and I pull the refrigerator door open. I know I'll never be able to answer any of those questions for myself. I'll just continue to pretend I already know based on what others have experienced. Luckily, there are no shortage of travel vloggers and bloggers out there sharing their own adventures and wanderlust-inspired emotions. Their actual first hand experiences help me create believable versions of my own imaginary ones.

Sighing, I exit the kitchen and make my way to the sales room. Most days, I'm able to suppress the guilt I feel about my lies...the longing that eats away at me to take the steps needed to actually travel myself. Other days, the weight on my shoulders is constantly present.

It looks like today will be one of the latter.

By the time I've made my to-do list and gathered all of the necessary files, it's already seven forty-five. I switch my computer on, rocking back and forth in my chair while I wait for it to boot up. Traffic sounds intensify outside as more and more people drive by, heading to various parts of the city for another work day. Soon I'll hear the slamming car doors of colleagues who are lucky enough to nab the street parking closest to the office.

Sure enough, the first footsteps sound in the hallway five minutes later. In a matter of seconds, Sherry and Lamar walk in, and my golden silence is interrupted. "Morning, Ellie," they call in unison as they drop their things onto their desks, Lamar's voice much more chipper than Sherry's per usual.

"Good morning," I say, turning to smile at Sherry before she sits down.

Over the next few minutes, the office continues to come to life. The front door opens and closes. People filter down the hallway, sharing morning greetings before splitting off to go into the kitchen or up the stairs. Computer monitors chime as they're turned on. Petra verbally ticks off her list of most important tasks. Whether or not she's speaking with someone or saying them to herself, I'm not sure.

I wait a few more minutes before getting up to walk back towards the front, taking a right into the sunroom that serves as a reception space. Jade is perched on the edge of her chair, using a compact mirror to carefully apply a mauve lipstick that perfectly sets off her dark skin tone. She fluffs her naturally curly hair before snapping the mirror shut and looking up at me.

"Oh, hey, Ellie. You look exceptional today." She grins, looking my outfit up and down.

I pull my oversized sweater further down over the fake leather leggings I've paired it with. Jade is my office go-to for talking about clothes, and a compliment from her always results in a blush because she knows way more about fashion than I could ever hope to. Her emerald green pantsuit makes me feel massively underdressed, even though I'm still a few steps above what our very casual dress code requires.

"Thank you. Just trying to keep up with you," I joke.

"Don't flatter me. Did you need something or were you stopping by to gas me up?"

"Both?" I smile. "Just letting you know that I have a scheduled call with James Arden at three o'clock today. Could you hold off on sending any new prospects to me around that time?"

Jade peels a new sticky note from the pad on her desk and jots a quick note down before sticking it on her monitor. "You got it, babe."

"You're the best. Now tell me about this suit, where did—"

"Happy Tuesday, ladies." Rick appears in the doorway, giving us both a quick wink before he continues on his way. He's gone before either of us can respond. Jade arches an eyebrow at me as if to say "Who gives him permission to look so damn good all the time?" before diving into her suit details.

Freaking Rick Williamson.

Eren comes through the door just as I'm leaving reception. He's holding two paper coffee cups and his tattered messenger bag is slung over one shoulder. Despite the cool weather, he isn't wearing a jacket. His signature button-up shirt is covered in little tiny airplanes today (very on brand) and his long hair is down. In true Eren fashion, a grin is plastered on his bearded face. He seems normal, but my gaze is automatically drawn to the bags underneath his eyes.

"One cinnamon dolce latte," he announces, passing over the larger of the two cups. I wrap both of my hands around it, soaking in the warmth.

"Thank you. Are you...okay?" I ask, fighting the look of concern that wants to overcome my face.

"Do I look that bad?" He rakes a hand through his hair. His cheery demeanor falters for a split second before he pulls it back together.

"No, not bad. Just tired," I tell him honestly.

"So, bad then." He laughs. "I just didn't sleep much last night. Kristen and I—well, it's a long story."

He's made a few comments over the past month or two that have made me wonder about things between him and his girlfriend. I've never pressed him on it, because he's usually the first person to offer information. He's never afraid to tell his life story. As we stand here in the entry way though, I sense that, for the first time, he doesn't want to talk about it.

"I'm sorry." I take a step to the side as he goes around me to start up the stairs. "Let me know if you need someone to chat about it with."

On the third step, he turns to smile down at me. "Thanks, El. Lunch at the usual time today?"

I nod and he departs. I stand in the hall until I can hear his heavy footsteps on the floor above my head, then return to my desk. Lucia and Sherry are already yelling back and forth about something. Lamar is slurping his coffee. Rick is talking loudly on the phone. "Yes, ABSOLUTELY Mrs. Francis. That won't be an issue at all."

Taking my first sip of latte, I check the clock on my computer. It's only 8:04 a.m.

CHAPTER 6

EREN

I temporarily tuck the photo of Kristen and I away in my bottom desk drawer because I can't stand looking at it. Once again, it's been nothing but radio silence from her since last night. Her voice has been playing on a loop in my brain, preventing me from taking the initiation to reach out.

You're too much sometimes, Eren!

It's not the first time in my life I've been accused of this. Although, "pushy" isn't my favorite adjective that people have used. I prefer "overzealous," or "assertive." Hell, I'd even prefer to be called "bossy." What confuses me is I always feel like my obtrusiveness comes from a good place. It's almost like I'm missing the sensor that tells me when I've stepped over the line between just enough and too much.

Work is only distracting me from about half of my worries today. When I tell someone that I book air travel for a living, they tend to assume it's a piece of cake job. Even my co-workers who don't have a hand in booking the flights think this. It's not true at all, but I don't argue. I know how much attention to detail it actually requires, and that's all that matters. Unfortunately, over the past couple of hours, focusing on even the most challenging schedules hasn't kept my thoughts from holding me hostage.

Which means it's time to move to Plan B of my extrovert coping mechanism: ranting to a friend. Logging in to the office's instant messaging system for the first time today, I double-click Ellie's name. She's the only person in my contact list who hasn't updated her profile picture. A straightforward "E" inhabits the space where a photo would be.

Eren Polat:
'Ello Ellie!

Ellie Amos:
Your message came at just the right time. I was about to throw my stapler over the wall at Rick.

I laugh, which makes me feel better immediately. Scrappy Ellie is my favorite Ellie.

Eren Polat:
Sounds like a sure fire way to lose your job. And maybe even get arrested for assault. No offense, but I don't see you doing well in prison.

Ellie Amos:
Thanks for single-handedly saving me from jail. You're a true friend.

Eren Polat:
Plus, you'll never win his heart if you're throwing office supplies at his head.

She responds with three middle finger emojis. My grin doubles in size. Joking with Ellie about Rick is my current favorite way to pick on her. And even though she won't admit it, I'm positive she's into him. She's always a good sport, but what if she secretly can't stand it?

Oh shit, I really am too damn pushy. My grin falters.

Time to change the subject.

Eren Polat:
Sorry if I was sort of rude this morning. Kristen and I have been fighting lately. She's walked out the past two nights.

Ellie Amos:
It's okay, I'm sure that can't be fun. I bet things will be back to normal in no time!

Eren Polat:
I'm not so sure...

Ellie Amos:
You don't have to tell me specifics if you don't want to. But what's going on? Normal relationship stuff?

Ellie may be just a work friend, but I trust her. Perhaps even more than some of the lifelong friends I've kept in contact with. She's gentle with her words, and a great listener. A pushy guy like me could learn a thing or two from her.

Eren Polat:
She's been distant for a while now, which I could understand at first because she works long hours. Then two nights ago she backed out on our Thanksgiving trip to Colorado—said she wasn't ready to meet my parents and she'd rather be with her family. Which isn't a big deal in theory, but we had an extensive conversation about this when I booked the flights back in

August and now I'm out about $500. And since then, every-
thing between us has been shit.

Ellie Amos:
That's not cool. I do understand wanting to be with family on
the holiday, but why doesn't she want to meet your parents?

Eren Polat:
She keeps saying she's too nervous, but that makes no sense.
They were excited to meet Kristen. Hell, they've sent her more
care packages than me over the past year. I'm pretty sure it's
the only bogus excuse she could think of to start ending things
between us.

I send the message and rub my hands over my face. Walt
passes my office door, holding a fresh cup of coffee. He must
notice my slumped shoulders and mussed hair because he
doubles back to peek around the door frame. "You doing
alright there, Polat?"

"I'm good, thanks. Just one of those days." I force a
smidge of lightheartedness into my voice.

"Okay, as you were then." He gives me a mock salute and
leaves me to myself.

Ellie Amos:
That's tough. I obviously can't relate, so I don't have any
advice. I do agree that Kristen should have been honest about
this sooner though. Maybe she will come around before you're
set to leave?

Eren Polat:
This is where things get more confusing. After my sleepless
night of thinking, I'm no longer sure I want her to come

36

around. But I also don't want to break up? God, what is my problem?

Ellie disappears from the chat and I worry I've disclosed too many of my feelings. Looking over at my phone, I see that her line lit up green, signaling that she's on a call. Saved from my worry of oversharing, I slump back into my chair and reopen my booking system. The half-complete schedule from Washington-Dulles to Miami sits right where I left it and I quickly add in the returning flight.

It's another twenty minutes before she gets back to me.

Ellie Amos:
I'm no love expert, and I hope this doesn't sound too harsh, but if you've felt like you don't want to patch things up for even a second, you need to explore that feeling deeper. Thoughts like that don't just go away. I'm sure the last thing you want is a partnership that has resentment on both sides.

Fuck. She's right.

Eren Polat:
Wow. You're deep, Ellie Amos. And also 100% correct.

Ellie Amos:
I love being right. (But if it makes you feel any better, I wish I didn't have to be right about this particular situation. I know you love Kristen.)

She's right again.

Eren Polat:
Would you mind if I don't eat lunch with you today? I think

I'm going to take a walk and have some much-needed (but not wanted) time to myself.

Ellie Amos:
Not at all. I'm the world's biggest advocate for alone time.

Eren Polat:
Maybe you can have lunch with Rick instead?

She logs out of messenger, giving me a head start on sitting with my thoughts.

CHAPTER 7

ELLIE

"Delivery!" Uncle Rob is standing on my tiny front porch when I open the door. He holds out a saran wrap-covered plate of chocolate chip shortbread.

My mouth waters at the sight. His shortbread is straight out of the best dream you've ever had—so buttery, crisp, and delicious that the cookies practically melt right on your tongue. They're a rare treat, only coming out to be devoured once or twice each year.

"Yesss," I squeal, taking the plate from him. "Did you make these tonight?"

"They're as fresh as can be," Uncle Rob says proudly. "I always get a craving for shortbread when the holidays start approaching."

"I'm so excited. I wish I had some—"

"Milk?" He turns and magically produces a carton of whole milk from the banister behind him. "I know you too well."

Opening the door wider, I move so he can step inside. He slides his slippers off and walks over to the couch. I sit the cookies on the coffee table and grab a couple of glasses from my tiny kitchen. Uncle Rob fills each one to the brim and we settle in with our treat.

"I'm surprised Uncle Sai didn't eat them all," I joke.

"It's your lucky day. He's in bed already."

"But it's only seven thirty." I dunk my first piece of shortbread and bring it to my mouth.

"He's been tired lately." Uncle Rob inhales an entire cookie. "He's having a stressful time at work these days."

"That's new." Uncle Sai is a finance manager. I still have no idea what exactly that entails, but I've always thought it sounds stressful. He's consistently loved his job over the years, though.

"He and I are unfortunately entering that period in time where some people have the famous midlife crisis." Uncle Rob falls into his Dracula impression, speaking as if he's telling a ghost story.

"Spooky," I snort, nearly choking on my last bite of shortbread. "Are you having a midlife crisis?"

He considers my question. "No. But my job is also much less brain numbing."

"Fair." I place my half-empty—or as Uncle Rob and Eren would insist, half-full—glass of milk on the table and tuck my legs underneath me on the couch, summoning a mental picture of Uncle Rob working as a sociology professor. I've always imagined that his bald head probably shines underneath the study hall lighting. I wonder if it's distracting to his students.

"Anyway, how was your day?" he asks, changing the subject. He pierces me with a gaze that is so similar to mine it's often unsettling. I've somehow always looked more like him than my own mother, down to his green eyes instead of her hazel.

"Unremarkable," I tell him truthfully. "The usual work stuff. Listened to Eren's relationship drama. Had a consultation with a new client that I'm pretty certain I'm going to send to Australia. Ate leftovers for lunch."

"Oooh, relationship drama. Do tell." He polishes off his third cookie and sits his glass on the table next to mine as if that will serve as a barrier to prevent him from grabbing a fourth.

"You're so nosey. I'm not telling you his business."

"I don't even know him," he argues.

"That's besides the point." I give him a sly smile, leaning forward to wrap the plate of cookies back up. Standing, I collect our glasses and walk them to the sink.

"You're no fun." He pretends to pout. "At least tell me something new about Mr. Rick Hunkyson."

Freezing, I blink across the room at him. As close as I am with my uncles, I've never been super open about my love life with them. It's just who I am—some things feel better left inside my head. Seeing as I've only had one boyfriend, back when I was nineteen, I know they must wonder why I choose to stay away from anything serious. They know I go on the occasional date. As much as I hate to admit it, they've probably seen a man or two come up to the guest house with me, too.

And if I'm being honest with myself, I don't even know why I haven't committed to anyone yet. It could be as easy as nothing has felt right. It could be that my expectations are just too high. At 28, it's my own personal romantic cold case.

"What the hell does that mean?" I try to sound nonchalant but a scoff escapes at the end of the question. The glass I'm washing slips out of my too-tight grip, clattering into the sink.

"Come on, Ellie Smellie, I'm just using context clues." He pushes up from the couch and comes to rest his elbows on the bar across from me. "You know how parents tell their children that bullies only target kids they secretly admire? That's bullshit if you ask me, by the way, some kids are just assholes. But, what I do believe, is when a grown adult can't stop complaining about stupid things a colleague is doing, it's probably because they're harboring some fondness."

I finish drying the glasses and turn to put them back in the cabinet, grateful for the brief opportunity to hide my expression. Uncle Rob is like a hunting dog sometimes. He can sniff secret feelings from miles away when he wants to. He'll know he's right if I don't take a moment to alter the look on my face.

"Can you send me the research on that hypothesis?" I ask, feebly meeting his eyes again. "Do you teach that in your sociology courses? Because I think I totally disagree."

"Ellie and Rick, sitting in a tree..." he sings.

"Okay, sir, you're cut off. You can go now." Walking around the bar, I grab his elbow and guide him back to my front door. "But the shortbread stays with me."

He pokes his feet back into his slippers, chortling under his breath as he does so. Chilly evening air rushes in when he opens the door and we both shiver dramatically. It's tough for Floridians to handle anything below 75 degrees.

"I hope you know I'm only joking." He affectionately pinches my cheek. "Always around to hear about it when you're ready though."

One corner of my mouth lifts against my will. "Goodnight, Uncle Rob. Thanks again for the cookies. Can't wait to polish them all off tomorrow."

He skips down the steps. I watch until he makes it to his back door, where Brat's squishy face waits for him in the window. With a final wave, he slips into the house. I lock up before returning to the couch.

Rick Hunkyson, huh? Why are my uncles always right about everything?

CHAPTER 8

EREN

KRISTEN

I need some space.

That's what the text that Kristen sent me at 6:28 p.m. said. Not *Can we meet up to talk?* Not *I know what I want, but I'd rather tell you in person.* Definitely not the *I'm sorry and I love you and I'm bringing ice cream to your place later* that I was kind of hoping for.

Just a written request for time away from me.

I didn't text her back right away, because I figured that would result in me saying something I don't mean. She's going to have to give me more than that at some point, though. I need details. Does she need space just for tonight? For a few days? Forever? And while we're at it, what do *I* want? I can't decide that until I have a better idea of what she's thinking. More time apart is the last thing we need—we need to work through this together.

I've been wandering around Avondale since I left work. I didn't want to go home without hearing from Kristen, and

43

after I finally did hear from her, my need to busy myself with any activity available tripled. I had a drink at one restaurant. Then I moved to a new one for dinner and a second drink. Since I can never end the night without something sweet, I walked to Verve for a pastry and a shot of espresso. Now, my feet are leading me back to where my car is parked near the office, and going to my apartment is still the last thing I want to do.

But I'm running out of options. What I really want is to talk to someone about all of this. Dropping down onto the curb next to my car, I consider calling my brothers. What good will that do though? They'll only say, "I told you, you're cursed."

I scroll through the other names in my phone. None of them feel right. That's another difficult thing about being social...I have hundreds of contacts right at my fingertips, but hardly any of them feel safe to go to with heavy stuff. For a beer or for game night, sure. Never for my emotions though. I toss my phone onto the ground beside me. The cold concrete beneath me seeps through my jeans, slowly freezing my ass.

Stretching my legs out in front of me, I use the tie around my wrist to pull my hair back into a ponytail. Mom and Dad won't be happy to see how long it's gotten when I see them in a few weeks. Maybe they won't even notice if I have news of a breakup to distract them with instead.

Footsteps pull me from my sorrow fest. Looking up, I see two women nearing me on the sidewalk. When they spot me, they make a feeble attempt to discreetly cross over to the other side of the street. I'm a giant hairy dude sitting on the ground, so I should understand. For some reason though, their action makes my heart fall further. A single tear pricks the corner of my left eye. I blink it away, staring up at the dark windows of TST in front of me.

Ellie.

Her name bombards my brain like a random song lyric and I know she's who I want to talk to. Strange...it only took one missed lunch hour to feel like I haven't talked to her in ages. Grabbing my phone from where it fell, I locate her in my contact list. When I tap on her name, the message screen is blank. Have we really never corresponded outside of work before? My fingers pause above the keyboard, thinking maybe she wants to keep it that way.

My impulsiveness still wins.

EREN

Hi.

I keep it simple and add a classic smiley face emoji for flair. Now I wait. What if she ignores me? What if she responds and asks me not to talk to her outside of work?

Why is this making me so nervous? What if Ellie is a completely different person outside of the confines of TST? The *Mean Girls* quote about seeing teachers outside of school comes to the forefront of my mind. For some reason, the current situation has the same vibes.

A few minutes pass with no reply. I know I should stop staring at the screen, but I can't help myself. Ages later, three little dots appear, showing that Ellie is typing. My spirits immediately rise, then plummet just as quickly when the dots disappear and no message comes through. Several more minutes pass before I give up, pushing myself up from the curb and stretching. I grab my keys from my pocket and slide my phone into their place.

This is a sign to go home, Eren, the rational part of me says.

Send her another text, my brash side argues.

Agreeing with the responsible side, I unlock the car and fold myself into the front seat. I'm just about to turn the keys in the ignition when my phone vibrates against my thigh. My legs are so cramped in the floorboard that I can't remove my phone while sitting down. I push the door open again, climbing out to retrieve it.

Ellie's name is on the screen.

> **ELLIE**
> Hey, are you okay?

How did she know? Should I jump right into what's on my mind? Or do I make small talk first? Why do I feel like I'm texting a crush for the first time instead of talking to someone I've known for years?

> **EREN**
> I'm fine. What's up?

Liar. Her response is immediate this time.

> **ELLIE**
> You've never texted me before, so something must be wrong.

I type out three other messages filled with small talk and delete them before I figure it's best to just jump in. It's not like I wasn't texting her to rant anyway. My impulsiveness has faded away now though, leaving my negativity to tell me that all I'm doing is bothering her.

> **EREN**
> It's official. Kristen wants to take a break.

I hit send. Tucking myself back into the car seat, I shut the door and rest my head against the steering wheel while I wait for the next text's arrival.

ELLIE

> Can I call you? These conversations are usually best had in person. Or, verbally, at least. You know what I mean.

In person, huh? This gives me an idea. Ellie lives somewhere around here. I check the time. 8:23 p.m. That's not too late, right? Ellie does seem like the type of person who goes to bed at nine sharp though, so I could be completely off base.

EREN

> Actually, I'm still in Avondale. Want to meet up for a drink or dessert or something?

ELLIE

> I'll be real with you, the idea of getting dressed and leaving my house again seems like the worst.

I deflate a little even though I know it's not personal. I tried though, and will be equally thankful for a phone call. I'm about to tell her so when I receive a second message.

ELLIE

> May have a better idea though. Do you like shortbread?

Not even five minutes later I'm parked on the street in front of one of the many picture-perfect homes in the area. I've always just assumed that Ellie lives in an apartment, but this is no rental. Does she live with her parents? Are they going to wonder why this guy who may or may not look like he's been crying is knocking on their door on a Tuesday night? What if they get the wrong idea?

A dark figure emerges from the side of the house and makes its way down the front path. Ellie clearly comes into view as she draws closer. She stops just inside the front gate and waves at me. I clamber out of my car and lock it before moving around to meet her.

"This place could be in a magazine," I tell her, shoving my hands in my pockets and peering around at landscaping so perfect it should be unattainable. A giant oak tree protrudes from the left side of the yard, its branches creating a natural frame for its surroundings. It's one of the few houses in the neighborhood still decorated for fall instead of Christmas, complete with pumpkins on the front porch steps.

"Don't tell my uncles that. It will make their heads even bigger," she jokes, opening the gate for me. It screeches on its hinges, igniting a deep bark from somewhere within the house.

"So you live with your uncles, then?" I look down at her through the darkness. Her face is free of makeup and she looks different yet also the same.

"Yes and no." She starts walking and I follow awkwardly behind. "I live in the guest house around back—with them, but not with them."

"Sweet..."

We follow the walkway around the house and pass beneath an archway covered in ivy. The backyard opens up, revealing a large wooden deck off the main house and a detached garage just a few steps away. Another muffled bark comes from inside, closer this time.

"Don't worry Brat, it's just a friend," Ellie calls.

I follow her gaze to the back door and can't help but grin at the sight of a black and white face in the window. The dog stops barking immediately and perks its ears. The serious look on its face is replaced with a toothy dog smile. Its tongue drops out of one side of its mouth as excited pants form clouds of condensation on the glass.

"Brat?" I ask, making my way up the stairs to the guest house in Ellie's wake. "What a cutie!"

"Short for Bratwurst," she tells me, one side of her mouth tilting up as she looks down at him one last time. "He's a pittie mix, and basically my best friend."

"I love it." I follow her inside, appreciating the warmth. "Learning things about you is fun."

"Don't get used to it." She arches her eyebrow at me as she takes my jacket and hangs it on one of the hooks beside the door. "This is about you. Make yourself comfortable!"

Turning, I assess Ellie's house for the first time. At work, Ellie is friendly, but no-nonsense. Her desk is organized, but bare—not a personal trinket in sight. I've always imagined that her home is just as minimal.

Don't get me wrong, it's one of the cleanest living spaces I've ever set foot in...as organized and functional as any type-A personality could ever hope for. But it's also warm and personalized. A blue velvet couch sits atop a jewel-toned rug. White shelves covered in books and knick knacks line the far wall. A folding room divider separates her bed from the rest of the studio-sized space.

"This is so nice, El." Sitting down, I can't help but run my hand over the silkiness of the couch.

"Thank you." She changes the subject quickly, pulling plastic wrap from a platter of cookies and offering me one. "Uncle Rob brought these over earlier. Have as many as you'd like."

"Do you have any milk?" I ask as the first piece of shortbread crumbles against my tongue.

"I knew we were friends for a reason." She winks at me and stands to go to the kitchen. She's wearing sweatpants and her short brown hair is messy. Between that and her lack of makeup, it's nice to see her in a more relaxed state.

She hands me a glass of milk and I settle in with my second cookie. (The best fucking shortbread I've had, maybe ever.) Everything about her home feels cozy, and the comfort I feel when hanging out with her at work covers me in this new territory of our friendship as well. I've almost forgotten why I'm here when Ellie breaks the silence.

"So what happened?" She props her elbow on the back of the couch and rests her head in her palm. "I'm all ears."

The events of my evening come rushing back and I ramble in circles, giving her maybe a little too much detail. And while the subject is quickly becoming a sour one for me, Ellie's company already makes me feel the tiniest bit better.

CHAPTER 9
ELLIE

"S omeone must have been up late last night."

I clamp my mouth shut, cutting both my yawn and stretching short. Pulling my arms from the air, I pin them to my sides and spin around to face Rick. He's standing just outside my cubicle, arms crossed with a smirk on his freshly-shaven face. I have to force my eyes away from his biceps, made more apparent by the taut fabric of his black polo shirt.

"Nope," I fib, refusing to tell him that 10:30 actually is late for me. "Is there something I can help you with?"

He takes a step forward and leans against the flimsy wall. It moves slightly under his weight. I hate when he does this. At least...I think I hate it. I try to relax, but my shoulders rise slowly, growing closer and closer to my ears. Every moment shared with Rick seems to be filled with tension. For me, at least. I don't think he would know what anxiety is if it kicked him in the khakis.

"Yes, please." He smizes at me in a way that makes me positive he used to binge watch *America's Next Top Model*. "I was hoping you'd loan me some of your stock images for Glacier National Park. I'm working on a planner."

"Sure, I'll share the folder with you," I say evenly, turning to send it to him before he leaves and I forget. "You've never been there? I'm surprised you don't have any of your own pictures."

The genuine question sounds condescending as it rolls off my tongue. I honestly didn't mean for it to. Even my tone of voice is full of the pressure I feel when I associate with him.

"I could say the same about you, Miss Travel Expert." He laughs, uncrossing his arms and backing around the corner to his desk. "Thanks for the help."

I stick my tongue out at him through the wall. It's immature, but makes me feel better. Refocusing on my own tasks, I take a big gulp of cold coffee and hold my eyes open as wide as possible, refusing to blink until I absolutely have to. I can't remember when I started doing that to make myself feel more awake, but it's now a habit. And it works.

10:30 really is a late bedtime for me. It's not the reason I'm so exhausted today though. That would be because I laid awake for hours after I crawled underneath the sheets. Eren's visit interrupted my usual schedule and I was so worked up by the time he left that my brain wouldn't power down. I couldn't stop thinking about how sad he was over Kristen. I couldn't stop thinking about what it must be like to feel so deeply about someone.

I couldn't stop thinking about how strange, yet oddly, comfortable, it felt to have Eren in my home; a personal boundary that I never envisioned myself crossing.

For god's sake, I've turned down every social invitation he's ever extended. In all fairness, I also never thought I'd see Eren so...down. He's the friendliest, most positive human I've ever met in my life. Unfairly, I assumed he was immune to the negative pressures of existing. And though I am somewhat flattered that he trusts me to share his emotional burdens, I have to wonder—why me? The man must have more friends than he knows what to do with. And family, for that matter.

A two-day reminder for Friday's meeting populates on the screen in front of me, snapping me out of my episode of disassociation. "As if we could forget about this damn mystery meeting," Sherry grumbles beside me.

"Oh, I'm sure there's someone in this building that benefits from being reminded every five minutes," Lucia says sarcastically.

"Like Ellie, for example. We all know how much she appreciates a good, structured calendar," Rick pipes in. Everyone but me laughs. Once again, I view the joke that others heard as something more sinister. Uncle Rob's theory about feuding co-workers finds its way back to me. On the outside, I force amicability, but on the inside, I'm over-analyzing everything.

"That's why we love our El, though," Lamar adds. "She's there to keep us all on track when needed."

Lamar is what can only be described as a "workplace peacemaker." I don't know if it's because he's an empath, or if, like Eren, he just sees the world through rays of sunshine at all times. Either way, his presence on the sales staff is crucial to preventing fights that would probably put mixed martial arts to shame.

"You always have my back, Lamar." I grab my coffee mug and hop to my feet. It's time for a refill.

The break room is empty, but so is the coffee pot. I go through the process of changing the filter and adding new grounds and water. Then I wait for it to brew. It's rarely this quiet here, so I take a few minutes to decompress and mentally prepare for the rest of the day. Walking over to the refrigerator, I run my finger across the familiar photo, tracing the outline of Big Ben while coffee splatters into the pot behind me.

"Looking at that photo every day makes me want to go back to London." I turn at the sound of Eren's voice. His shirt is covered in tiny pumpkin spice lattes today. "I'm sure you can relate."

"Sounds about right," I lie.

Can't relate, is what I should say.

Eren trusts in our friendship so much. And half of what he does know about me isn't true. Does it bother him that I can be so closed off? Would he even want anything to do with me if he knew I've been pretending to have experience that I actually don't have? Or if I was more open with him about my past and anxieties?

"Oooh, fresh bean juice!" Eren sits his cup on the counter beside the coffee maker. He sounds more like himself today. "It's my lucky day."

"Calling it bean juice makes you sound about sixty years old," I tell him.

"Just practicing for my future role as TST's office grandpa," he quips. "Do you think I'll be bald by then?"

I assess his hair, fighting to avoid getting sucked in by thickness and shine that most people only dream of. Even his beard gleams in the kitchen lighting. "For some reason, I don't think so."

"Cool," he says simply, leaning against the counter and looking at me in his way that always makes me feel scrutinized, but in a good way. "New dress?"

"No, I just haven't worn it in a while." I run my hands down my sides, smoothing the plum-colored shift dress. "You seem to be in higher spirits today."

"Thanks to you I was able to go home and get a decent night's sleep." The last of the coffee filters into the pot and he retrieves the carafe. He fills my mug, then his. "By the way, your uncle could make millions selling that shortbread he makes."

"I'll let him know," I snort. If I can get a word in later when he's giving me the third degree about Eren's visit, that is.

"I also took your advice." He moves to the fridge and pulls out a carton of half-and-half with his name written across it in capital letters. "I texted Kristen before I went to bed. Told her I understand and want to respect her decision, but still think I deserve a face-to-face conversation so I know what to expect long term."

"And?" I press.

"She's coming over later. I'll keep you posted."

"Good!" I back slowly toward the door, the magnetic pull of my desk becoming stronger and stronger. "I'll send you a bill for last night's session."

"I hope you take insurance," Eren jokes. "And Ellie, thank you, seriously. I hope you know I'm always here if you ever need to talk about anything."

"I know." I smile, giving him a wave and moving out of the room before he can see my face fall.

Eren has proven himself trustworthy from the beginning. Over the past week, our friendship has unlocked a new level, and with that upgrade, my guilt has intensified. On top of that, I'm feeling a different desire for the first time—the desire to have someone I can be completely sincere with, to have someone that I can turn to besides my uncles.

Most of my old friends have pulled away from me in my adult years. My parents have never been present enough for me to depend on. I've used my fears, my perfectionism, my cautiousness, to convince myself that getting too close to people is problematic.

But Eren gives me a hunger for authenticity.

"You were gone an awful long time," Rick points out as I re-enter the sales room.

I ignore him, sitting my fresh coffee on the desk and tucking my right leg underneath me as I sit down. His comment presses none of my buttons at the moment. I'm distracted by a new mission, one that may be the first hasty decision ever. My coffee is fueling a fresh new impulse—the impulse to come clean.

Not to everyone, not yet. But to one person for sure.

CHAPTER 10

EREN

She should have been here forty-five minutes ago.

As I sit on the back patio nursing my second beer, I'm not surprised. I'm not even annoyed. Kristen hasn't gotten off work at a decent hour in months. Serious, potential breakup conversations are no exception to the rule. She'll let me know when she's on the way.

I sit the bottle on the table next to me and lean my head against the back of the chair, closing my eyes. The usual sounds of apartment living surround me. Dogs bark. Babies cry. Loud music plays and someone yells at the culprit to "turn the fucking volume down." When you've lived in close proximity to others long enough, anything can serve as relaxing background noise.

Minus a few moments of spiraling, I've felt strangely calm since Kristen walked out the second time. In my heart, I know the issues are nothing new. I've already been dealing with this for weeks. The majority of the emotional damage is done. I've been through this eleven times before. And with Ellie's added perspective, I feel prepared for any result.

If it's a permanent break, I'll be okay. If it's a temporary break, I'll be okay. Both outcomes will give Kristen what she wants, but I'll also get the time I need: The time to heavily consider not entering into a thirteenth relationship in the future.

Unlucky thirteen. The superstition makes me laugh out loud. My next partnership is doomed before it's even started.

Ten more minutes pass without a word from Kristen, and my beer is gone. Standing, I walk inside and drop the bottles in the recycling bin. There are dishes in the sink so I wash them. The floor looks dirty, so I sweep it. Before I know it, I've deep cleaned the entire kitchen, and my phone is still silent.

My pride won't allow me to be the first to reach out to Kristen again, but I'm officially feeling twitchy.

EREN

She's an hour and a half late. I have a bad feeling she's going to bail on me.

Keeping the cleaning momentum going, I gather the laundry from the couch into a bear hug and move it to my bed. I've never been one to sort my laundry, so I have a good variety of socks, towels, and work clothes to distract me for a while longer. I'm hanging the last shirt in my closet when Ellie replies.

ELLIE

Sorry, Brat and I were on a walk and it's tough to text while handling him. Fingers crossed she's there soon!

As if Ellie's words are magic, there's a sudden knock at the door. It takes everything in me to walk to it instead of sprinting. Taking a deep breath, I turn the knob and open it slowly, revealing Kristen bit by bit. Then she's there fully, solid in front of me, wearing her usual black pantsuit, blonde hair professionally blown out.

"I know, I'm late and I should have updated you," she says.

"It's fine." I try to be nonchalant. "Come in."

Inviting her into my apartment feels strange, considering she was letting herself in with her own key just a couple nights ago. She makes no move to enter, staying rooted to her spot on the front porch instead. Her fingers are twisted in a knot. I can feel the anxiety coming off of her in waves. She looks down and I follow her gaze, noticing a cardboard box next to her feet.

"Maybe we can take a walk instead?" she asks. "Get some fresh air?"

"Yeah, let me grab my jacket."

I find my windbreaker and keys. When I return to the door, Kristen has the box in her hands. She holds it out to me and I take it, confused.

"Just a few things that you had at my place." She won't look me in the eye, focusing instead on the door frame above my head. "I think I got all of mine from here the other night."

If I wasn't already suspicious about what direction this conversation is going to take, she just gave me the ultimate form of foreshadowing. Forlornly, I place the box in the hallway and join her on the porch, turning to lock up. Didn't I tell Ellie that I wasn't even sure I wanted to work things out? Wasn't I just thinking about how I feel mentally prepared for whatever decision Kristen should make?

The fact of it is, the actual event is always going to be more difficult than the anticipation beforehand. It's like when I go to the dentist. (Which I hate. More like, *loathe* entirely.) I can hype myself up the entire drive over, so much so that by the time I park in front of the dental office I'm no longer dreading it. But then, I sit down in that cold, leather chair and see the silver torture instruments on the table beside me. And I proceed to hold back tears for the entire cleaning because I'm a wimp.

We walk in the direction of the apartment's dog park. The evening is gray around us, with just enough breeze to chill your hands and face. We're silent for the first couple of minutes, the sounds of Kristen's heels on the concrete the only noise. The smell of her shampoo swirls in the wind. It's a smell that is so ingrained in my mind that I know I'll still think of her when I catch a whiff of something similar one, or even ten, years from now.

"I know I haven't handled all of this in the best way," Kristen speaks, and we make eye contact for the first time when I look over at her. "It's just...this is the first time I've ever been the one to end something. Both of my previous relationships were ended by the other person."

"I get that." It's kind of a lie. I've also never been the one to concede first. So, how do I know how I would handle it? I'd like to think I wouldn't give the other person the silent treatment and communicate solely through sporadic texts, but maybe I would?

"Every bit of energy I have has been sucked up by my job lately," she continues. "And as much as I hate that, I can't convince myself to give a shit about anything outside of figuring out how to be a good lawyer."

"Ouch." It's all I can think to say.

"It's not fair to keep dragging you along with me." She uses the toe of her shoe to kick at the grass as we come to a stop in front of the dog park. It's empty—too dark and chilly out for any games of fetch.

"I appreciate that. But why didn't you ever talk to me about this? When you first started feeling overwhelmed, I mean." I turn to face her. With her work shoes on, our eyes are nearly level. Despite the conversation, the same blank, expressionless look covers her face. It's her courtroom presence, which has leaked into her personal life drip by drip, eventually becoming a full-force flood, drowning everything.

"At first I didn't want to hurt you. I assumed things would eventually go back to normal." She shrugs. "Plus, I know you. You wouldn't have rested until you thought the problem was fixed."

"Am I really that exhausting?" My defense goes up. The familiar wound of being deemed a pushy person opens itself once again.

"Not exhausting. But you trying to fix everything while I don't have the energy to help would only prolong the cycle that we've been stuck in. Or even make things worse." She takes one of my hands in both of hers. The gesture is surprising, out of character for her recent persona. She rubs her thumbs across my knuckles, then releases my hand like it never happened.

The breeze blows a strand of hair into her face. Out of habit, I reach up and tuck it behind her ear. She shrinks away. Her reaction is one I know well, and the faces of everyone else I've ever loved flash over Kristen's. How can you go from craving someone's touch to being repulsed by it?

"Do you think after some time, you'll want to give this another shot?" I ask the question I already know the answer to; the question I want her to say both "yes" and "no" to, so that both halves of my confused state of being are satisfied. "Yes" would give me hope, hope that I'm not actually cursed. "No" would allow me to breathe without being driven crazy by the questions of "When?" And "What if?"

"Neither of us can predict the future." She turns and begins walking back in the direction of my apartment. "Right now, I don't think so. But who can say?"

How did she manage to produce the most vague answer possible? I stand rooted to the spot, jolting forward when she looks over her shoulder to see if I'm following. I fall into place beside her, but don't say anything else. Loud people are often the quietest in the most serious times.

She makes nervous small talk on the walk back: asking about TST and about Thanksgiving like it isn't the beginning of the end. It's surface-level conversation, but also the most we've chatted in weeks. We arrive back at my apartment and she stops in front of her car. She looks at me expectantly, as if waiting for me to say the final words of our time together. Having nothing to add, I step forward to wrap her in a hug instead.

"It was a good year," I say into her hair. "I'm here if you need anything."

"I know." She gives me a final squeeze before pulling out of the hug. Taking my face in her hands, she gives me a short kiss on the lips. A lump forms in my throat as I watch her climb into the car.

She backs out of the space and waves at me through the open window. Then she drives, leaving me behind for the last time. Leaving me to tend to my twelfth case of a broken heart.

CHAPTER 11

ELLIE

Thursday arrives faster than usual this week.

Normally, when a week is passing quickly, it's because I've been drowning in work. I've only been moderately busy the past few days though, so that only leaves one other option: the Eren-related events. He's added some spice to my routine; changed up my everyday order of events.

I'm in the bathroom, washing my hands for lunch, when Jade comes out of one of the stalls. Joining me at the sink, she turns the other tap on and pushes the sleeves of her black turtleneck up to her elbows. She grins at me in the mirror.

"How's your day, El?"

"Not so bad, just about to have lunch. How's yours?" I wash the last bit of soap from my hands and reach for a paper towel.

"One step closer to Friday," she jokes. "You eating with Eren?"

"Yeah, per usual. It's somehow become a tradition around here."

"If it wasn't for him having a girlfriend, I'd say he's crushing on you."

A wave of bewilderment crashes over me, leaving me feeling like I've been punched in the stomach. I go to discard my towel, moving in slow motion. My pulse creates a rushing sensation in my ears.

No one has ever said that before. *I've* never even thought about it before.

"You know him." I giggle nervously. "He treats everyone like his best friend."

"True. He once spent twenty minutes at my desk talking to me about this bakery downtown. Somehow I wasn't totally bored to death."

"That's the Eren we all know." I back into the bathroom door and hold it open for Jade to exit in front of me.

"How about the meeting tomorrow, huh?" She changes the subject, steps syncing up with mine as we head down the hall. "Wonder what it's all about.'

"I know! We haven't had a full office meeting in...well, maybe ever, since I've been here," I answer, even though my thoughts are still tied up in her previous comment.

"We'll know soon enough!" She leaves me at the break room entrance and hurries off to the front of the building.

I continue to obsess over Jade's observation as I put my Tupperware of leftover chili in the microwave. The soup pops and sizzles in front of my eyes. My brain pops and sizzles along with it. It's not that I actually think Eren would ever feel that way about me. He's simply a friendly guy...maybe the friendliest ever.

What has frazzled me is the brief feeling of excitement that overtook my body when Jade verbalized the possibility. I've never thought of Eren and I as anything more than work friends until yesterday. Even then, thinking of him as a friend in my personal life was an epiphany in itself. Is this going to ruin that?

More importantly, will it reverse my decision to come

clean to him at some point? A point I haven't even plotted on a definite timeline yet?

The beep of the microwave pulls me back to the present. I grab a spoon and a bottle of water and head out to our usual picnic table. The sky is blindingly blue and patches of sunlight fall onto the patio between the trees. Eren is already there, scrolling through his phone with one hand and shoveling chips into his mouth with the other. I freeze for a moment, feeling strange about seeing him after he's just been the subject of my thought spiral.

"Yum, chili," he says before I've even sat down.

"How did you know?" I ask, swinging my legs over the bench across from him.

"I could smell it as soon as you put it in the microwave."

"That's a talent." I laugh and my shoulders relax. There's no reason to be freaked out. Jade was just making a silly joke. She doesn't know that he actually doesn't have a girlfriend anymore (as confirmed during my phone conversation with Eren last night), but that doesn't change anything. Eren is my friend. He may even be on track to becoming my best friend.

"How's your first official day back in the world of singleness?" I ask around a bite of chili. "You can borrow my single people handbook if you need a refresher."

"Hilarious." He rolls his eyes even though he's smiling. "*You* wouldn't be single if you'd just let me introduce you to one of my brothers. Or if you'd stop being scared and ask Rick out."

This helps me relax further. Would Eren be advocating for *Operation Get Ellie a Date* if he was pining for me behind the scenes?

"No, thanks. And no, thanks."

He throws his empty chip bag into his lunchbox and unwraps a sandwich. He seems pretty good today. With the sun beaming down on him and a ham sandwich in hand, I'd even go so far as to say he looks pretty carefree. I know that can't be the case because a broken heart doesn't heal overnight, but at least he appears to be heading in the right direction.

"Do you ever just feel like a total idiot?" Eren asks randomly around a mouthful of bread.

Okay, maybe he isn't doing so well.

"Fairly often. Doesn't everyone?" I use my hand to shield the sun from my eyes so I can get a better look at his face.

"Of course. But I mean *really* feel like an idiot. Like in the sense you think you may never feel normal again."

Every day of my life, I think.

"In what sense? Talk to me," I say instead.

The door to the kitchen opens briefly and we both look over to see who's coming out. Before anyone exits, it shuts again. We shrug at each other.

"I've come to the conclusion that there's this innate part of my brain that sabotages everything. My heart will think 'Wow, I'm so happy,' then I get too excited over being happy and start doing stupid shit." His words come out in a jumble.

"Are we talking about your breakup here? Because if so, you're being too hard on yourself. It's not solely your fault."

"Do you think I'm too pushy?"

"Huh? I don't think pushy is a good word..." I say, trying to keep up with him as he jumps from subject to subject.

"I don't mean to unload all of this on you." He finishes his sandwich, looking into my eyes as if it helps him refocus. "It's just hard to silence a certain thought sometimes, ya know?"

I know. Every second of every hour. For example, he doesn't know I was freaking out in the kitchen just before I came out here. He doesn't know that my entire job depends on a lie that I told at an interview for a position I was certain I would never get. He doesn't know that I can't think of the good memories of my parents without being overwhelmed by the bad. He doesn't know that I feel like the worst person on the planet, because others out there have it so much worse than I do yet I can't stop throwing myself pity parties.

It's the perfect time, my subconscious tells me. *Get one thing off your chest. Let him know he's not alone.*

My pulse is thundering in my ears again. My hand starts to shake, and the spoon I'm holding clatters against the edge of my Tupperware. If there was ever a right time to dive into this, it's now. I drop the spoon and take a swig of water, allowing it to slowly trickle down my throat while I gather the last bit of needed courage.

"Would it make you feel better if I told you something that makes me feel like a total idiot? Something that no one knows, and I'm actually kind of terrified to tell you because I'm afraid you'll hate me, but I want to tell you because you're such a good friend to me and I only want to be honest with you like you are with me?" The words come fast and faster, and by the time I finish Eren looks concerned.

"Have you murdered someone or something?" He tilts his head and narrows his eyes at me.

"Would you unfriend me if I did?" I ask, just out of curiosity.

"I mean, we'd have to talk about why you killed them." A snort escapes his nose. "Are you going to finish that chili, by the way?"

I push the half-eaten bowl across the table to him. Having no qualms about germs, he picks my spoon up and starts eating slowly. He looks at me after each bite, patiently waiting for me to continue.

Taking a deep breath, I glance around the deck. There's no one out here, but I'd rather check and be safe, than open my mouth in front of Petra, or worse, Yuke. The door is still closed. Whoever opened it earlier must have decided to stay inside. Once I'm satisfied that we're truly alone, I look Eren in the face seriously. I rest my elbows on the table and lean forward like I'm about to question him within an inch of his life.

Except, I'll most likely be the one answering questions in the end.

"I'm giving you permission to judge me all you want. But please don't tell anyone. Especially anyone here at TST," I plead.

"You're starting to scare me. Spit it out." He wipes a bit of chili from the corner of his mouth, and my eyes follow the motion of the napkin. His lips are smooth and pink against his dark beard. I find myself dazed, staring for a second too long.

Focus, Ellie. What is wrong with you?

"So, you know how I'm a travel agent?" I return to the subject at hand, splaying my fingers out and staring down at them. It's a rough start, but it's a start.

"Duh. And a great one too."

I'd love to bask in the glory of the compliment, but it'll have to wait. "Thank you," I say shortly. "But...um...the kicker is..."

Eren's thick eyebrows shoot higher and higher as my voice falters. "Go on," he urges.

Leaning closer, I drop my voice to a whisper. "The kicker is...I've never actually traveled."

His eyebrows plummet, furrowing so low they nearly touch the tops of his cheeks. "What are you talking about? Yuke doesn't hire people who don't have first-hand experience."

"She does if they tell really good lies during their interviews," I admit flatly.

Eren drops the spoon into the empty bowl. His eyes never leave my face. "So you mean you've only been to a few places? That's fine. As long as you have the basic experience you have the resources to plan anything. Y'all do it all the time."

"No," I argue, my voice rising in an attempt to gain his

understanding. "Eren, when I say I've never traveled, I mean I've never traveled. Anywhere."

"Internationally, right? That's not so—"

"I've never left Jacksonville!"

Struck by the element of surprise, Eren's mouth falls open. His expression doesn't scare me. If anything, I feel the opposite of regret. It's out in the open. One person knows, and he's one of the people I trust the most. Whatever happens from here, I at least have the satisfaction of knowing the guilt-laden weight on my chest has lightened a little.

"I have questions." He runs a hand through his hair. "So many questions."

"And I have answers."

The kitchen door swings open. This time, Lamar steps out, followed by Rick. The two of them sit at the picnic table on the other side of the patio. Lamar waves in our direction and Rick grins at me. "The two E's! Beautiful day out, don't you think?"

Our conversation has come to an end, whether I like it or not. I pull my empty container away from Eren and screw the cap back onto my water bottle. We're no longer alone, and with that, I feel the need to run. There's no way Lamar and Rick know anything just by looking at us, but I feel unsettled, like my secret is fluttering around in the air and they're going to pluck it from flight with their lunch-covered fingers.

"Ellie," Eren says, forcing my attention down to him as I stand up. His fingers have found their way to my wrist. The gentle touch sends sparks up my arm and I pull away, growing more nervous by the second. "It's fine. You're okay. We'll talk more later."

And like always, I believe him.

CHAPTER 12

EREN

You really think you know people.

At the beginning of the week, I thought I knew Kristen. I thought I knew Ellie. Four days later, both of them have surprised the hell out of me in completely different ways. It's mind-blowing. I have to wonder, do I really know anybody? Are my brothers harboring big secrets? My parents?

Am I harboring something that I've somehow suppressed into non-existence? It's far- fetched, but I entertain the thought anyway. No wonder I've only accomplished the bare minimum at work this week. Unfinished flight schedules are piling up like unused firewood in Florida.

Ellie hasn't messaged or emailed me at all this afternoon. I'm sure she's embarrassed. And nervous. She's probably biding her time, waiting to see if I go running to Yuke's office to rat her out. Hopefully she knows me better than that, though. I'm more curious than anything. And far from mad at her. If I know Ellie as well as I think I do, she lied for a good reason.

She's never left the city of *Jacksonville*. How is she so fucking good at her job?

My butt leaves my chair soon as 5:00 rolls around. Ellie most likely won't leave for at least another ten minutes, but I don't want to risk missing her. I'll hang out at reception and bother Jade for a few, then bombard Ellie at the front door. It's a full proof plan.

Except Jade has already peaced out by the time I make it downstairs.

Plan B, then.

Hoisting my messenger back higher onto my shoulder, I march toward the sales room. All five of the agents are still there, wrapping up who knows what. Just like they don't actually understand what I do, I also don't understand exactly what they do. Performing a quick observation, I note that no one is on a phone call.

"Ellie!" Everyone looks up at me as I enter. "It's time to go."

"Are you two going on a hot date or something?" Lucia jokes. I happen to look in Rick's direction in time to catch the briefest flicker of jealousy pass over his features. Bingo. Another clue to confirm my hidden suspicion that Rick is in love with his cubicle neighbor.

"Nope, she just works too much and I want to annoy her with some flight details as she tries to escape the premises."

AKA: I want to get all of the *dirty* details I didn't get at lunch.

"I don't know about Ellie, but *I'm* out of here," Sherry announces, standing up to collect her purse. "Eren, you know better than to ask *me* questions after five so don't try it."

"Wouldn't dream of it, Sher," I quip, giving her an ass-kissing grin as she approaches the exit. She pushes her way past me and disappears.

"If any of us called her Sher she would smite us." Lamar stares at me in awe.

"I call her Sher," Rick jumps in.

71

"You called her that *once*," Lamar lectures. "She told you to never do it again."

Lucia giggles in the corner. Rick's cheeks flush red and he shrugs at me before settling back into silence. Ellie is gathering her stuff and silently watching the events play out over the top of her cube. She looks in my direction and I tap my imaginary watch, pressing her to hurry. When she eventually walks toward me, she moves with the rigidity of someone who suspects they're potentially going to fall into a trap.

"Goodnight, everyone," she says over her shoulder.

"See y'all t'morry, ya hear?" I add in my best faux Southern accent, tipping an imaginary cowboy hat as I back into the hallway. Lamar laughs, which lessens the burden of the steely gaze Rick fixes me with.

Damn. Maybe Ellie's right and he is somewhat of an asshole underneath that charming exterior.

Ellie stays silent as she shrugs on her jacket, then exits the building, holding the door open for me to follow. I breathe deeply, enjoying the freshness of the air after being holed up inside for hours. The sun is rapidly falling in the sky and shadows have already cloaked the car-lined street. Goosebumps form on my arms, but I don't mind. When you're a big guy, the chill is often welcome.

"Are you planning to follow me home or something?" Ellie breaks the silence, squinting up at me as we turn on to the sidewalk.

"Possibly." I stop in front of my car. "Unless I can convince you to get a drink with me and confess all of your secrets?"

I study her face, waiting for a response. A single freckle sits on the top of her right cheek, just below her eye. Has that always been there?

Obviously it has, but why haven't I noticed it? It's cute. For some reason, I want to run my thumb across it.

"I can't." Her voice breaks the freckle spell.

That was...new. What are we talking about again?

"That's okay," I say once I remember, trying not to look too disappointed.

"It's not that I don't want to. But I have to get home to let Brat out and give him dinner. Neither of my uncles will be home for another hour or so."

"I completely understand." I smile and unlock my car, opening the passenger door to put my bag in the seat. "I'll just look forward to chatting more about 'you know what' at lunch tomorrow."

"That won't work either. Tomorrow is the meeting, so everyone will have lunch together," she reminds me.

"Dammit, I forgot." I fold my arms over the top of the open car door, leaning into it.

"Eren." Ellie takes a step closer to my car and absent-mindedly runs a finger through the dust on the side mirror. "I told you my secret because you're a good friend and I trust you. I'm happy to explain further whenever you have questions—whenever we have time away from listening ears."

Right on queue, Rick and Lamar burst out of the TST building. They amble off in different directions, calling good-byes to each other. Rick is parked behind me and he gives us a final wave before settling behind the steering wheel of his truck. He pulls away from the curb, glaring at me through the window as he passes.

Does he always scowl at me like that when he thinks I'm not paying attention?

"So...never then," I joke.

"Drama king." She backs away, heels pointing in the direc-tion she needs to go. "There will be plenty of time. I'll see you tomorrow for our *super fun* meeting day."

With a final sheepish grin, she turns and begins her trek

home, heels clicking on the sidewalk. "Have a good night!" I call after her.

She's barely made it a few feet when she comes to a stand-still, turning to look at me through the deepening evening darkness before she stares down at her shoes. "Eren..." Her voice is softer, similar to the customer service tone she uses with clients on the phone. "Do you view me any differently?"

Since I've known her, I've learned that Ellie's vulnerable moments are few and far between—almost non-existent really. Her question makes my heart swell a little. There's something about knowing that a person legitimately trusts you. Sharing a secret is their way of saying, *Hey, I'm choosing you to help me carry this, because you're important to me.* With as many people I've met over the years, as many "friends" as I have, it's still rare that I bask in the feeling of being needed by someone.

Kristen would tell me I'm looking too far into the situation, but her opinion is no longer one that I should value so highly.

"Not even a little bit," I tell Ellie.

Her cheeks redden. She pulls a hand from her pocket and runs it once through her short hair, then continues on her way with the slightest bit more pep in her step. I stare after her, somehow still thinking about the freckle.

I eventually shut the passenger door and slump against my car. Another night of being without someone to share it with stretches before me. I've never learned how to appreciate alone time.

Outside of traveling, I can't say I have any hobbies to keep myself busy. I rarely read. I'm the least coordinated person I know, so I don't go to the gym or do any other form of exercise unless my brothers force me to. (Even though I probably should, since I'm not getting any younger and my doctor, who also happens to be my older brother, stays on my back about potential health decline in my thirties.)

The only thing I occasionally do is get sucked into a television show, and even then I prefer to enjoy it with someone sitting next to me. Maybe it's time to call my brothers. I won't be able to avoid their endless questioning about Kristen forever, and it may as well occur sooner rather than later.

Imagining one or both of them on the couch with me is better than no one. The chill of the evening is seeping through my shirt. I lift myself to standing and get in the car, starting it and embarking on my normal drive to I-95 while I go through a mental list of shows I've been meaning to start. I carefully consider each option.

What types of shows does Ellie like to watch?

The thought comes out of left field, but I entertain it. Before I know it, I'm imagining Ellie on the couch next to me, laughing at some over-delivered one liner, the light of the TV illuminating the freckle underneath her eye. She's focused on the screen, but I'm focused on her.

I pull into the parking spot in front of my apartment door. It's not until I shut off the car's engine that I realize I just spent my thirty-minute drive thinking about Ellie Amos. And none of the thoughts had anything to do with what she told me earlier today.

Good Morning TST-ers,

Happy Friday! As you all know, we have our office-wide meeting today. We'll start with lunch at noon, and then the phones will be shut off for the remainder of the day so we can gather without interruption.

I hope to finish up around 2:00, and you'll all be free to go for the day unless you have something you need to finish up.

You may want to bring something to take notes with, but other than that nothing is needed!

Looking forward to having everyone together for a couple of hours.

Best wishes,
Yuke Tanaka
President
Top Secret Travel

CHAPTER 13

ELLIE

The world feels brand new today.

For the first time since being hired at TST, I wake up feeling the slightest sense of peace about the lie that got me there—the lie that allows me to stay there. With Eren being my friend, telling him may have technically been the easy step forward. But the confession was enough to lighten the burden and prove to myself that I'm capable of making things right in the future.

Am I the only person who has ever lied to get a job? No. But do I also feel weighed down by dishonesty more than the average human? Absolutely. I learned that very quickly.

I practically float across the floor as I move around my apartment to get ready. I spend an extra five minutes in the shower with a hair mask. I shave my legs, even though I know I'll be wearing pants. I don't gag while brushing my teeth. I carefully wing out my eyeliner while applying my makeup, which I never do. I treat myself to a bowl of Cinnamon Toast Crunch for breakfast.

Even the process of hopping and wiggling into my new Good American jeans—that I landed on major sale—can't crush my spirit. I'm a freshly unencumbered woman. The waistband of my denim will not get me down today.

The uncles are leaving through their backdoor as I reach the bottom of the stairs. "Oooh, a little leather jacket look today," Uncle Sai says, looking my outfit over. "I'm into it."

"Thanks!" I place a hand on my hip and give them my best model spin.

"It's a bit edgy for my taste." Uncle Rob turns to lock up, giving Brat a kiss through the window as he does so. "But you do look nice."

"I bet Rick Hunkyson will like it." Uncle Sai gives me an evil grin. In his black suit he looks like the villain character from a white-collar television drama.

"And...that's my cue to head out!" I roll my eyes at them as I walk away. "Happy Friday, I hope you have a terrible day after that comment!"

"I bet Eren will like it, too!" Uncle Rob calls after me. "Have a good day, we love you!"

Luckily my back is already turned so they can't see the redness that creeps up my neck and into my cheeks. Somewhere behind me, the garage door opens and I hear their cars start up and back out to leave around the other side of the house. They're probably both still chortling at their little jokes behind the steering wheels.

Just as I suspected, they did indeed give me the third degree about Eren's visit on Tuesday night. *So that's the famous Eren Polat!* Uncle Rob had said. *You've never mentioned how tall, dark and beautiful he is.*

He looks like a broad-shouldered vampire, Uncle Sai had added. *If vampires were adorable and cuddly.*

After they had gotten the gossipy compliments out of their systems, they seemed somewhat disappointed about why Eren had actually come to visit. They also refused to believe that I've never had a romantic fantasy about him. If they knew what Jade had mentioned to me in the bathroom yesterday, they would really have a field day, especially now that they know Eren is single.

Damn, I really need to go on a date soon or these two are never going to lay off the constant commentary of the males in my life. Thank god said date won't actually be with Rick or Eren. Then they'd really have something to hold over my head.

I've fantasized about going on a date with Rick so many times. But what would it be like to go on a date with Eren? Is he a dinner and a movie type of guy, or does he prefer something more involved? Does he like to hold hands? Does he kiss on the first date? Does he—

Fucking stop it, Ellie! I shake my head to clear my thoughts as I come to a crosswalk. A driver in a blue van stops to wave me forward, and I almost wish they would hit me as I traipse across the road. Maybe that would set my brain back onto the straight and narrow. When I turn into my usual coffee shop, I stand in the entrance to take a few deep breaths of fresh espresso. It calms me down, reviving my predetermined decision to have a good day.

At the last second, I decide to grab a coffee for Eren too. As a thank you for yesterday, of course. I know he'll drink it even if he's already had one.

It's warmer out today. So much so that I almost wish I had removed my jacket before making the second leg of my walk. Between the leather sleeves against my skin and the two steaming lattes in my hands, I feel like I'm going to melt before I make it to TST's front door. I curse Florida for the rapid weather change, fighting to hold tightly to the final thread that my positive mindset is hanging by.

"Hold on, I'll get that for you!" Rick's voice floats over my shoulder as I ascend the office steps. He takes the stairs two at a time, rushing to open the door for me. A cloud of his cologne forms around us and he smiles down at me as he steps to the side for me to enter first. His grin is so sincere and his action so kind that I find myself dopily twinkling back at him. He's wearing a Jacksonville Jaguars t-shirt and a pair of dark jeans. His casual appearance makes me weak in the knees.

"Thank you," I say, setting the coffees on the entry table long enough to remove my jacket. My body temperature immediately begins to drop to a more comfortable level and relief washes over me.

"Is one of those for me?" Rick jokes, side-eying the coffees.

"You wish." I mean for the statement to have an heir of sarcasm but it definitely sounds more flirtatious instead.

"Well darn." He hangs his head in mock disappointment, peering at me through his eyelashes. This one-on-one attention from him is certain to make me drop the two piping beverages on the floor. Perhaps that's what he's aiming for? He would probably think of it as a funny little office prank.

"Maybe one day you'll be lucky enough to receive a morning treat from me," I offer.

"I look forward to it, El." He leaves me standing by the coat rack.

Once I'm out of shock and able to move, I take the stairs to the second floor. It's still dark, the only bit of light coming from underneath Yuke's closed office door at the far end of the upstairs hall. Faint typing sounds escape from the crack. Her "Do Not Disturb" sign hangs from the door knob.

I shuffle into Eren's tiny excuse for an office and go around to the other side of his desk. Stealing one of his sticky notes, I draw a smiley face and adhere it to the lid of his paper coffee cup. Curiosity overcomes me and I can't help but take a quick survey of his desk. It's not messy, but not exactly overly neat either. The framed photo of him and Kristen has disappeared. On his desktop calendar, COLORADO is written in giant letters across the dates of our Thanksgiving break.

Colorado.

I imagine snow-capped mountains covered in elk and moose. To me, it seems like another world. To Eren, it's his home away from home, now that his parents live there. My own parents sent me a postcard from Keystone, Colorado once. I'm sure it's tucked away in the box in the back corner of my closet, with the rest of the postcards they've sent me over the past 26 years.

It's one of the few thoughtful things they've managed to do for their only child.

On the way downstairs, I pass Walt and we exchange morning pleasantries. He barely looks up from the article he's reading on his phone. After peeking into reception to say hello to Jade, I finally make it to my own desk.

It's almost 8:00. I may as well be running late. Rick makes a nearly word-for-word comment of the same observation. Is he a mind reader now? Because that's something I can't put up with.

The morning progresses rapidly. Everyone seems to be procrastinating more than usual. A collective mindset of, *We have a meeting soon, so what's the point?* is wafting through TST. I'm half-heartedly working on a new travel planner for Belgium, switching over to my browser every few minutes to search eBay for new name-brand clothes that I wouldn't be able to afford otherwise.

An I.M. pops up on the screen, blocking the vintage Dooney and Bourke purse I had been inspecting.

Eren Polat:
Thanks for the coffee! I was already one deep, but a second never hurts.

Seeing his name makes my heart give an odd little lurch inside my chest. My fingers pause above the keyboard. I can't decide what makes me more weirded out—diagnosing myself with a heart murmur, or having chest flutters at the mere thought of Eren.

Jade and my uncles should be ashamed of themselves for planting such outrageous ideas in my head.

Ellie Amos:
No problem! I owed you one from the other day.

My cardiovascular health returns to normal and I click back to the travel planner. I type a single sentence and pivot back to eBay, where I place a bid on the bag to reward myself for a job well done. Another pop-up appears, this time a one hour meeting reminder that arrives in time with everyone else's. On my right, Sherry makes an irritated sound that isn't all too different from a growl.

"One hour, everyone!" Lamar designates himself as our human alarm.

"We KNOW!" Sherry and Lucia bellow.

To my left, Rick laughs quietly. It's one of his genuine laughs, the type that makes me want to be responsible for whatever he found humorous. The type that makes me want to curl up next to him and stare at him while the sound escapes his lips. I wonder what he would think if he knew I was smiling at him through our cubicle barrier.

My computer chimes for a third time and I assume Eren is replying. My insides are free of butterflies this time and I breathe a sigh of relief. The calm doesn't last long though, because this I.M. is not from Eren Polat, but from someone who is less than five feet away and usually prefers to bother me with questions face-to-face.

Rick Williamson:
Hi

My motor skills malfunction. Unable to type properly, I tap out a response with my index fingers. The action ages me by at least twenty years.

Ellie Amos:
Are you really messaging me instead of breathing over my shoulder right now? Lol

Rick Williamson:
Is it illegal to tell you hello or something?

Ellie Amos:
Only in a few states.

He laughs again and I glow from the inside out. What have I done to deserve this honor? I lean forward onto my elbows and stare at his name on my screen. Taking a quick peek over my shoulder, I confirm that he's not sneaking up to catch me basking in the glow of his conversation. I calm down as I listen to him typing, accepting that something work-related is bound to burst my bubble. But it doesn't. At least not yet.

Rick Williamson:
How is your day going? What are your thoughts on the meeting?

Ellie Amos:
It's fine. I'm working on something for Belgium. How about you?

Ellie Amos:
Honestly, I haven't thought about the meeting much. I assume it's just basic office overview stuff.

Rick Williamson:
Cool. I haven't done anything for Belgium yet. And same here, I'm mainly excited we'll get to go home early. Don't tell anyone though. ;)

He's sent me my own personal winky face. I consider taking a screenshot, emailing it to myself, and setting it as my phone's lock screen background. That would be a completely normal thing to do.

Ellie Amos:
Your secret is safe with me. Any plans for the weekend?

Rick Williamson:
I have tickets for the Jags game on Sunday, but that's about it. Do you like football?

I scrunch my nose in distaste.

Ellie Amos:
Not in the slightest. No offense!

Rick Williamson:
That's too bad.

Ellie Amos:
Why do you care? :)

Rick Williamson:
Because maybe I was going to ask if you'd like to go to the game with me on Sunday. I have an extra ticket.

My brain completely shuts down. And not just my ability to process information. The signals that allow me to move my fingertips (or any part of my body, for that matter) are blocked. Caput. Defective. I'm frozen with my hands hovering above the keyboard. Whether it's been ten seconds or ten years, I couldn't tell you.

Yuke will have to have me physically removed from the vicinity. Where will I go? Perhaps I can be a statue in the *Museum of People Who Were Blindsided by Their Crush Asking Them On a Date.*

Or is it a date, in his mind? Perhaps he's asked everyone in his life. And in the office. And I'm simply the last resort.

Yeah, that sounds more like it.

Rick Williamson:
Ellie? Are you still alive over there? Sorry if I made you uncomfortable.

I watch Rick's new message populate on the screen. The timestamps show that there's a three minute window between this one and his last one. I've been sitting here contemplating my entire existence for three minutes. I need to reply before he decides to check on me in person.

Ellie Amos:
Why would you want me to go with you?

My sarcasm is still buffering so I choose to be blunt. My heart beats in time with his fingers on the keyboard, slightly muted by the thin wall between us. There's no nervous clambering in the gait of his fingers, just pure Rick Williamson confidence.

Rick Williamson:
I don't know...I guess I thought it would be cool to hang out with you. Get to know you a bit outside of the office.

Ellie Amos:

Don't take this the wrong way, but I've always assumed you've viewed me as barely tolerable.

Rick Williamson:

Hm. In my mind we've been caught up in a prolonged flirting episode.

Oh my god.

Uncle Rob's theory has just been proven fact. And hasn't Eren been telling me this for months, too? Haven't I been harboring some fantasy version of this myself? Secretly dreaming up make-believe conversations similar to this one that I just assumed would never happen because I have so little confidence in myself, let alone the possibility that the hottest man in the office could ever look in my direction for anything other than work advice?

Ellie Amos:

I'm...not good at this stuff. I don't know what to say. Let me get this straight, you are asking me on a date, right?

Rick Williamson:

Yes. If you're open to it. But since you hate football let's nix the game idea and come up with another plan. I don't want you to be miserable.

HALLELUJAH.

Ellie Amos:

Um...ok. Why not? Question though...why has it taken you this long to bring this up?

Rick Williamson:
I don't know. It's Friday. It's a short work day because of the meeting. I'm feeling confident. No time like the present I suppose.

Ellie Amos:
And this isn't a prank?

Rick Williamson:
No! And to be honest even further, I figured asking now would give me some idea of whether or not you and Eren are more than friends.

Ellie Amos:
NO!!! Eren and I...it's not a thing. Why does everyone all of a sudden think that? We're good friends.

Rick Williamson:
I'm glad I made my move then. :) Can I have your number? I'll text you this weekend if that's cool.

I've officially gone from barely being able to move, to vibrating with energy. I'm shaking, and I don't know if it's from nervousness or sheer disbelieving excitement. It takes a few tries to correctly type out my cell number and send it to him. He responds with a simple smiley face, ending the conversation.

Then the real panic sets in. I'm suddenly aware of how full my bladder is, but terrified to get up and go to the bathroom because that will put me in the position of having to pass behind him. What if he turns to look at me? I'll collapse onto the floor. How am I supposed to physically exist in his proximity for the rest of the day?

I can't wait to tell Eren. He's going to flip.

CHAPTER 14

EREN

Ellie walks into the conference room and I hold my hand up to beckon her to the empty seat next to me. She squeezes past Lamar and I and drops into the chair, her leather jacket rustling as she settles in. The leather smell mixes with her usual perfume in the air around us and I want to bury my face into her neck and breathe in deeply.

That's so fucking weird, Eren, I chastise myself.

"How's your day been?" she asks. She seems slightly jumpy, tapping her heel on the ground and running her hands across the top of her jeans. Her usual serious expression has been altered somehow. I study her face and realize the corners of her lips are both turned up, like she's in a constant state of trying to suppress a grin. Is she overstimulated by the crowded room? Or maybe just in a good mood?

"The usual," I answer, still scrutinizing her. "You seem... excited? Did you make a big sale or something?"

"Or something. I'll tell you about it later." She crosses her legs and settles her notebook onto her thigh, which I can't help but notice looks amazing in her form-fitting jeans, before uncapping her pen. She writes the date, followed by the word

MEETING in giant letters across the top line. My single, crumpled sheet of notebook paper looks lazily unprepared in comparison.

People continue to trickle into the room, filling the seats around us. Rick pauses to give Lamar and I a fist bump before claiming the chair directly behind Ellie. It seems whatever was souring his mood yesterday has passed. Beside me, Ellie stiffens. She reaches up to tuck her hair behind her ears. I try to catch her eye but she stares straight ahead.

Yuke makes her entrance with a notebook in one hand and a steaming cup of coffee in the other. Petra flits in behind her, bombarding her with questions in that nerve-inducing way that only Petra has. Yuke's calm demeanor never falters, an encouraging smile on her face to counteract the unnecessarily panicked one on Petra's. Yuke arranges her things on the podium at the front of the room and politely guides Petra to the only empty seat in the front row.

"Here we go. Two hours of TST fun," I whisper to Ellie dramatically, even though I know it won't be that bad. She continues to stare at her notebook but one corner of her mouth quirks further upward.

"Do we seem to be missing anyone?" Yuke's gentle voice elevates slightly when she addresses the room, glancing around the crowd and comfortably holding eye contact as she connects with different faces.

"Not that I can tell!" Petra pipes in over other randomly mumbled replies. "I think we're all accounted for, Yuke."

Sometimes I forget that Petra isn't actually Yuke's assistant. She just seems to step into the role, even when help is never requested. Any boss less patient than Yuke would have put Petra in her place a long time ago.

"Good, good." Yuke takes a careful sip of her coffee and smooths the collar of her shirt. "Did you all enjoy lunch?"

The room fills with nods and a chorus of thank you's.

She'd provided pizza from a favorite local spot a couple of blocks away. Free pizza is never a bad thing. And when the pizza is anything above mediocre, the excitement over it reaches the equivalent of being rewarded for reading a certain number of books in elementary school. Pizza enthusiasm never falters at any age. Did I have to eat it at my desk in order to finish my work for the day instead of joining everyone else in the break room? Sure. But did I enjoy it any less? Nope.

"We're going to try to make this as quick as possible so everyone can get out of here and enjoy their weekends," Yuke continues. "I just ask that you all stay focused because the few things we'll be discussing apply to each person in this room, in one way or another."

Ellie elbows me in the side and points to something she's written on her notepad.

Do you think we're about to get fired?

Smirking, I scrawl a quick reply on my own paper and angle it in her direction.

I don't think she would make that a public event, ha ha.

We return our attention to the front of the room. Petra has angled her chair slightly, giving herself a better vantage point to glance around the room with her beady eyes and make sure everyone is paying attention. She really missed her opportunity to have a career as a spy, or something else that relishes in the art of butt-kissing.

"First, I want to go over the numbers for 2019, since we're coming up on the end of the year." Yuke gives a thumbs up to Marvin, our resident I.T. guru. He points a remote to the projector on the ceiling and a PowerPoint fills the wall to Yuke's right. I look at the list of figures on the slide and immediately zone out. I can't help it.

Kill me.

I write it in my smallest handwriting and show it to Ellie. She covers her mouth to hide a grin and tries to stay focused on the presentation.

I attempt to follow her lead. Through my zoning out, I do manage to hear what are probably the most important pieces of this segment of the meeting. Phrases like "our highest earning year so far" and "you'll be seeing some nice holiday bonuses" enter one ear and momentarily pique my interest before they escape out the other. I'm in the midst of dozing off when Ellie elbows me again.

You-know-who asked me on a date.

Energy jolts through my veins and my slowly-dying body boots back to life. I'm pretty sure there's only one person who could be "you-know-who," but I have to fact check.

R.W.?

I become increasingly aware of Rick's presence behind us and making sure to shield the paper with my body. I stare at her out of the corner of my eye. She nods, so slightly it wouldn't even register as movement to anyone not looking for it.

My stomach falls. The sensation is so unexpected I wonder if I'm about to have a pizza-induced episode of diarrhea and I quickly map out my potential escape route. My heart thuds against my ribs and I take a couple of deep breaths, willing my digestive system to calm down. This isn't the reaction of excitement that I should have for my friend right now. I wipe my clammy palms on my jeans.

This feels a lot like...envy? But how could that be? Maybe in the sense that Ellie is about to have all of the goodness that comes with the start of a new relationship, while I continue to wallow in self-pity over the loss of mine? Yeah, that has to be it. Deep down I'm actually thrilled for her. Right? She's been dreaming about this since she first laid eyes on Rick.

I know he is into her too. And now that I have confirmation, I swear I can feel heat on the back of my neck from Rick's laser beam eyes. He wants to be the one writing secret messages to Ellie during this meeting.

Get in line, pal. The thought confuses me further.

"Any other questions or comments on this? You should all be very proud of yourselves!" I tune back into Yuke's voice, mentally re-joining my co-workers and making the mistake of glancing in Petra's direction. She's staring at Ellie and I with narrowed eyes. We've essentially been caught passing notes in class. With my confidence returned to its usual level, I stare back at her until she looks away. A couple of hands pop up and Yuke begins taking questions.

That's the best news ever.

I add with a quick flick of my pen. I think I mean it.

So why does it still feel like a lie? I've been begging Ellie to make her move with Rick since he started at TST.

"Moving on—the next item on the agenda is especially important for our sales team—our Secret Travel Agents." Yuke clasps her fingers together and leans forward onto the podium, propping herself up on her elbows. Ellie's attention diverts completely away from me and she slides to the edge of her seat, pen poised over her paper. Our Rick conversation is over. At least for now.

"If our numbers from the past couple of years prove anything, it's that TST is growing. With that growth, I imagine that we'll be ready to hire a few more agents over the next year as our clientele expands—probably one or two more air specialists too, so we don't burn poor Eren and Walt out." She glances at me briefly and smiles.

"And as the team grows, I plan to create a sales manager position. That way I can focus on the other aspects of the company and ensure our agents are getting all of the support and attention they require and deserve."

The energy in the room stills completely. All of the sales team members in my line of vision have taken up the same edge-of-their-seats stance as Ellie. Nothing grabs a person's attention as quickly as discussion of impending change. Especially when the change most likely involves a raise.

"Obviously I want to hire someone internally, and would like to do so by the first of the year. But we'll advertise on the job boards, too. Think it over, and if you're interested, email me or come see me." Yuke ends the announcement abruptly and doesn't even ask if anyone has questions. Ellie bristles beside me. Behind me, Rick's breathing pace has quickened. I don't have a clear view of Sherry, but I don't have to see her to know that she has already entered battle mode.

Yuke doesn't realize that she's just started a war. Or maybe she does, and that's why she shared the information so casually. I'm willing to bet most agents in the sales department will want that job. Not to mention, the future of sales kind of plays a pivotal part in how the company continues to progress, i.e., every other person in the office is going to want the absolute best person for the job. As if the holidays aren't already stressful enough.

Personally, there's no doubt in my mind that Ellie is the

right person to manage that department. Even knowing the secret that she just shared with me. She's unstoppable without actual travel experience. I can only imagine where she could take us once that changes. Or rather, *if* that changes.

This job has your name written all over it.

I angle my paper in her direction again. She doesn't respond, only gives me the tiniest shrug. Yuke continues on, covering various topics such as the annual holiday party and on-call protocol for the upcoming Thanksgiving break. A quick peek at my watch shows we're steadily creeping towards that 2:00 p.m. quit time that was informally promised to us. My leg begins to jiggle. I've been sitting here for too long.

"We're almost finished, I promise." Yuke flips to the last page of her agenda. "And you'll be happy to know, I've saved the best announcement for last."

During the course of the meeting, everyone has slowly slumped further into their chairs. Now, the group of bodies sits straight back up in unison, hopeful that the "good news" will be more than just another announcement of donuts in the breakroom.

"Some of you will remember this." She motions to Sherry, Walt, and a couple of other TST old-timers. "Back in 2008, we were forced to cut our annual employee travel perks. With the recession, we just couldn't keep it in the budget."

At the phrase "travel perks," we all sit up even straighter. Certain employees get to travel occasionally for business purposes, but the annual personal travel stipend for employees has been nothing more than a myth since I've been here. Is she really about to say what I hope she's about to say?

"I'm so excited to tell you, we'll be bringing this back. Every year, each employee will get a stipend to go towards a personal trip of your choice. Flights aren't included in that—

we'll keep those in a separate budget. So the entire stipend can go towards lodging, in-country travel, food, and so forth."

The room erupts with claps and cheers. We're all pumping our fists, giving each other high fives, and yelling thank-you's to Yuke. Petra has a proud look on her face. With her hands directly on the company's money, she's probably known about and been holding this in for some time. Yuke is beaming. She must be thrilled to be in a place to offer this to her employees again.

I turn to Ellie to give her a fist bump, but she isn't celebrating. She's staring straight ahead, wide-eyed, her fingers twisted together on top of her notebook.

"At the beginning of January, we'll get started on a travel schedule, so we don't have more than one or two people gone at the same time. This obviously won't eat any of your other assigned vacation time up. However, there is one person who I would love to give the opportunity of being the first to go, and that is our current top-of-the-books agent, Ellie Amos."

More claps erupt. Rick reaches forward to give Ellie a little squeeze on her shoulders. For a moment, I want to slap his hands away. Instead I reach over to pull her into a side hug, feeling Rick's hands recoil from beneath my arm. Ellie is stiff as a board beneath my embrace, barely pasting a half-assed smile onto her otherwise terrified face.

What's wrong with her? There may be more to her recent confession than I previously thought.

"Start thinking about your trip, Ellie," Yuke tells her with a proud grin. "You can travel as soon as you'd like, even before the year is over. Maybe over your Christmas break?"

CHAPTER 15

ELLIE

My butt is frozen to the chair. I can sense the excited chaos around me, the happy smiles and congratulations from my co-workers, but I can't react with any form of communication other than a fake, dead smile. Everyone's voices sound like they're coming through three pairs of ear muffs. My vision has tunneled. I can only see Yuke and her excitement over being able to give every employee in this room the ultimate gift.

If only I could return the enthusiasm. How do I tell Yuke that I can't accept this perk? How do I tell her that I don't want to go? That I *can't* go? I took this job knowing that the travel perks were on hold. But I've failed to prepare for what I would do if they were ever returned to us.

My brain is flooded by nausea-inducing dread. Just a couple of hours ago, I walked into this conference room with a brief high that only confessing your biggest secret to your best friend, and being asked out by your crush, can bring. The sales manager announcement alone was enough to flip my small world upside down. And now this.

I can't tell Yuke I don't want to travel without telling her everything else. If I tell her everything else, I'll never be the new sales manager. I probably won't even be a part of the TST team anymore. I'll be back on the job hunt, with the only career that has ever made me happy slowly fading into my past.

I'm going to have to quit. The entertainment of the thought brings tears to my eyes. The room is emptying around me. Everyone is leaving to go enjoy their weekends. I still can't move.

"El?" Eren stands and steps in front of me. "Are you coming?"

I look up at him. A single tear rolls down my cheek before I can stop it. Eren's face falls, concern taking over his features. He says nothing else, just holds a hand out to help me stand up. Cautiously, I look around to see if anyone else is here to witness my embarrassment. To my relief, we're alone.

"Come on." Still clutching my hand, he pulls me towards the door. "Get your stuff. Let's go somewhere to talk."

Back in the hallway, Eren releases me and heads up the stairs to collect his things while I go to the sales room for mine. Upon entering, I receive more exclamations of congratulations. "Where are you going to go?" Lamar asks. "I don't know when it will be my turn, but I already have a plan in mind."

"Oh. Um, I'm not sure yet," I reply, shoving my phone deep into my bag and avoiding eye contact. "I hope you all have a good weekend!" I call with fake sincerity as I go to leave the room.

Rick's hand gently catches my wrist as I pass his cubicle. My breath catches in my throat at his touch—the first physical contact we've had since he first started and I shook his hand. "I'll text you this weekend," he says under his breath, smiling up at me from his rolling chair.

"I'll be looking for it," I say, rushing away before he can see the blush in my cheeks or the remaining tears in my eyes.

Eren leads us out to his car and opens the passenger door for me. Every emotion in my body seems to be pooling in my brain and I don't have the energy to try and shake him off, so I plop into the worn leather seat. He closes the door and I'm enveloped by the smell inside of the car—the smell of Eren. It's spicy, with a hint of floral that I recognize from his shampoo. I always mean to ask him what he uses, but he would probably tell me, "Oh, it's just Suave" and then I'd be really annoyed that he has the most perfect head of hair I've ever seen in my life.

A fresh breeze flows into the car as he slides into the driver's seat. He fastens his seatbelt and turns to look at me, silently searching my face. The air feels thick between us. I don't think our faces have ever been this close. His dark eyes keep flicking to a spot on my cheek, and I reach up to touch it self-consciously. Shaking his head, he licks his lips and my heart gives a little flutter. Instinctively, I scoot away and press myself against the door.

What is going on with me?

"I wish you knew how much restraint I'm practicing in not immediately begging you to tell me what's wrong." Eren's voice fills the silence before he puts his keys in the ignition and starts the engine. "I can only assume that it's something to do with your recent confession."

"More like a deeper level of my recent confession," I say. "Is this the part where you kidnap me, by the way?"

He checks his side mirror before pulling away from the curb and grins at me devilishly. "I was just going to take you home, but kidnapping works too."

"Home is great." I fasten my own seat belt even though the drive can't be more than two minutes.

Eren's presence has momentarily calmed me, but by the time we reach the first stop sign my thoughts are back in full force. What am I going to do? I can't go on this trip. I can't continue working at TST. Should I spend my weekend drafting a resignation letter? My breathing quickens and the belt sits too tightly against my chest. I pull it away from me in a panic.

"Hey," Eren says calmly. He reaches over to place a hand on my knee, and the warmth of his palm seeps through my jeans. It's not meant to be sexual, but my heart gives another weird lurch. I've never noticed how lithe his fingers are—like a pianist, or a surgeon.

TST. Rick. Eren.

It's becoming very difficult to differentiate between all of the confusion in my life.

"Ellie," he continues softly. "You can talk to me. I'm not going to rat you out to Yuke, or judge you, or whatever else you're afraid of."

I roll the window down and let the breeze cool my face. Eren retracts his hand and I immediately miss the comfort. Familiar houses appear and then disappear as we drive, and I know we're only seconds away from our destination.

"Here's one positive," Eren says with a little more pep in his tone. "I know you've never traveled before, but now you'll have the chance to!"

Oh, sweet Eren. He just doesn't get it.

"It's...not just that I haven't had the opportunity to travel." My voice cracks. "It's a lot to explain."

"So help me understand." He stops in front of my uncle's house and puts the car in park. "I have all the time in the world. Well, some time anyway. I'm supposed to meet my brothers for burgers and beer."

Another beat of silence passes and I hear Brat bark inside

the house. I look towards the front door, where his smooshy face smiles at us from one of the entryway windows. I smile back at him out of habit before turning to the equally eager face in the car with me. Eren's dark eyes stare through my soul, his thick eyebrows raised in hopeful anticipation.

"Okay, I'll try." So I start at the beginning of getting hired at TST.

I tell him about my extensive preparation for the interview—about the research skills that continue to allow me to be successful in the job. I tell him that I accepted the job knowing there were no travel perks at the time, without giving thought to the fact it could be a possibility in the future. I tell him about the guilt that I carry every single day; the guilt that still doesn't outweigh how happy I've been at TST.

He listens quietly, interjecting only with the occasional nod or hum. I finish rambling and twist my fingers together in my lap, squeezing so hard I'm surprised none of the bones snap.

"I always knew you were smart," Eren says with a smirk. "But now I think you might possibly be a fucking genius. Ellie, that's a lot of extra effort to put into a job. You must really be happy in this position."

"It gets easier as time goes on. And I am happy. So happy. Or at least, I was. Now I don't know what to do."

"What do you mean?" he asks.

"I can't stay at TST, Eren. I can't...travel. And I'm afraid we're at the point where I can't keep my job if I don't." Tears fill my eyes as the realization sets back in.

"Why can't you? This is the perfect opportunity to start. And no one at work has to know the truth about everything up until now!" He attempts to twist in his seat to face me, but his large frame makes it difficult.

I have to tell him everything.

Eren and I have only recently reached a more personal level in our friendship. Typically, when you're getting to know someone, you're allowed to do it at your own pace, admitting hopes, fears, and traumas only when you're ready to. You can take your time, and decide when you're ready to provide them access to your vulnerability.

At least that's what I think. I've never really had the opportunity to build that type of friendship with someone, and it feels like Eren and I have suddenly jumped in full force, traveling at the speed of a runaway train. So all I can do is ask myself if I truly trust him.

And to my surprise, I do.

"Alright." I draw a deep breath and release it shakily. "I've lived with my uncles full-time since I was about 5 years old. My parents have always been a bit...nomadic."

"Okay," Eren says, his eyes never leaving my face.

"They don't like to stay in the same place longer than they have to. They've never even owned a house. They've lived in a travel camper full-time since they were married. And for this reason, because they love freedom so much, they never wanted children."

Realization washes over his features as he realizes where I'm possibly going.

"Anyway, along came me, obviously. The excitement of having me, of having something new, was enough for them for a little while. We lived together in their camper, here in Jacksonville. My Uncle Rob thought maybe I was the fix to their spontaneity, that maybe they would learn how to live an adventurous life, but with me included."

"So what happened?" Eren asks, invested.

"When I was five, they dropped me off with Uncle Rob and left for a trip to the Grand Canyon. They were only supposed to be gone for a couple of weeks, but on day seven they called and said they were going to extend the vacation. Sure, no big deal, right?" I say sarcastically.

"Maybe it wouldn't be a big deal if you didn't have a 5 year old waiting for you across the country."

"It gets worse." I swallow the lump in my throat. "A couple of days after that, I ended up in the hospital with acute appendicitis. It was really serious. I was so young, but I can still remember everything...the pain, the I.V., the smell of the hospital. Uncle Rob was beside himself. By the time he reached my parents, I had been out of surgery for two days."

"Please tell me they came straight home," Eren begs.

I answer him with a blank stare, which delivers the same impact as a "No."

"They finally made it home another three weeks later, bringing me back nothing but a t-shirt that was four sizes too large. They tried to brush the whole situation off, like it wasn't a big deal. That's when Uncle Rob lost it on them."

She's your DAUGHTER!

She needed you!

If you don't want to give her what she deserves, I will.

To this day, parts of the conversation randomly flow through my head. More than 20 years later, it still hurts. I swear I occasionally get phantom appendix pains, although it could actually just be the pain of being unwanted by your parents.

"When Uncle Rob offered to let me move in with him, they didn't even argue. They were almost...relieved." I shrug my shoulders.

Eren takes my hands, unraveling my fingers and holding them between his palms. They seem to fit perfectly, and I wish I could leave them in his comfort forever. "I'm so sorry, Ellie. You didn't deserve that. No one deserves that, especially you," he says.

"Now I just receive postcards." I stare at the roof of the

car, fighting the tears. "And every now and then they'll visit. But I stopped expecting the family reunion that I used to hope for."

"So your parents...they've given you a fear of travel?"

I consider his question. "It's not so much a fear of travel. It's a fear of leaving and having something bad happen. My parents left and I could have died while they were gone. I can only think of all the things that could happen if I leave—what if something bad happens to someone else?"

It's the first time I've verbalized the thought, and in words it's even deeper than imagined. In my mind, travel has always been intriguing and terrifying. A blessing and a curse. It's the thing that ripped my family apart, that could have led to a much worse situation if it wasn't for Uncle Rob.

Yet, in another way, I want to experience it more than anything. My parents must love it for a reason.

I look back at the front window of the house. Brat is gone and there are now lights on inside, which means someone is home. I want to go inside, but I also don't. I feel safe here... with Eren.

"I wish I had more words, Ellie. But I don't, and you know that's rare for me." He smiles sheepishly and I laugh. "But...maybe I can help you? Maybe we can work through this together. Maybe you can go on that trip Yuke offered, and stay at TST in the process."

I look at him skeptically, but don't dismiss him right away. There's so much hope in his expression. It makes me want to feel hopeful too.

"Perhaps you can start by traveling with me to get dinner and drinks with my brothers?" He releases my hands and holds his together like he's praying, pleading with his eyes.

"Fine. But only because you're catching me on a very confusing day where I would normally say no," I quip.

EVERYWHERE WE'VE NEVER BEEN

He slowly claps and starts the car. A strand of hair falls into his face and I almost reach out to tuck it away.

"And Ellie?" He looks at me one more time before turning to the steering wheel. "Thank you for trusting me with this. I've got you. I promise."

"I know you do." I let my shoulders relax as we get on the road, once again feeling a little less of the weight of the world on my back.

CHAPTER 16

EREN

I spot my brothers the second we walk into the dive bar, but that doesn't stop Tanner, my younger brother, from standing up and waving his arms at me like an over-caffeinated air traffic controller.

"Eren, over here," he yells, drawing the attention of every other patron in the room. "We got our favorite table!"

"I can see that, Tanner," I say through a laugh as I pull the chair across from him out for Ellie. She sits down awkwardly, a polite close-lipped smile plastered across her face. Tanner immediately hones in on her.

"And who is this?" he asks, sitting back down to stare at her like he's never seen a woman in his life.

"This is my friend, Ellie." I take my seat across from Adem, placing a hand on her shoulder when I say her name. "Ellie, these are my brothers—"

"Wait, THE Ellie?" Tanner interrupts. "TST Ellie?"

"In the flesh," Ellie jokes, extending her hand to Tanner. "Nice to meet you."

"Hey Ellie, I'm Adem," the eldest Polat, and calmer of my

two brothers, speaks for the first time. "We've heard a lot about you."

"Oh, you have?" she asks playfully, raising her eyebrows at me. "Good things, I hope."

"Only the best," I assure her with a wink.

"To what do we owe this pleasure?" Tanner takes a gulp of his beer before passing Ellie and I a menu to share. Her shoulder presses into mine as she leans over to look at it. I could just let her hold it—I've been here so often that I know my order by heart. But her close proximity and the smell of her leather jacket and perfume have me frozen in place, intoxicated before I've even had a single drink.

"It was a long day, so I invited Ellie to join us for a drink," I respond simply, forcing myself to stay still so she doesn't move her arm.

What is happening inside your head, Eren?

"How's it going, guys? You having your usual?" Ned, our typical server, asks as he comes to a halt at the end of our table.

"You've got us all figured out," Adem tells him. "Ellie, do you know what you'd like?"

"What are you having?" she asks me, looking up through her eyelashes.

"I always get a chocolate stout. And a double cheeseburger with mayo and pickles. They have the best burgers in town."

"That sounds great, I'll have the same." She takes the menu and passes it to Ned. My shoulder feels cold the second she pulls away.

A moment of silence passes between the four of us. Ellie twists her fingers in her lap nervously. Tanner and Adem keep their attention glued to her, smiling between sips of beer. I suddenly wonder if bringing Ellie along was the best idea. Just like I've joked about setting her up with one of my brothers, I've also told them how cool Ellie is more than once. Maybe they think this is finally their opportunity to battle it out for her hand in marriage. Or, at least for a date.

I can't think of anything I'd like less right now. Because, that would make Ellie uncomfortable. I would be fine with it, obviously.

Liar, says my new inner Ellie-related monologue.

"So, did you two have a good day?" I ask, pushing the thought away and settling on a safe subject.

"Meh...same old, same old." Tanner shrugs and runs a hand through hair the same color as mine, but much shorter.

"It's Friday, so no complaints." Adem raises his beer in cheers to the weekend.

"I don't think I've ever been more happy to see a Friday." Ellie's lips quirk slightly as she rests her chin in her palm.

"I bet Eren agrees with that," Tanner says. "After the week he's had with all of Kristen's shit..."

"Ellie, do you know about the Kristen shit?" Adem asks, pushing his glasses further up onto his nose.

"I do," Ellie confirms.

"I don't really think it's fair to call it that," I interject. "It was technically my shit too. 'Our shit,' if you wanna be super accurate."

"Has Eren ever told you about his curse, Ellie?" Tanner moves further into territory I was hoping to avoid and it takes everything in me to not kick him beneath the table.

Ned returns with mine and Ellie's drinks, not a second too soon. I down half of my pint in one gulp and suppress a burp. Why, why, WHY have I willingly put myself in this situation? I seriously need to start being a little less spontaneous. Maybe I'll actually start thinking ideas through instead of acting on instinct. It's going to be at the top of my New Year's resolutions a couple of months from now.

"Curse? Please, tell me more." Ellie leans forward, grinning at me before her attention returns to the two traitors I call family.

"It's the 'Twelve-Month Curse,'" Adem begins to explain. "All of Eren's relationships have ended around the one-year mark."

"All of them?" Ellie asks, turning to me again. She notices my flushed face and her smile falters out of concern.

"All twelve of them." Tanner adds more fuel to the fire that is my dating life.

"Twelve one-year relationships," Ellie says—more of a statement than a question.

"What can I say?" I lift my shoulders and try to force a bit of amusement into my tone. "I just really love being in love."

"But with love comes heartbreak," Adem interjects. "One heartbreak was enough for me. I can't imagine multiplying that. By *twelve*."

"This time next year it will be thirteen." Tanner laughs.

"Oh my god, the unluckiest number." Adem elbows Tanner and they continue to guffaw, once again attracting attention to our table.

"Hey, don't say that." Ellie's smile is completely gone now. "Maybe that's actually Eren's lucky number. No one ever said finding your soulmate was easy."

I'm used to the constant heckling that comes with having brothers, but Ellie obviously isn't. She's staring daggers through both of them. Their laughter dies and their cheeks redden as Ellie reprimands them, most likely realizing they are no longer making the best first impression. I wipe my sweaty palms on my jeans, secretly enjoying the show of two six-foot-three jokesters being put in their place by a five-foot-four woman with a pixie cut and freckles that make her look deceivingly innocent.

"Thank you, Ellie." I find my voice through her support.

"Plus, at least I'm trying to find my soulmate. You two are still dicking around like you're in your fraternity days."

Ellie finds my forearm under the table and squeezes gently, lingering for half a second before she moves her hand back into her own lap. Being the middle brother, I usually have to hold my own when this type of banter breaks out. This is the first time someone has stuck up for me. I could kiss her for it.

In a completely platonic way, of course.

"Touché…" Adem nods and downs the last of his beer.

"You're right; fair enough." Tanner raises his palms in mock surrender.

Ned stops by to drop our food off and we're all momentarily distracted by greasy fries and ketchup bottles. Ellie bites a hunk out of her burger, holding one hand to her mouth and giving me a thumbs up with the other while she swallows. "You were right, this is really good."

A dollop of mayonnaise rests at the corner of her lips, and before I can stop myself I've reached over to wipe it off with my thumb. My fingers graze her cheek and she flinches before making a dive for her napkin to wipe the remaining residue off. Her face is beet red against the white of the paper.

"S-sorry…" I laugh. "Instinct, I guess."

"No worries…"

We awkwardly return to our dinner. Tanner and Adem look back and forth between Ellie and I. Adem's gaze meets mine and he raises his eyebrows at me questioningly. I grab a fistful of fries from his plate to distract him from whatever his obnoxious older brother brain is thinking.

Because whatever it is, he's wrong.

"Can I ask one more Kristen question, then I swear I'll leave it alone?" Tanner asks me.

"If you pay for my dinner," I bargain.

"You wish."

"Okay, then no more questions." I grin smugly.

"What if *I* pay for your dinner?" Adem attempts to make a trade. "And I'll pay for Ellie's too, for putting up with all of us this evening."

"I don't know about Eren, but I accept," Ellie jokes, tucking a leg beneath her as she sits taller in her chair. We all laugh.

"I like her, she's cool," Tanner says to me while poking a thumb in Ellie's direction. "Bring her along more often—she makes you tolerable."

Back off, I think, rolling my eyes at him.

"Fine. What's your question?" I ask, preparing to think about Kristen again.

"What are you going to do about her plane ticket?" he prods. "Are you just going to take the loss?"

"I think that's my only option." I shrug. "It's non-refundable."

"Who knows? There are still a couple of weeks before Thanksgiving. Maybe you'll have number thirteen by th—" Adem stops short and I look over to find Ellie staring at him through narrowed eyes.

Fuck, she's amazing.

"I'll take the loss," I reiterate. "Unless one of you wants to bring a friend. Since we all know neither of you have anyone special in your life."

"Look at you, making comebacks," Ellie compliments me. It makes me feel all fuzzy inside. It must be the single beer I've had.

"Ellie, you should come," Tanner tells her. "Have you ever been to Colorado? We can show you around Estes Park. It's always a great time...a nice change from Florida."

Ellie stiffens beside me and I'm transported back to our conversation in the car. She purses her lips and shakes her head, attempting to politely decline. Today is making it impossible for her to get away from her predicament.

"I'm sure Ellie has plans with her own family." I assist her away from the line of fire.

"Yeah, sorry. Thanks, though." Ellie dumps the last of her beer into her mouth.

Ned comes with our checks, and as promised, Adem pays for Ellie and I. I stand and push my chair in, hoping she will follow my lead. She does, and we say our goodbyes to my asshole brothers, who I will most *definitely* not be playing matchmaker for in the future.

I hold the door to the bar open for her and we walk into the night, her a few steps ahead of me as we find our way back to my car. Her short hair flutters in the breeze, and I'm once again surrounded by her scent—a scent that has somehow only just developed a chokehold on me, even though I've known Ellie for years now. She sticks her hands in her pockets and turns to smile at me over her shoulder. The events of today filter through my brain, and it's then that I think...

What if Ellie *did* come to Colorado with me?

CHAPTER 17

ELLIE

I've never been more exhausted.

Today drained me. And as much as the pessimist in me would like to, I can't even say that all of the events of Friday have been terrible. There have been terrible moments, but also...great ones, too? I need a long period to reflect. I need a new life plan. I need to be alone for at least eight uninterrupted hours.

I fall onto my couch and rub at the back of my neck, adding a massage to the list of needs I'm building. I've unzipped one boot and kicked it across the room when my phone buzzes. I groan at the sight of Uncle Rob's name on the screen and consider ignoring it. I'm not sure I can handle any more human interactions today.

"Hi," I grumble into the speaker before taking on the task of removing my second boot.

"Wow, great to hear your voice too, Ellie Smellie," Uncle Rob retorts. Brat lets out a bark in the background. The sound is immediately followed by the sound of his little toenails tapping in circles on the hard flooring.

"What are you doing to my poor baby?" I ask. "It sounds like he's tattling on you for something."

"He's actually cussing you out. He heard me say your name and asked me to tell you that he's pretty pissed about not getting his evening Ellie walk today."

"I'm so sorry, Brat. I went to dinner with a friend. How can I make it up to you?" I pretend to grovel.

"Wait, who did you have dinner with?" Uncle Rob pries, dropping the Brat charade.

"You're nosey."

"I saw you get dropped off, but couldn't tell who was in the car. Was it Eren? Rick?" he persists.

"Why are those the first two people to enter your mind?" I reach up to massage my temples.

"They're the only two people I hear you talk about lately."

He has a point.

"I think it was Eren," Uncle Sai joins the conversation. "Who do you think, babe? Let's bet on it."

"Am I on speaker?" I ask even though I already know the answer.

"Always," they sing in unison.

"It was Eren." I decide to put myself out of my misery.

"I knew it," Sai jests. "Ellie, come over for some tea. We miss you."

"Before I commit, are we talking about the tea you drink, or do you just want to know every detail about my night?" My left eyebrow quirks on its own accord.

There's a brief silence before Uncle Rob says, "Um...both?"

"Fine," I sigh loudly. "But just for a few minutes. I'm dying to go to sleep."

"Don't worry, I'll make caffeinated tea. See you in a few." Uncle Rob ends the call.

Hauling myself up from the couch, I walk to the bathroom to splash some cold water on my face before changing into my pajamas. My bed calls to me from the corner. It's so close...five large steps and I could be beneath the covers, shutting my eyes and letting my brain power down. It would be that easy to give myself an escape from the events of the day.

That is, until I wake up in the morning and have to start pondering everything all over again.

"Ellie, I have a proposition for you."

Eren's voice enters my head again and I squeeze my eyes shut and try to shake it away. It doesn't work.

"Maybe you should come to Colorado with me. We can work on your travel fear. You can use my extra ticket. It's a win-win situation all around."

I think of the way Eren's face, lit red by the brake lights of the car in front of us, had been filled with anticipation as he turned to look at me. I think about the nervous flutter of his thick eyelashes against his cheeks. I think about his large hands on the steering wheel, long fingers thrumming to pass the time while he waited for my response.

He really does have amazing hands—strong, capable ones. They're the type of hands that look sensual doing everyday things, like operating a vehicle. The type of hands that would wrap around many different parts of the body just as beautifully as they wrapped around that steering wheel...

Jesus, Ellie.

Finding my slippers, I walk back into the night and skip down the stairs. The evening chill clears my head and I breathe a sigh of relief. It'll be difficult enough to make a decision about Colorado without having confusing thoughts about my best friend. Between tonight's dinner and car rides, I've had more of them in the past few hours than the rest of our friendship combined. A girl should only be allowed to have confusing thoughts about one man at a time, and right now, Rick should hold that spot.

While I'm on the subject, I try to conjure an image of Rick's hands (for research purposes of course), but the image in my mind is blurry. Instead, I move on to imagining his devilishly handsome face. But for some reason, it's fuzzy too.

Weird. It must be the exhaustion.

"The party has arrived," I yell as I burst through the back door. "Bring on the caffeine!"

Brat comes slipping and sliding into the kitchen and I bend to scrub him behind the ears.

"We're in here," Uncle Sai yells from further down the hallway.

Brat leads the way to the study, where Rob and Sai are snuggled beneath a blanket on the couch. A low flame burns in the fireplace, warming the room to the perfect temperature and casting a golden glow on the opposite wall of built-in bookshelves, which are stuffed to the gills with everything from Uncle Rob's very first sociology textbook to the latest Kristin Hannah novel.

"Grab a blanket, make yourself comfy," Uncle Rob tells me.

"I would have done that anyway." I stick my tongue out at him.

"I know, and I would be offended if you didn't."

Tucking my legs beneath me on the loveseat, I spread a fluffy blanket over my lap and pat the empty space next to me. Brat hops up and curls into a chubby little donut against my side and rests his head on my thigh. A content groan escapes from his mouth as he settles.

"I'm really glad the whole 'no Brat on the furniture' rule is holding up." Uncle Sai turns to stare at the side of his husband's face. Uncle Rob makes a dramatic show of gazing wide-eyed around the room, resting on every surface except Sai's eyes, which I can't help but notice are framed by dark circles. Work must really be getting to him these days. Sai gently elbows Uncle Rob.

"In my defense, I would just like to remind you," Rob says jokingly, "that you were the first to break this rule that night you invited him to sleep in our bed."

"He was cold and lonely on the floor! How could I say no? What am I, some kind of animal?"

Brat and I look back and forth between them, watching the ping pong of a silly argument I've heard the two have at least five hundred times before.

"No, you're a sensitive softy with a big heart and that's why I love you." Uncle Rob pulls Sai's head onto his shoulder and strokes his hair. I look down at Brat and I swear he rolls his eyes at me.

"How was dinner with Eren?" Sai asks me. "Did his girlfriend join?"

"The girlfriend is no more. They officially broke up," I fill them in quickly. "We went with his two brothers. It was...fun, I think."

"You *think*?" Uncle Rob furrows his brow at me.

"There was a lot of picking on each other and what I can only describe as 'boy banter,'" I explain.

"Three brothers? I would imagine so," Sai laughs.

I almost bring up Eren's love curse, but decide at the last second it's not my place to discuss it with people he doesn't even know. Besides, it's not the part of the evening I'm hung up on. Neither is the sibling rivalry, for that matter.

"Maybe you should come to Colorado with me..."

Brat scoots even closer, as if he can feel my anxiety and wants to suck it out of me. I trace a finger along the white stripe that runs down the center of his head and he grunts in approval before closing his eyes. I never knew a dog could exude such love and support before Brat.

What do you think, Brat? I ask internally. *Should I talk to your dads about the Colorado invite?*

He doesn't answer, of course. But if he could, I think he would tell me to go for it. I lean forward to grab the mug of tea that is cooling for me on the coffee table. It has a splash of almond milk in it, exactly how I like. Between the warm drink and the warm dog, I have the support to continue.

"Since Eren and Kristen broke up, he has an extra plane ticket to see his family in Colorado over Thanksgiving." I stop to take a sip of my drink. "He invited me to go with him. As a friend, obviously. But if you'd rather me be here I completely understand..."

Neither uncle speaks right away, although their eyes widen considerably. They study each other's faces, silently conversing. It's impossible to determine their feelings. Are they upset that I would think about leaving during the holiday?

"You have to go, Ellie," Uncle Rob says bluntly, returning his attention to me. "It's a great opportunity."

"But what about Thanksgiving? I wouldn't be here with y'all."

"Ellie, we love you more than anything, but I'm begging you, please do this for yourself." Uncle Sai slowly sits up to perch on the edge of the couch.

"Yes, we've been waiting for you to express even the slightest interest in traveling. And you're a travel agent, for Pete's sake," Uncle Rob exclaims.

The knot of guilt in my stomach begins to claw its way up my esophagus. I've not only been lying to everyone at TST, but to my family as well. When I got the job, I told them travel wasn't required. In the age of the internet, they never questioned it.

They know I have trepidation when it comes to traveling, but I don't think they know how deeply rooted it is in Mom and Dad. They've just always assumed it's a fear of the unknown, or of airplanes, which is part of it, but the smaller part for sure. Seeing their excitement over my announcement makes me wonder how long they've been waiting to approach the subject.

"I'm sorry," is all I can think to say. Tears threaten to fill my eyes.

"Sorry? What is there to be sorry about?" Uncle Rob throws the blanket off of his lap and comes to sit beside me on the arm of the loveseat. Sai cringes at the furniture abuse and I smirk at him.

Uncle Rob wraps an arm around my shoulders and looks down at me. "Ellie, believe me when I tell you—you deserve the world. Is it big? Sure. Can it sometimes be scary? Yes. But it can still be yours for the taking."

"He's right, you know," Uncle Sai agrees. "If there's one good thing you can learn from your parents, it's that there is so much out there to experience. And not giving it a try would be doing yourself a great disservice."

I've never looked at it that way before.

But do I want to look at it that way? It's so much easier to be here, in my bubble, where I know I, and everyone around me, are safe.

"But Colorado is so far. What if I hate it?" I ask.

What if something happens to one of you while I'm gone?

"And what about Thanksgiving?" I ask again. "I've never missed it." I'm looking for any reason for them to tell me not to go.

What if something happens to Brat? What if I can't get home? I wrap my hand around one of Brat's paws and hold tight.

"You won't hate it," Uncle Rob reassures me. "And of course we'll miss you, but we'll be having the same dry turkey that Sai makes every year. And we'll save some leftovers just for you."

"Hey, you love my dry turkey." Sai pokes his lower lip out at his husband.

I look up into Uncle Rob's face. The crows' feet around his eyes soften the rest of his features, and I'm reminded for the millionth time how different my current life might be if he hadn't been there for me all of these years. There's no one I love more. There's no one I trust more.

Which means...maybe I need to trust him on this too.

CHAPTER 18

EREN

I didn't hear from Ellie all weekend.

Now, it's nearly 10:00 a.m. on Monday, and she hasn't made it to the office. Each time I check the clock, no more than two or three minutes have passed. In terms of actual work, I've completed absolutely nothing. More nervous sweat beads on my upper lip and I swipe them away.

Where is she? Did she decide everything is too much for her? Did she quit without notice? Would she do that without letting me know?

Out of respect for her space, I decided it was best not to text her after Friday night. I wanted her to have the time to make the decision on her terms, without my influence. But that was two days ago, and now I'm starting to worry. I pull my phone out of my desk drawer and check for messages.

Nothing.

Ellie, where are you?

I push away from my desk and stand. I might not know where she is, but someone else in this office could. And I can't think of a better place to start asking questions than the sales room. Up first: Rick Williamson.

My face rapidly heats at the mere thought of him knowing where she is when I don't.

Footsteps sound outside of my office door and I freeze, preparing for Walt to come by and make his morning small talk. If only he knew that, for the first time in my life, I'm not in the mood to chat about, well...anything. Unless he knows where the hell Ellie is.

A shadow falls through the doorway, followed half a second later by a body. Ellie hovers at the entrance to my office, wearing a baby blue sweater and wringing her hands in front of her. She smiles sheepishly and relief floods my insides. Coming around the desk, I take two giant steps forward, ready to wrap her into a hug. But I stop just short, not wanting to seem too desperate to make sure I'm not imagining her.

"Hey! Where have y—" I start to ask.

"Yes," Ellie says at the same exact moment.

"Huh?" I squint down at her, so close that I can practically see the arteries transporting the blood to her pinkening face.

"Yes," she says again. "I'll come to Colorado with you. I had to say it before I chickened out."

I exhale slowly through my nose and let my shoulders relax for the first time all morning. "Really? Are you sure?"

"No? But I'm going to do it anyway." She shrugs and lowers her voice to a whisper. "I don't want to leave TST, Eren. I'm happy here. I love this job. If I can get past the negative feelings about having my own adventures, I know things will only get better. For work, and for me personally."

"I'm so proud of you!" I reach out and pull her to my chest, ruffling her hair with my palm before I release her. She reaches up to smooth it, then absentmindedly trails her hand down the side of her face and neck before letting it fall to her side. I watch every movement as if it's happening in slow motion, admiring the creaminess of her skin against the pale blue sweater.

She's beautiful. I've always known it, of course. But lately, little things keep jumping out at me that make her beauty even more apparent. Like the contrast of her dark features with her complexion. Like the way she smells slightly different every day, even though I know she's wearing the same scent. Like the way the freckle on her cheek inches closer to her eye when she smiles or laughs.

It's because you're single again, Eren. This always happens. Don't mess around and fuck up this friendship.

I take a step back, from both Ellie and my inner demon, and sit on the edge of my desk.

"Why are you late?" I ask, changing the subject. "I thought you quit or something."

"Don't get me wrong, I thought about it. All weekend, actually, while I was trying to make up my mind," she says. "But I had a dentist appointment this morning. It was on the office calendar."

"You know I don't look at that thing."

"Maybe you should start." She grins. "I have to get back downstairs. Lunch at the usual time?"

"I'll put it on the office calendar," I joke.

She scrunches her nose at me, then spins on her heel to head to her desk, leaving my office painfully empty. I add "nose scrunch" to my mental list of "reasons Ellie is stunning," then slink back to my chair to work.

The flights will have to wait, though. I have something more important to do.

THE TWO E'S TAKE THE CENTENNIAL STATE

JACKSONVILLE, FL —> ESTES PARK, CO

Monday, Nov 25 - Saturday, Nov 30, 2019

Overview

Mon 11/25: Fly from Jax to Denver. Rent car. Drive to Estes Park and check into The Polat Estate AKA: Eren's Parent's House.

Tues 11/26: A day to explore...endless possibilities.

Wed 11/27: Rocky Mountain National Park sightseeing, featuring a giant thermos of Eren's mom's famous hot chocolate.

Thurs 11/28: EAT, EAT EAT. Thanksgiving feast, and Eren's dad's famous Donër Kebab.

Fri 11/29: National Hibernation Day.

Sat 11/30: Fly home to Jax.

CHAPTER 19
ELLIE

The next few days pass fairly quietly. Then, on Thursday morning, two things happen.

First, after an awkward week of the two of us avoiding each other (which is very difficult when you sit five feet apart), Rick I.M.'s me:

Rick Williamson:
Sorry I haven't texted you yet. To be honest, I started over-thinking. I realized I don't know what Yuke's opinion on workplace relationships is. And that's kind of a hard thing to just go knock on her door and ask.

Ellie Amos:
Wait, wait, wait...Rick Williamson OVERTHINKS sometimes?

Rick Williamson:
When it comes to the sanctity of his job, he does.

Ellie Amos:
I can appreciate that. I'm not sure if there's a formal policy, but I think she's cool about it as long as it doesn't cause any drama.

I re-read my message after I've already sent it, and realize that it sounds like I'm vouching for him to pursue me. Have I been dreaming about this since I met him? Secretly, yes. But, to be totally transparent, his lack of communication has been the very least of my worries. Other than work, I've been more focused on Colorado, and what to wear in Colorado, and airplanes, and possible *snow*, which I have never seen in my life.

Which brings me to the second thing that happened.

When I walked into the sales room this morning, my eyes were immediately drawn to two foreign objects sitting next to my keyboard: a to-go cup containing my favorite cinnamon dulce latte, and beneath it, a manila file folder with no label.

Eren, I had known immediately, based on the latte alone.

With the rest of the room still empty, I had settled in with my drink and flipped open the folder to find a packet, laminated and even binded. The heading at the top of the first page jumped out at me: *The Two E's Take the Centennial State.*

He'd made me an itinerary.

A post-it note was stuck to the inside of the folder.

Next, we plan the trip you're going to take over Christmas break. :)

I'd closed the folder and hugged it to my chest with tears in my eyes. To anyone else, it would have been *just* an itinerary; a glorified schedule. To me, it was the start of taking myself to places I've never been, both literally and figuratively.

Now, the folder sits securely in my bag, which is tucked

beneath my desk next to my feet. I can't wait to get home and pour over everything in uninterrupted peace. For the first time, it won't be about what my client is doing on their trip—it will be about what I'm doing on mine. What Eren and I are doing on *ours*.

As friends, of course.

Next week is the last week of work before TST is closed for Thanksgiving. There's still so much actual work to finalize before then. Add preparing for my first trip to my responsibilities, and my to-do list is officially overflowing. It's safe to say I have no, or very little, Colorado-approved clothing. Or shoes. Or even pajamas. So some shopping will be in order. But, I'm pretty good at that. A little excited about it, even.

Not to mention, I don't own a suitcase.

"Hey, Ellie?" Jade's voice comes through my phone's speaker and I pick it up.

"Yeah, what's up?" I ask.

"Do you want to take this call? New client, never traveled with us before. In their words, they're looking for a 'Christmas with the Kranks' experience in December. Which I take to mean, they want to go somewhere warm and far away from their family." She lets out a forced little laugh.

"Sure, send them over. Thanks!"

The day continues like this; I take more calls than I've had the rest of the week combined, ask questions, and email off detailed surveys for the clients to complete so I can make a final decision on their secret destinations. When I look at the clock for the first time, it's almost 2:00 p.m. I've missed my lunch hour with Eren.

My heart sinks a little at the realization. I haven't even had a chance to thank him for the itinerary yet.

As if summoned, Eren walks into the sales room. He grins at me before stopping to chat with Lamar. I sit a little taller in my chair and take a moment to adjust my top and smooth my hair, freezing in the process when I realize I'm checking my appearance for Eren. Has that ever happened before?

"How's your day?" A deep voice asks from behind me. I spin my chair around to find Rick leaning against our cubicle in that way that either enrages me or completely turns me on —sometimes both at once. He's wearing a navy blue polo that deepens his tan. His arms are crossed over his firm chest and I let myself sneak a look at his hands. His fingers are shorter and thicker than Eren's, but his nails are clean, trim, and obviously well taken care of. Just like the rest of him.

"Busiest I've had in a while," I tell him. "I think I've talked to six new clients today alone."

"Everyone is trying to accomplish things before the holidays come into full swing." Rick holds eye contact with me and I force myself not to look away. "Speaking of, what do you and your family do for Tha—?"

"Am I interrupting something?" Eren appears, standing to create a triangle between the three of us. He sticks his hands into his pockets and rocks back and forth on his heels. A brief flicker of irritation passes over Rick's face and I make note of it, confused.

"Just having a midday chat with Miss Ellie here." Rick tilts his head at me and stands up straight. He still only comes just above Eren's shoulder. An energy I've never picked up on before fills the space in our triangle. It's a strong tension...and not a good type either.

"Anything interesting?" Eren asks him, taking a step closer to me in the process. I furrow my brow and look up at him, wondering where the hell this weird alpha male personality is coming from. And, why?

"Mostly pre-holiday chit-chat. Although, Ellie..." Rick steps closer to me as well and I roll my gaze from Eren to him. "I was going to see if you'd like to join me for a drink after work tomorrow."

It feels as though the air gets sucked out of the room. The workplace scurry in the other cubes stops and Lucia pauses mid-coffee slurp, coughing and sputtering in the process. Sherry picks the worst possible moment to re-enter the room with her own coffee. She does an awkward little side step to pass between Eren, Rick, and I, looking curiously between the three of us as she goes.

I know the only way to end this special form of torture is to answer the question, but it's almost impossible to make myself speak in the deafening silence surrounding us. "Um..."

Eren and Rick lean one inch closer; their eyebrows quirking one inch higher.

"Sure. That sounds fun." I fight to keep my voice as low as possible.

Rick's shoulders relax and he smiles. Out of the corner of my eye, I see Eren's face crumple into a frown. It quickly transitions to a smile as I turn to face him. The room slowly begins to bustle again.

"Cool, y'all have fun." Eren shuffles backwards out of my cube. "Ellie, I'll catch up with you later." He walks quickly out of the room.

What has gotten into him?

CHAPTER 20

EREN

So, Ellie has a date with Rick after work tomorrow.

Great. I'm happy for her. Haven't I been wanting this for her for ages?

I have to keep reminding myself of this. Because it's how I *should* feel. My insides shouldn't be twisting and turning with something that feels a little too close to jealousy for comfort. And, what reason is there to be jealous anyway? Ellie is my friend, and nothing more.

She can never be anything more.

When did I even start entertaining the thought that she could be more than just my best TST pal? This is all coming out of nowhere.

You're just vulnerable right now. Kristen is gone. The "curse" is running rampant. You're confused.

Yeah...confused.

I'm only human. It's okay to be confused every now and then.

It's just incredibly frustrating, considering Ellie and I will be taking a trip together in a little over a week. What if the entire trip is uncomfortable? What if she notices I'm acting differently and has a terrible time and decides traveling really isn't for her? What if I'm the one to ruin this, and Ellie does leave TST?

I don't want any part of a TST that doesn't involve her.

Come to think of it, I don't want to imagine a life that doesn't involve her.

Fuck me.

A knock sounds on my apartment door and I quickly sit up from my spot on the rug, where I've been laying and staring at the ceiling in silence since I got home from work an hour and a half ago. I can feel my hair shooting out in every direction, but I don't bother to fix it as I push myself to my feet. "Just a second," I call.

I amble to the door and fling it open. Adem is standing on my stoop with a twelve pack in his arms. His eyes disappear beneath his dark brows at the sight of me. "What the hell is wrong with you? You look like you've been electrocuted. You really need to cut your hair before we leave for Thanksgiving. Mom is going to hate it."

"I think I'm starting to have feelings for Ellie!" The word vomit tumbles out of my mouth and lands at Adem's feet. The look on his face would be the same if it had been actual vomit.

"Wow." Adem's mouth forms a little "o" and we stare at each other in silence for a few seconds. He eventually pushes his way past me and I follow him to the couch, forgetting to shut the door in the process. Adem goes back to kick it shut and then we're trapped in silence once again.

"Eren, don't do this to yourself." Sighing, Adem walks to the kitchen to grab the bottle opener from my junk drawer. "You always do this to yourself. It's okay to be alone! Look at me, I'm 32 and single and I'm fine."

"I know, I know. I promise, I was so prepared to work on myself this time. Now everything is weird." I slump into the couch and press my palms into my eyes.

Adem pops the cap off a bottle and thrusts it at me. "Drink this and take deep breaths through your nose."

I do as I'm told, focusing on the way the crisp beer feels as it trickles slowly down my throat. My heart rate slows and the tension between my shoulder blades dissipates. Then Tanner bangs through the front door and pulls me out of my meditated state.

"Whoa, what the hell is wrong with you?" Tanner repeats the same questions Adem asked, squatting to perch on the edge of the coffee table even though I've asked him a million times not to do that. "Your hair is out of control. You really need to cut it bef—"

"I'm not cutting my hair." I sit the beer next to Tanner on the table and use the elastic around my wrist to pull my hair back into a low ponytail. "I like it. It's fine."

"Eren thinks he's falling for Ellie," Adem tells Tanner.

"Shit, here we go again..." Tanner grabs a beer and takes the bottle opener from Adem.

I ignore them and continue to sip, my head full of too many emotions. Confusion over Ellie. Annoyance at my brothers and their lack of sympathy. Anger at myself. The aforementioned jealousy over stupid Rick.

He's good-looking—yeah. But, so what? I've dated good-looking people too and it never took me long to realize that being attracted to someone's inner workings is more important than the initial enchantment with their outward appearance.

How do you know he's not a great person, Eren? Stop being a dick.

"Do you want to step out of your head for a few minutes and talk to us?" Adem asks, startling me.

I roll my head along the back of the couch to stare at him. "Why, so you can laugh at me and joke about the stupid curse?"

"No," Adem says just as Tanner answers, "Basically."

Tanner dodges the kick I send in his direction and slides down to sit on the floor.

"Stop it, Tanner. Can't you tell he's having a hard time?" Adem chastises.

"Sorry, okay? All I'm saying is we go through this roughly once a year, and I'm running out of advice," Tanner defends himself.

"Like I need your advice. You've never even been in a relationship," I spit.

"Why do I need one when you've had enough girlfriends for all three of us combined?" he lashes back.

"Okay, both of you need to chill out." Adem continues to play his role of eldest sibling.

"Besides, this isn't like all of the other times," I say. "It's... different somehow."

"How?" Tanner presses.

Scrambling, I try to figure out how to put what I'm feeling into words. I push myself off the couch and begin to walk a slow lap around my living room. My brothers stare after me, waiting in silence.

"Well, it's Ellie." I lift my hands helplessly before letting them fall heavily to my sides. "Not some random guy or girl I met on Tinder, or at a bar on Saturday night and decided to pursue. Ellie is someone I know. Someone I have a non-romantic history with. Someone I've always thought was beautiful and amazing, but I still viewed with a veil over my eyes. Because of Kristen. Because of Monica, before Kristen. And now that veil has been lifted, and I'm drowning in these new emotions."

"How do you know it's not just the factor of convenience? You two spend a lot of time together. That could be confusing for anyone," Adem says.

"It doesn't feel that way." I shrug. "Usually I'm addicted

to the feeling of 'new.' This feels more like I'm freaking out because I'm discovering I've always wanted the familiar. And now it might be too late."

"How is it too late? Just talk to her," Tanner pushes.

"She has a date tomorrow. With a guy from the office. Rick." My top lip curls and I start pacing again.

"The Rick? Hunky Rick?" I confirm Adem's question with a single nod.

Why, why, WHY did past me encourage this and allow this to happen? Shouldn't I have somehow known better? I've completed three laps around the couch before Tanner stands to grab me by the shoulders and guide me back to my spot on the couch.

"It's a first date, Eren. Not a marriage proposal." He releases me and gives my ponytail a gentle tug before patting me twice on the cheek. "Besides, you already have a leg up on Rick: two years of friendship."

"Damn, Tanner. That's actually a good point." Adem pops a top off of a second beer.

Yeah, I think. He's not wrong. My thought spiral slowly begins to unfurl itself and I feel somewhat normal for the first time since leaving Ellie's cube.

"I just thought about something," Adem says. "Maybe this isn't a total surprise. At the bar last week, I could sense something between the two of you, but I wasn't sure what it was at the time."

"Really?" I perk up a little more. "Did you sense anything from her, or just from me?"

"Considering the way she came to your defense, I'd say the tension was mutual. New—but definitely mutual."

I think back to that night at the bar, to the way she wasn't in a hurry to remove her arm from mine while we were looking at the menu. To the way she stood up for me with these two buffoons. To the way her hand found my forearm beneath the table to help ease my nerves.

"Fuck. You could be right." I stare straight ahead, replaying all of the events in my mind for a second time.

"You want this? Then go for it, Eren," Adem encourages. "Don't worry about it being too soon. Don't worry about the stupid curse we made up to get on your nerves. You want to find your forever more than anyone I've ever known. And, shit, this might be getting too sappy, but I think you deserve it more than anyone I've ever known. Keep putting yourself out there. Sometimes I wish I could give myself permission to do the same."

"You can, you know," I tell him. He brushes me off with a smile and we fall into silence for the first time all evening.

Can I do this? It feels so fast, but is it really? Like Tanner said, Ellie and I already have two years of history. Will I be able to live with myself if I don't try? If I don't try, what if I miss my chance? She could end up with Rick instead, and I would have to watch it play out firsthand every day.

I have to do this. How I'm going to approach it, I have no idea. But I have to test the waters.

Falling for one of my best friends—it's somewhere I've never found myself. Somewhere I've never been before. It's somewhere I, newly without a doubt, want to go.

"I'm guessing this means it's probably not a good idea to ask you for Ellie's number like I was planning to, then," Tanner breaks the silence.

Laughing, I grab one of the couch pillows and hurl it at him

November 15, 2019 8:22 AM
FROM: y.tanaka@topsecrettravel.com
TO: TST SALES TEAM
SUBJECT: Sales Manager Application Deadline

Good Morning Secret Travel Agents,

The posting for our new sales manager position went live on all of the public job boards today. I plan to keep it live through the week before Christmas break.

If you're interested in applying internally, there's no need to fill out the application on the job boards. Just send me your most up-to-date resume and a cover letter.

I'm always here for any questions.

Have a great weekend!

Best wishes,
Yuke Tanaka
President
Top Secret Travel

CHAPTER 21

ELLIE

"You ready to go?" Rick finds me at the reception desk chatting to Jade and I sneak a peek at the time on her computer monitor. "I can't believe it's 5:00 already! Just let me go grab my things."

I wave to Jade and she wiggles her eyebrows at me. "Have fun you two."

Everyone else in the office is also filing out and I have to press myself against the hallway wall until they pass. I hurry into the sales room and begin throwing stuff into my bag. Footsteps make their way in the direction of my cubicle but I complete my task before turning to see who it is, expecting Rick.

It's Eren. He's wearing his usual short-sleeved button-up shirt. Today's is patterned with tiny stacks of books.

"Hey, you." I can't stop the grin that spreads across my face. "I haven't seen you much today. Actually...have I seen you at all today?"

"No, I've been slammed," he says. "This pre-holiday rush is killing me. I can't tell you how many times I've had to explain to someone that there is no such thing as an early 'Black Friday' deal on flights."

"Imagine how many calls you would be getting if there was a deal like that."

"Ugh." He clutches his stomach like he's going to be sick. "I can only conjure terrifying ideas such as that in my nightmares."

Throwing my bag over my shoulder, I place a hand on his forearm to skirt around him. "I hate to cut this reunion short after our whole eight hours apart, but Rick is waiting for me in the foyer."

He gazes down at my hand before turning his eyes to mine. Suddenly aware of the feeling of his bare skin beneath my palm, I let my hand drop to my side. Where have all of these little semi-awkward moments between Eren and I been coming from lately? We've been friends for two years and things like this have never happened until recently.

"Have fun." He smiles but it doesn't reach his eyes. "If you're not too tired when you get home, maybe you can text me?"

"Sure. Do you want to chat about Colorado?" I ask.

"Colorado will be a given subject, yes. We're just over one week away." A blush enters his cheeks and he falters as if he's questioning what he's about to say next. "I really just like talking to you, though. About...anything."

Maybe it's a trick of the fluorescent lighting overhead, but his dark eyes brighten to a shade of brown slightly lighter than his usual color. His hands actively twist together in front of him, making him appear less confident than usual. His expression, though calm, feels forced. For the first time ever, he seems shy. I never even knew that was possible for him.

Eren has always been a bright light in the room, but lately, I've been finding him more and more magnetic. My hand reaches for his without my permission. "I really like talking to you t—"

"Ellie!" Rick's voice comes from the door. "You coming? Happy hour ends in thirty minutes."

Instinctively, I take a step back to put more distance between Eren and I. His shoulders slump and he glares at Rick over his shoulder. The friction between us dies just as quickly as it was created.

"Coming," I yell, backing away. "I'll text you later," I say to Eren. He nods solemnly.

"See ya, Polat," Rick says, guiding me toward the exit with a palm on my lower back. I would expect his touch to light me up from the inside, but instead his hand just feels heavy against my spine. I turn to take one final look at Eren and he waves. Why does he look so...sad?

Why do I also feel a bit strange? I'm going on a date with *Rick Williamson*. I've been secretly pining for this for nearly a year. I shouldn't be able to contain my excitement right now.

Rick holds the door open and flashes his signature smile.

No butterflies.

His smile *always* gives me butterflies. Where are they? And why have they left?

Eren, my mind quickly says, unfortunately with no further explanation. I skip down TST's steps and walk ahead of Rick down the sidewalk, thankful for a brief second to think without him being able to see my face.

Eren? That makes no sense. Hasn't he wanted this for me, too? At least, he used to want this for me. The expression I left him with says otherwise, though. What has changed? And again, why?

"My truck is over there." Rick beckons to a blue Ford a few feet down the street. "I don't know about you, but I'm starving! Hope you like tacos."

"Who doesn't like tacos?" I joke, forcing a smile and trying to clear my head.

We drive to a popular Mexican spot a couple of streets over and Rick squeezes his giant truck into a compact parking spot while I cringe internally. We're so close to the Prius next to us that I have to suck my stomach in when I open the door to slide out. We haven't even made it inside the restaurant yet and I'm already marginally annoyed. What if things only go down from here? Maybe this wasn't such a good idea.

We claim the last two seats at the bar and Rick orders us a pitcher of margaritas. "Cheers to Friday. And to this," he says, passing me a glass shaped like a cactus.

"Also to five more days before we get a whole week off," I add.

"Yes, definitely to that." He takes a gulp of his drink and slides the basket of chips and salsa closer to us.

"What are you doing for Thanksgiving?" I ask him.

"My dad lives in Tampa, so I'm going down there for the week to spend time with the fam. I can't wait."

"Is your mom in Tampa too?"

"She actually passed away a few years ago. Breast cancer." His voice shakes a little on the last word.

Dammit Ellie. Tread lighter.

"Oh, I'm sorry, Rick. I didn't realize." I want to punch myself. I understand how difficult it can be to talk about parents. I should have known better.

"Don't apologize." He shrugs and places a hand on my knee. "You couldn't have known. She fought hard. We had a lot of good years before the bad ones."

Now I remember one of the reasons I don't love going on dates: the personal conversation. The "getting to know each other." The expectation to share deeper things about yourself than the other person already knows.

I'm not a fan. Of asking the questions, or of giving the answers. But it's too late to escape it.

"How about you?" He squeezes my knee gently and I study the way his tan skin looks against my jeans, waiting for the butterflies to return. "What are you doing for the holiday?"

Shit. More dangerous territory. Do I tell him about my trip with Eren?

"Normally I have a quiet day with my uncles. I live in their guest house," I explain. "My Uncle Sai always makes turkey that's slightly too dry and mashed potatoes that are slightly too runny. We dress up for lunch, then change into pajamas to binge watch *Gossip Girl* and snack on the couch for the rest of the day."

It's always one of my favorite days of the year. Will I miss it?

"*Gossip Girl*?" Rick chuckles. "Why *Gossip Girl*?"

"I was obsessed when I was a teenager. The two of them slowly became invested along with me, and now it's somehow a tradition." I finish off my first margarita and reach for the pitcher to give us both a refill, my shirt lifting slightly in the process. Rick's eyes immediately drop to the inch of exposed skin.

It's been a while since I've felt desired. Given the person who's admiring me, I should be nervous with anticipation for the rest of the evening. But half of my mind is focused on going home to think about Colorado. On going home to text Eren.

Maybe I need to flirt a little harder.

The bartender takes our food order and I return my attention to Rick, ready to up the ante. His cheeks are flushed from the margaritas, his eyes alert and shiny. He undoes the top button on his polo, exposing the tiniest bit of light chest hair. I scoot my stool closer and let my knees rest against his.

The evening continues this way—asking questions, laughing about office gossip, sharing bites of chimichanga and street tacos, finding reasons to touch one another. I'm relaxed and enjoying myself, and so is Rick. His hand has settled further up my thigh now, and I lean into the touch.

Rick is nice. Sure, he purposely parks his giant truck in spaces that are far too small. He tries to steal sales at work. He even uses his flirting power to make his daily life a little easier. But, I can tell he's a good person. I can tell he is being genuine with me. Which has allowed some of my attraction to return.

It could also be the margaritas, but I'm choosing to go with the former.

"What season of *Gossip Girl* will you and your uncles watch? Or do you start from the beginning?" he asks, bringing the conversation back to Thanksgiving.

"It would be four," I answer, feeling the liquid courage push me unwillingly into providing further information. "But, I'm actually not going to be home this year. I'm going somewhere. I meant to say that earlier and then we changed subjects."

"Do tell." He finishes his drink and switches to water, preparing to sober up.

"I'm going to Colorado. Estes Park. With Eren."

He visibly stiffens. His fingers shift, loosening the clutch on my leg.

What is the deal with him and Eren?

"Sounds...fun. I didn't realize the two of you were that close outside of the office." He removes his hand from me completely to run it through his hair.

Holy shit. He thinks Eren is into me.

Just like Jade. Just like my uncles.

"Yeah, we're friends," I clarify. "Only friends."

Not the tiniest bit more. Regardless of what people think.

Regardless of the change between him and I lately.

Regardless of the fact that I can't wait to get home and text him all night.

Regardless of the way I think about running my hands through his hair far too often lately...

"It's a long story, but he had an extra ticket," I tack on.

"I don't know anyone that would turn a free flight to Colorado down." He leans his elbow into the bar, visibly relaxing once more. "I'm sure you've been before. But I hope you have a great time."

"I love it out there." The lie slips out, smooth as butter.

What I should have said is, *I hope I will love it out there*. But I'm not about to risk opening an even bigger can of worms.

The bartender drops our bill off and I make a dive for it. Rick beats me, producing his credit card before my fingers have even brushed the check folder. I thank him, wishing I had another pitcher of margaritas to push me back into the warm comfortability I was feeling before Colorado came up.

Rick signs the receipt and slides off the stool, undoing a second button on his polo as he does so. "Wanna walk outside? It's warm in here. Margaritas always do that to me. Or maybe it's you." He smirks.

Finally, some more content to help Flirty Ellie out.

"We made it through most of the evening before you used some lame pickup line," I joke, elbowing him gently in the ribs. "I'm proud of you."

"It's an art. You have to wait for the right moment."

We walk outside, passing his truck and continuing down the street. Darkness has fallen, the sidewalk lit by early Christmas lights in the windows and patios of various restaurants and bars. Parking spaces continue to fill as everyone seeks out Friday dinner and drinks. Laughter and music flow intermittently through doors and windows into the night, and the air holds just a hint of chill.

The atmosphere is screaming for the addition of a perfect, romantic gesture. As if reading my mind, Rick's arm brushes mine, and he takes the opportunity to thread our fingers together. His hand is warm, and a tiny bit clammy. I spread my fingers a little, trying to find a more comfortable position.

It still doesn't feel right. Perhaps I've spent too long romanticizing this in my head. It's the only explanation that makes sense. Why else would I be on a date, holding hands with the beautiful Rick Williamson, and feeling close to nothing?

I think back to last week, in the car with Eren, when I told him my TST secret. He had wrapped my hands in his, and it felt...safe. Secure. Like the perfect fit that you hear about so often in books and movies. The perfect fit that I've never quite believed in. And now that's being put to the test.

Do I really have feelings for Rick?

More importantly: *Do I have feelings for Eren?*

Now that's a question I never thought I'd be asking.

"Did you see Yuke's email about the sales manager position today?" Rick asks, startling me.

"Huh? Oh, yeah..."

"Is it too nosey of me to ask if you're going to apply?" he says. "Because you should. Everyone knows you're the best agent."

Ignoring his compliment, I press my mouth into a tight line. The margarita buzz is gone, and multiple anxieties are finding their way to me at once. Do I even like Rick? What the heck is happening with Eren? Do I want to be the new TST sales manager? Do I deserve it? Oh yeah, don't forget I also have a giant secret that could ruin my career if made public.

Halting in the middle of the sidewalk, I release Rick's hand and turn to face him. "I don't know yet. Maybe."

"Just so you know, I might apply too. For the hell of it. I

hope that doesn't mess anything up here." He gestures between us.

It's the out I need. The out I've been secretly searching for all evening.

"Rick, I don't think we should do this right now." I stare at him directly in his piercing eyes, waiting for regret to make a quick appearance. It doesn't come.

"What do you mean?" he asks.

"I think you're nice. And, hot, obviously." He puffs his chest up at the compliment. "But we're in dangerous territory right now. We have the same job. We sit five feet apart. We're possibly going after the same promotion. Adding romance into the mix could be sticky."

Plus I also might be falling for one of TST's flight investigators, but I digress.

He wipes a hand across his mouth and stares up at the sky, sighing. I can't imagine this happens to him very often, so I have no idea how he's going to react. He might still try to sell himself. But you can't outsale TST's top earning agent. Even when it comes to relationships. Or love. Or wherever this was going.

"You're smart, Ellie." He sticks his hands in his pockets. "I don't want to admit it, but you're right."

"So you're not upset, then?"

"Disappointed, yes. Upset, no." He looks somewhat peeved, but I take his word.

"I'm sorry," I offer. "I did have fun tonight, though."

"No, I had fun too, Amos." He puts a friendly arm around my shoulders and turns us back in the direction of his truck. "Come on, I'll take you home. I'm sure you have some *Gossip Girl* to catch up on."

Any other night, maybe. Tonight I have better plans.

CHAPTER 22

EREN

M y family thinks I'm afraid of being alone.

But, it's really not as simple as that.

I grew up as the middle child in a family with a mostly healthy dynamic, which means not only was I never really "alone," but I was also fiercely loved by my parents. Both of them. That's not something many people can say anymore, so I *am* thankful.

The truth is though, while I have spent my life surrounded by people, there has always been a little loneliness-shaped hole in my heart. Maybe it's middle-child syndrome, and I'm harboring the anxiety of being on the back burner in everyone's life. Maybe that's why my personality has developed the way it has, and I live in a constant state of needing everyone I meet to like me. To love me, when possible.

College was my first real test. Freshman year can be brutal on anyone. You're away from your family. You're away from your friends. Just because I looked like I was 30 at the age of 18, didn't mean I had the emotional intelligence to understand why I was so depressed. To suppress that feeling, I became "Eren the fun guy." The guy who would always get invited to parties or hang-outs because I was nice. The guy that glued groups of different personalities together and made sure everyone was having a good time. Eventually, once the excitement wore off, I was the guy who still felt unfulfilled when his head hit the pillow every night.

After college came the unease of true adulthood. I quit my first job after two weeks of going absolutely stir crazy entering data into spreadsheets. Turns out a degree in data analytics wasn't a particularly great fit for me. So, I took the savings I had been harboring since I started receiving allowance as a kid, and I traveled. I spent an entire gap year jumping countries. Trying new things. Meeting new people. Eating a lot of new foods. I even got certified to teach English as a foreign language along the way, which helped me earn money while traveling. That income turned one gap year into three.

Turkey marked the fiftieth country I visited, and the most important. My dad's parents immigrated from Turkey when he was a teenager, and having the opportunity to learn about my roots organically solidified some of the unease within me —enough of it to return home and try again, anyway.

When I returned to the States permanently, I decided to pursue a career in travel. TST was the only well-established agency in Jacksonville at that time, so I reached out to Yuke about a job. They were in need of an air specialist, and even though I knew nothing about the software or the logistics of booking travel for anyone but myself, she took a chance on me. She paid for my training and provided support every step of the way. I can't imagine not working at TST. If we ever go under, they'll have to drag me out by my hair.

I'm still searching for the same balance in my personal life. Which would explain my continued dependence on being in a relationship over the years. While at the root of things, I do love love, and I am afraid of being alone, I'm more so terrified that maybe I'm strictly the type of person people only want for surface-level satisfaction; that maybe I'm always going to be more than someone bargained for at the end of the day.

Now, I can't stop thinking about the fact that Ellie could be the exception to this rule. Which must be why I feel like I'm going to jump out of my skin while waiting for her date with Rick to end. I even accepted an invitation from Adem to join him at the gym, where I'm now speed walking on the treadmill because running would probably kill me and my gym-avoidant body.

"Are you going to get off that treadmill any time soon? It's been like an hour. You look like you're training for the local suburban mom walking club." Adem walks over to check on me, a dumbbell in each hand.

"Have you ever watched a suburban mom power walk? It's both horrifying and impressive, so I'll take that as a compliment," I pant, wiping the back of my hand across my sweaty brow.

"Fine." He laughs. "I'm just happy you're here. It's good for you."

"Thanks, Dr. Polat, I didn't know that."

"It's about time you start referring to me by my formal title." He puffs his chest out and starts alternating bicep curls.

"Ah, yes, the golden Dr. Polat. Perfect eldest child. Medical doctor. Highly-esteemed pain in my ass," I joke. "I pity anyone who doesn't have a brother so cool."

"I never hear any complaints from you when you're obsessively texting me at 3 a.m. because you're convinced you have Yellow Fever," he says in between deep breaths.

"We live in Florida. There are a lot of mosquitos and you know it's plausible," I defend myself.

"You probably have a higher chance of being eaten by an alligator."

"*Again*, we live in Florida. That's not entirely out of the question, either." I shiver, my sweaty body chilling from head to toe. "We should have moved to Colorado when Mom and Dad retired there."

"Why, so you can worry about being trampled by a moose 24/7? Or maybe hypothermia?" He drops the dumbbells, quirking a thick eyebrow at me over the top of his round-rimmed glasses.

"Yeah, yeah...go lift heavier weights or something." I shoo him away and look down at the treadmill's timer.

Only twenty-four fucking minutes. Are you kidding me?

With Adem gone again, I'm back to forcing myself not to check my phone for messages from Ellie for the billionth time. That will be my reward at the thirty-minute mark. No sooner, no later.

Too bad my phone feels like it's burning a hole in my pocket.

At 27:54, I cave and pull my phone out of my sweats, squinting at it as it comes to life. My stomach does a flip when I see the solitary notification on the screen.

1 Missed Call: Ellie Amos TST

I slap the stop button on the treadmill, forgetting to slow my pace and tripping forward in the process. I catch myself at the last second and a few people around me shoot concerned looks my way. Heat floods my cheeks and I give them a thumbs-up along with a closed-lipped smile to show them I'm okay.

This is why I don't work out.

Jumping off the treadmill, I grab my discarded jacket and pat my pockets to check for my keys before jogging off to find Adem.

"I gotta go," I say breathlessly when I find him on the seated cable row machine.

"What? You just got here."

"I missed a call from Ellie. I'm gonna call her back. I'll talk to you tomorrow!" I turn and run for the exit.

"Bye, I guess," he yells from somewhere behind me.

Sliding behind the steering wheel, I hit the call button. The ringing continues as I navigate out of the parking lot and Ellie's voicemail picks up.

"Hey, sorry I missed you, I was at the gym. I'm free now though, and will be around for the rest of the evening." I fumble through the message and toss my phone into the passenger seat. It remains silent on the drive home.

She calls again just as I'm getting out of the shower. "Is this our first game of phone tag?" I ask after accepting the call.

"I believe it is." A door opens and shuts on Ellie's end. "Sorry. I was at my uncle's seeing Brat."

"I haven't asked yet. Are your uncles okay with you missing Thanksgiving this year?" I wrap a towel around my waist and shuffle to my bedroom to rummage around for some sweatpants.

"Oh, they are practically pushing me out the door. I never knew they were so desperate for me to show interest in something like this." She pauses. "I really can't blame them, though. What twenty-something is happy just staying home and hanging out with her uncles all the time?"

"A very smart, ambitious, and beautiful twenty-something," I say, wincing as the words leave my mouth.

Ellie falls so silent I can hear the whirring of my ceiling fan in my ears. I put the phone on speaker and toss it onto the bed to pull my pants on, tightening the string a little too aggressively.

Dammit Eren...too soon.

I clear my throat, preparing to talk myself out of a hole but Ellie comes back to life just in time.

"Did...you just call me beautiful?"

"Errr, yes?" I choke. "Is that okay?"

"It's just different than your usual compliments," she tells me.

"I'm sorry if it was weird. I do mean it, though. I hope it didn't make you uncomfortable."

"No! No. It's just, well, thank you."

We push through the embarrassing moment and move on to other subjects. Colorado. What we're currently watching and reading. My brothers. Bratwurst the pittie. I roll across the bed to check the clock on my nightstand as we reach the office gossip segment of the night, and balk at the 12:00 a.m. glowing before me. The call time on my phone screen shows nearly four hours, and my battery is at 5%.

"Anyway, that's my opinion on Petra having a crush on Lamar—" Ellie is saying.

"You're right. They're total opposites which does some-times work," I agree as a thought hits me. "Holy shit, Ellie! I never even asked about your date with Rick! How did it go?"

I had been so full of jitters waiting for her to text that I forgot *why* I was so full of jitters in the first place.

"It was fun. We had margaritas and Mexican food. Rick is a good guy." She sounds like she means it and I hate it.

I suddenly want to have margaritas with Ellie more than anything in the world.

"Great, great." I force enthusiasm. "So, when is the second date?"

Did he kiss you? Did you kiss him? Did he invite you home with him?

Those are the questions I actually want to ask. But I can't. I won't.

"Honestlyyyy." She draws the word out, her voice pitching higher on the last syllable. "There's not going to be one."

Adrenaline floods my brain and I catapult off the bed and run into the living room, stopping near the couch to regain control of my body. My heart is beating faster than it was at the gym a few hours ago. "Why?" I ask, catching my breath.

"The topic of the sales manager job came up, and it made me realize that us pursuing a relationship while working so closely and also trying to nab the same promotion is a bad idea," she explains. "I already feel like I'm in hot water with the whole 'I'm a fake travel agent' thing. Dating a coworker doesn't need to be added to the agenda. Plus, him and I, we're too similar in a lot of ways."

Another adrenaline burst shoots me into the kitchen and I open the cabinet to grab a glass for water, smiling so wide the corners of my lips feel like they might split open.

If there's no Ellie and Rick, that means there is room for a potential Ellie and Eren.

The two E's. In a different context.

Except...I'm technically Ellie's co-worker too. Which makes me no more of an exception to the rule than Rick.

Fuck. I fill the glass and down the water in two gulps.

"There's also one more reason," Ellie says, bringing my attention back to her.

"What's that?" I ask.

"I think I mi—" She's cut off mid-sentence as my phone dies.

Growling, I stare down at the black screen and let my forehead fall against the side of the refrigerator for a second before I sprinting back to my bedroom to connect it to the charger.

For fuck's sake, Eren...

A few minutes later, it finally has enough charge to power back on and I find a text from Ellie.

ELLIE

I'm not sure what happened, but I should probably go to bed anyway. Goodnight!

Sighing, I lay the phone on my nightstand and gather my

hair into a bun on top of my head. What was her third reason? Will I ever find out?

I turn the lamp off and collapse onto my pillows, rolling over to decipher every second of our conversation before I eventually fall into a deep sleep.

CHAPTER 23

ELLIE

Somehow, TST makes it to the Friday before Thanksgiving break.

I say somehow, because the office has been a combination of a shit show and a wildfire for the past five days. On top of existing reservations, we've received a record number of calls. All sample planners and final itineraries have had to be sent out before we're closed for a week. Details for every existing trip had to be organized and documented for our on-call staff to refer to in emergencies during the closure.

The tips of my fingers feel raw from so much typing, and I've never spent so much of my home time researching. On top of prepping for Colorado. My eight hours of sleep a night have turned into roughly five-and-a-half. I'm going to have to binge nap all weekend so I don't immediately crumble when we get to the airport on Monday.

"Ellie?" Yuke's soothing voice comes through my phone's speaker. "Can you come up and see me for a minute?"

My breath catches in my throat as I shakily reach for the receiver. "Sh-sure. Be, uh, right up," I stammer.

Oh God. Does she know?

I stand up, knees quaking, and smooth my gray skirt over my butt, even though it already falls past my knees. Rick looks at me over his shoulder as I pass, but he doesn't smile or acknowledge me. He's been like this all week, which makes me think he was a little more upset with me on Friday night than he initially let on.

Normally, I only go up to the second level to visit Eren. I wish that's what I was doing right now. We've both been so busy this week, we've barely spoken since our phone call on Friday night. Which means I haven't even gotten to say the thing that I had been trying so hard to muster up the courage to say during our entire conversation.

I think I might have feelings for you, Eren.

Rationally, I've convinced myself that the phone died just in time to save me from making a mistake. I was obviously moving too fast. I need more time to make sure this is how I really feel.

At the top of the stairs I turn right and knock gently on Yuke's door. "Come in," she calls.

"Hi," I say with a grin, closing the door behind me and moving to sit in the chair across from her desk. "Happy Friday."

"Yes!" She stops typing and slides her glasses down to the end of her nose. "I know everyone is ready for a week off."

The wall behind her is covered in framed photos of her travels over the years. In the top left picture, she's in Iceland's blue lagoon, teeth gleaming from a clay-covered face. In the bottom right, she's standing at the edge of the Grand Canyon. In the one just behind her, she glowing gold in the sun on the Amalfi Coast.

There are so many places. So many of her memories.

I want that too, I'm surprised to hear myself think.

"I wanted to check with you," she continues and I snap to

EVERYWHERE WE'VE NEVER BEEN

attention. "Do you plan to use your travel stipend before the end of the year, or wait until after the first?"

"I'm–I"m not really sure yet," I say truthfully.

So much has happened since the meeting that I've honestly completely forgotten about it. And how do I commit without knowing how Colorado will make me feel? We're talking about potential international travel. Solo, *international* travel. Will I be ready for that after a single trip?

"No pressure to answer now, I'm mainly asking for end-of-year tax purposes. You know, the boring side of stuff." She runs a hand through her short, black hair and smiles.

"When would you need to know?" I ask. "Is after Thanks-giving too late? I need to take a look at my schedule and see what works best."

Thank goodness she has no way of knowing how empty my schedule is after next week. How empty my personal schedule always is.

"That would be fine," she confirms. "Just let me know, and we can get the ball rolling. You'll get to be the first to retest the travel perk waters."

"I can't wait!" I force enthusiasm into my voice.

Yuke stands and I follow her lead. "Thanks for coming up to see me. I have to go put a fire out in accounting. Enjoy your holiday, Ellie."

I open her door just as Eren is coming out of his office, his messenger bag thrown across his shoulder. He raises his eyebrows at me questioningly. Once Yuke has made it halfway down the stairs I slump against the wall and slide down to the floor. "I thought I was about to get canned. But she only wanted to ask when I'm using my travel stipend."

"What reason would she have to can you?" he asks, staring down at me.

I cock my head and narrow my eyes at him.

"Oh, right. That." He smacks his palm against his forehead. "No need to worry about that anymore. We have it all under control."

He holds a hand out and I take it so he can pull me to my feet. Chills race up my arm at the contact, and he provides so much leverage that I stumble forward and my nose bumps into his chest. He gently places his other hand on my shoulder to steady me. Our upper bodies press closer together and I peer up at him, trailing my eyes from his chest to his beard, pausing briefly on his lips before our eyes meet.

I need to take a step back. But then I would ruin whatever this is.

Walt's office door opens at the other end of the hallway and we shoot apart, faces red.

"Eren. Ellie. Have a great week off." He nods at us as he passes, and then we're alone again, afraid to look each other in the face.

"I should go wrap everything up." I point towards the stairs with my thumb.

"Yeah. Yeah, of course," Eren says. "Am I still good to come over on Sunday? To finish off Colorado prep 101?"

"Absolutely." I trot down the first flight of stairs and check to make sure he's following. "We can use my uncle's study. You can meet Brat."

"Fuck yeah!" He pumps a fist in the air. "I hope he likes me."

"He will love you," I tell him. "What's not to love?"

"You really mean that?" he asks at the base of the stairs, laughter in his voice even though his expression is thoughtful.

"I do."

With that, he walks away. The moment the door closes behind him, I already can't wait for Sunday.

CHAPTER 24

EREN

Even though I know it's not one, I feel like I'm going on a first date.

Ellie told me to ring the front doorbell of the main house when I arrive, and walking up the brick sidewalk to the picturesque wraparound porch deepens my nerves. What if Ellie's uncles are around? Will they like me? Would it be worse for them to hate me, or for Brat to hate me?

What if *all* of them hate me?

I walk up the steps, which are newly decorated for Christmas. Fake snowmen line both banisters and a hipster Santa with a beanie stares up at me from the door mat.

Quirky. I like it.

Lifting a shaky hand, I press the bell firmly, which sets off an eruption within the house. Deep barks make their way closer and closer to the door, along with mumbled shouts. "I'll get it," I hear Ellie say.

The door flies open and she appears, one hand on the knob and one wrapped around the collar of a meaty black and white dog. He's trying his hardest to claw his way closer to me, the biggest doggie grin I've ever seen plastered on his sweet face.

"As you can see, he's dying to meet you," Ellie says, pulling him back. "Please, come in."

I step into the foyer, momentarily enamored by my surroundings. A chandelier sparkles overhead. The rug on the floor has to be antique, and where the outside of the home is obviously Spanish-inspired, the interior is full mid-century modern. "This is so nice," I say, looking around appreciatively.

"This house is my Uncle Sai's baby," Ellie replies, placing a hand on Brat's butt to assist him into a sit position. "He's always making changes. He says it will be perfect one day."

"It already looks perfect to me." I kneel to Brat's level and hold my hand out jokingly. "Hi Mr. Bratwurst. I'm Eren. It's so nice to meet you."

To my joy, he lifts a paw and places it in my palm. Delighted, I look at Ellie. "'Shake' is the first trick we ever taught him." She grins. "I appreciate your shirt. It's perfect for the occasion."

I look down at my button-up, which is covered in dogs of various breeds wearing red-rimmed glasses. "I had to make a good first impression," I say.

Brat breaks his sit and slurps his tongue across my face in reply.

"I believe it worked," Ellie laughs. "Come on, I'll introduce you to my uncles. I also have a surprise for you."

"For me? What is it?" I ask, intrigued.

"You'll see!"

We walk down a long hall lined in expensive-looking artwork, which opens into a large, open kitchen and dining space. Two men stand behind the kitchen counter. The larger of the two has the shiniest bald head I've ever seen, and is moving cookies from a baking sheet to a plate. The other has short salt-and-pepper hair and is stirring something in a large pot on the stove. They both abandon their tasks when we appear.

"Eren, welcome." The bald man comes around the counter to meet me. His smile reaches all the way to his eyes as he grasps my hand. "I'm Rob. It's nice to meet you. This is my husband, Sai."

Sai sidles up and takes my hand from Rob. His grip is much lighter. "I can't believe we're finally meeting you in the flesh!" he says.

"Thank you for having me over," I tell them. "Your home is beautiful."

"No, what's beautiful is that hair of yours," Sai says. "There's so much of it. What shampoo do you use?"

"Oh, thank you. Just whatever is on sale, though. Nothing exciting."

"Whatever is on sale? Oh, Eren, no. I'll give you some recommendations before you leave." Sai returns to the stove to stir whatever is in his pot. "Otherwise you'll look like Rob here in ten years."

Everyone laughs, including Rob. "And here I've just assumed it was genetic this whole time."

Ellie slides onto one of the bar stools and pats the one beside her. "Here is the surprise," she says, opening her arms in front of her to display the cookies Rob is preparing. "Uncle Rob's chocolate chip shortbread. I know you really liked them last time."

"Liked? They're the best thing I've ever tasted!" I practically start drooling at the memory.

"Don't make me blush," Rob jokes. "And Sai is making hot apple cider. We love snacks in this house."

"Then I'm in the right place." I pat my stomach for effect. "I'm from a snackin' family myself."

Brat lets out a little bark, as if to agree.

Rob passes me a cookie and it's so warm it falls apart in

my hand. I shove half into my mouth and my eyelids flutter at the saltiness combined with the rich chocolate chips and buttery biscuit. This shortbread has ruined all other desserts for me.

Sai turns the burner down low and puts a lid on top of the cider. "That's all ready for you too," he tells Ellie. "I think I'm going to lie down for a bit, if that's okay. I'll be back soon. I'm exhausted today for some reason."

"Have a good nap." Rob pecks him on the lips before he leaves the room.

"Is he okay?" Ellie asks her uncle.

"Yeah, he…" Rob falters a little. "Sunday naps are his new thing."

Ellie's entire body stiffens on the stool next to me. I look over at her and she continues to stare at Rob, a look of deep thought on her face. He focuses intently on the countertop in front of him. I don't know what I'm missing, but something tells me that Ellie is out of the loop on it too.

"So, Eren," Rob changes the subject. "How did you end up in Florida if your parents are in Colorado?"

"Oh, I grew up here," I tell him. "My brothers and I were all born in Jacksonville. My parents retired a couple of years ago and decided to go back to Colorado, where Dad is originally from."

"Good for them. Most people do the opposite and move down here after years of cold winters," Rob jokes.

"My dad actually loves the cold." I laugh. "Mom…not so much. But she does love the mountains, and her and Dad agreed early on to raise us in Florida, and eventually retire back to Colorado."

"How did they meet?" Ellie asks. "That's a big distance."

"Tinder," I tell her, fighting to keep a straight face. Laughter booms out of Rob's chest and the sound causes Ellie and I to crumple into giggles along with him.

"I should have known the two of you would have the same sense of humor," Ellie says, rolling her eyes.

"That was a really good one." Rob wipes a tear from his eye and turns to pull a couple of mugs from the cabinet behind him.

"Really though," I say. "They actually met through work. At a sales convention in the early 80's. In Orlando."

"Workplace romance, then." Rob wiggles his eyebrows. "My favorite trope."

My neck warms at the mention of falling for a coworker. Pulling my shirt collar away from my skin, I sneak a glance at Ellie. Our eyes meet for half a second before she raises her eyes to stare at some invisible object on the ceiling. A soft whine fills the room, redirecting our attention to Brat, who is sitting patiently by the door to the patio, looking between the three of us with pleading eyes.

"Do you need to potty, Brat?" Ellie asks.

He sits upright on his haunches and paws at the air. His upper lip is tucked under, revealing a goofy little grin that unexpectedly fills me with serotonin. God, he's cute. No wonder he's Ellie's favorite thing on the planet.

"I'll take him," Rob tells us, pushing two mugs of cider in our direction. "Feel free to take your snacks into the study if you'd like. Sai and I set up the Christmas tree in there last night and it's looking mighty cozy, if I do say so myself."

"Thanks so much for this." I beckon to the steaming cup and the cookies. "That was really nice of you."

"Any time." Rob grabs a leash from the hook by the door and clips it to Brat's collar. "If y'all need anything, just let me know."

Standing, Ellie grabs her mug and the plate of shortbread. Carefully cradling my own drink between my palms, I follow her down the hallway, focusing intently to not spill a single drop on the rug running along the floor.

"Your uncles are awesome," I say to the back of her bobbing head.

"I definitely have no complaints." She smiles at me over her shoulder, her short hair enhancing the curved line of her neck. The skin there is smooth and inviting, and I couldn't dream up a better surface to press my lips against if I tried. I grit my teeth.

Get a grip, Polat.

A drop of scalding cider escapes the mug and trickles over my fingers, causing my teeth to clamp together even tighter. "Fuck," I whisper under my breath.

"Are you okay?" Ellie turns into the study and sets her drink and the cookies on a coffee table in the middle of the room, which is filled with such an heir of comfort that I immediately forget about my burnt fingers. Jewel-toned pillows and throw blankets cover two leather couches. Shelves and shelves of books line an entire wall. A tall, thin Christmas tree glows warmly in the corner next to the fireplace.

That's it. I'm moving in.

"Yeah…" I place my cup on the table beside hers. "I just spilled a little on my hand."

She steps in front of me and holds her palm out. "Let me see."

I let her take my hand, and she flips it over to inspect my fingers, flattening my palm against hers. She runs the fingertips of her other hand across my knuckles. Her touch is lithe and gentle, but I feel it all the way down to my toes. With her head bent, I have the perfect view of the top of it, and I wish I could rest my cheek against her hair and pull her into my chest.

"It's a little red. I'm sure we have some Neosporin somewhere." She releases me and backs toward the door.

"No, no. It's really okay." I laugh. "It just shocked me a little."

"Are you sure?"

"Positive."

I take a seat on one of the couches and pat the spot next to me. She flops down and grabs her mug and something else off of the table before tucking her legs beneath her and snuggling into the couch. She's less put together today than she tends to be at work...wearing jeans and a loose-fitting gray t-shirt. Her hair has a natural-looking wave to it, and it falls into her eyes as she grabs a blanket and tucks it around her bare feet.

"You look so cute and cozy," I say before I can stop myself.

"Cute, huh?" she asks after a beat of silence.

"Very." I stand by my choice of words and settle into the couch next to her, becoming distracted by the other object she grabbed from the table.

"My itinerary!" I exclaim, taking it from her lap. "How did I do? I feel like it's written pretty well, considering I've never put one together before."

"You're a natural. I especially appreciate the packing list you threw in at the end."

"I thought that was a nice touch." I flip the folder open to discover little hand-written notes in the margins of certain pages. Questions and comments and little mini to-do lists. Feeling intrusive, I close it and give it back to her.

"Sorry..." Her cheeks redden. "Those are all of my silly little anxiety notes."

"That's not silly at all, Ellie." I turn to face her, resting my elbow against the back of the couch.

"I'm just...nervous." She wraps her hands around her mug and stares into it before bringing her eyes to meet mine. She's different, here, in this environment. More vulnerable. More relaxed. More open.

"What can I do to help?" I ask. "Today is about making sure you're ready. I know you are, but I want you to know you are too. Ask me anything. Tell me anything."

She pulls her lower lip into her mouth and bites it gently,

deep in thought. My eyes follow the motion on their own accord. I would suddenly give anything just to know what her lips feel like. How they would fit against my own.

"How does it feel?" Ellie asks, and I wonder if she was somehow able to read my thoughts.

"Huh?" I ask, startled.

"To be so far from everything you know," she continues. "Can you feel it? Does your brain comprehend the distance?"

"Oh," I smile, relaxing. "Travel is weird, in that regard. Like you know you're somewhere different. When you think about it really hard, you are able to visualize how far from home you are. But none of that matters. Because when you're experiencing a new place for the first time, it also somehow seems familiar. Like you're meant to be in that exact place, at that exact time."

Her eyes soften as she listens to me speak. The corners of her mouth lift, and the worried crease between her eyebrows disappears. "Wow," she says. "That's beautiful."

"It's true." I shrug. "You'll see. And I can't wait for you to experience it."

"Thank you, Eren," she tells me. "I haven't said that yet, and I mean it. I couldn't do this without you."

"You could. But I'm happy to be a part of it."

I would do anything for you, is what I don't say.

"Now, for a more basic question." She sits up straighter and reaches for a cookie. "Can I bring a nail file on the plane?"

CHAPTER 25

ELLIE

"Thank you," I tell Uncle Rob as he stands from adding a couple of small logs to the study's fireplace.

"Let me know if it gets too low," he says. "It's chilly tonight."

He leaves and I turn back to Eren, who looks incredibly comfortable across from me. Evening has fallen and the sky is a deep purple outside of the window behind him. The fire casts a red hue on his dark hair as he reaches to grab another eggroll from one of the takeout boxes on the table. The day has flown by, and even though we have to be up abominably early to catch our flight, I'm nowhere near ready for him to leave.

"Don't think you can use your uncle as a distraction from what we were just talking about." He smirks, returning to the conversation we had been having before Uncle Rob came to check on the fire.

"I wouldn't dream of it," I reply, placing my hand on top of a sleeping Brat who is very tightly wedged between us on the couch.

"So what you were saying is, you didn't have a crush on

167

Westley, but on *Prince Humperdinck*?" He stares at me incredulously.

"That's what I said." I raise my eyebrows, challenging him to argue with me further.

"I'm honestly flabbergasted." He leans forward and pretends to whisper into Brat's ear. "Brat, Ellie grew up romanticizing *The Princess Bride* in the completely incorrect way."

"What can I say? Sometimes I like to go for the villain," I joke.

Eren stretches his arm along the back of the couch toward me and dramatically drops his forehead against it. I swat at him jokingly and he catches my wrist in a gentle grasp. "I'm not letting go until you admit Westley is the obvious and only correct person to crush on in that movie."

"I guess you're never letting go then." I laugh, attempting to pry his clasped fingers open with my free hand. Brat opens an eye and stares up at us momentarily before returning to his nap.

"We disrupted the baby's slumber," Eren jokes, releasing me. But I'm enjoying the feel of his touch too much, so I let my arm rest against his on the back of the couch instead of moving it.

We've been performing this same semi-flirty song and dance all day. Little touches. Deep conversations. Fun facts we've never shared before. All packaged up in the cloud of tension that has been slowly developing around us over the past couple of weeks. Until today, I thought it might just be me feeling this way. Eren is making it pretty evident that's not the case, though.

But I don't know what to do about it. What if he's using me as a rebound? What if I'm mistaking the kindness he's shown by helping me for something more?

The next week should be interesting.

"We have to be at the airport in roughly eight hours." He wipes a hand over his face before reaching to pet Brat, but his palm lands on top of mine instead of Brat's head. Neither of us moves a muscle.

"As much as I hate to say it, you should probably head home," I tell him.

"Why do you hate to say it, Ellie?" His eyes twinkle in the low lighting of the study.

I shake my head and sit up, letting the blanket fall from my lap as I begin to close up all of the half-eaten Chinese food. Eren sits up beside me. Annoyed, Brat jumps to the floor and stretches before leaving the room.

Eren scoots closer and helps me tidy the mess on the table. His thigh presses against mine, and my body considers being pressed against all other parts of him. He's so close that his hair tickles my cheek as it falls over his shoulder. I shiver and force myself to focus on the task at hand.

"Is it maybe because," Eren presses. "You like being with me?"

I shrug, committing to my stubbornness. I can't be the first to cave. I won't be the first to cave. What if I'm wrong? What if I voice my feelings, and he actually doesn't feel the same way? I have to wait until after Colorado.

He won't let go, though.

"Because..." He takes a box of orange chicken from me and places it to the side. His hands envelop mine and I instinctively turn toward him. "Lately I'm learning, I'm happiest when I'm around you."

My shoulders relax. Eren places a finger under my chin and tips it up, forcing me to meet his eyes. He trails his touch up my cheek to tuck my hair behind my ear. I can hear Uncle Sai singing to Brat from somewhere in the house, but it sounds muffled through the pounding of my heart in my ears.

He goes to remove his hand from the back of my neck, but

I grasp his forearm, holding him there. "Does this mean I can kiss you now?" I breathe.

We move at the same time, maneuvering around all of the confusing feelings and unasked and unanswered questions that have been building between us. His beard tickles my mouth briefly before giving way to the smoothness of his lips, which connect perfectly with my own.

The tension oozes out of me and I melt into him, wanting to be closer. Needing to be closer. He drops his hands to my waist and pulls, guiding my legs on either side of his until I'm straddling him, his mouth never leaving mine. A brief moment of panic pings around inside of my brain when I realize one of my uncles could walk in at any moment, but it dissipates the second Eren's tongue meets mine. I slide my fingers into his hair, becoming hungrier by the second as our lips continue to get to know each other, somehow gently and desperately at the same time.

A heat I haven't felt, well, ever maybe, courses through me faster and faster. If it wasn't for Eren and this couch, I would be in a puddle on the floor of the study.

I'm kissing Eren Polat. My coworker. My colleague.

My best friend.

The logical part of me, which is the largest part of me, knows it's complicated. But the tiny groans escaping from somewhere deep in Eren's body have me telling those doubts to shut the hell up. Life is full of reasons to be skeptical, but even I know that moments like this—feelings like this—don't occur just every day.

A high-pitched bark comes from the doorway. Startled, we shoot apart. I push myself off Eren's lap, knees shaking so hard that I almost fall back on top of him. Brat sits across the room, grinning that big dog smile, proud of himself for walking in on our little secret. I reach up to smooth my hair with one hand, bringing the other to my mouth. My lips are swollen, serving as proof that I really did make out with the man sitting in front of me.

The man, who with his mussed hair, flushed face, and wild eyes, could easily convince me to take him back to my tiny guest house apartment and discover other parts of him that I so desperately want to see.

The man I'm getting on my first airplane with tomorrow, to go to a place I've never been. Far from home. Away from what I know, and what is therefore safe in my eyes.

And with that thought, the confusion comes rushing back in.

"I'm sorry," Eren and I say at the same time, breathlessly. He leans forward, pressing his elbows into his knees and brushing his hair behind his ears. His hands seem to be quivering, probably from the same adrenaline that has my entire body wavering in the non-existent wind. He looks up at me, the lights from the Christmas tree casting a spray of glitter into his dark eyes.

"Not sorry that it happened..." he says. "I want to make that clear. More sorry for the awkward timing. I feel like a teenager who just made his first move in the basement of someone's house and got busted by a dad coming down the stairs. But in this case, the dad was Brat."

At the sound of his name, Brat trots over and rests his head on Eren's thigh. I'm sorry, his eyes seem to say. Eren and I burst into laughter.

I offer Eren a hand and pull him up from the couch. He towers over me. Has he always exuded this much heat? Or am I just drowning in the aftermath of the best first kiss I've ever had?

"I'm not sorry either," I tell him. "And hopefully neither of us are in the morning, since, well...you know."

"Since we have to spend the next week together and there will be no escape from me?" He grins and his white teeth shine through his beard. Subconsciously, I reach up and comb my fingers through the dark hair.

"Something like that..."

He grabs my wrist, moving my hand to his chest and holding it there as he dips his face toward mine. Instinctively, I rise onto my toes to meet him.

"Still doing okay in here?" Uncle Sai walks in and we jump away from each other a second time.

"Yeah, I was just about to head home," Eren tells him, his voice steady. Which is lucky for me, because I don't think I could speak actual words right now if I tried.

"I guess you two do have an early morning," Sai says. We follow him out through the hallway and into the kitchen, where Uncle Rob is eating more of his shortbread with a massive glass of milk.

"I'll send Ellie with a container of these for your travels," he says around a mouthful of chocolate chips, winking at Eren.

"Those will certainly beat out the plane snacks," Eren jokes.

"It was really nice to meet you," Sai tells him, putting an arm around my shoulders. "Have fun in Colorado, and take care of this one. We kind of like her."

Eren laughs. "She's going to love it. I have a feeling that after this trip, she'll be gone more than she's home. Happens to all new travel addicts."

I hug Uncle Sai before wiggling out of his grasp. "I'll walk you out," I tell Eren.

He follows me onto the porch and I shut the door behind us, breathing deeply as the comforting silence of the evening settles around us. "This is all going to be okay, right?" I ask, looking up at him through the darkness, trying my hardest not to appear as emotionally scattered as I'm starting to feel.

I'm in the midst of too much newness. Too much change.

And while I'm feeling optimistic about it now, I'm also waiting for the moment it will all come crashing down.

"More than okay, El." He reaches out to pull me against him, and I realize how much I've been longing to bury my face in his chest. He's solid against my cheek, and if I had to choose only one scent to smell for the rest of my life, I think it would be his combination of musky cologne and floral shampoo.

"I know this is all...crazy." He laughs, the vibrations in his chest tickling my cheek. "But I'm here. For you. For this fear you're facing. For us."

We stay silent for a few moments, learning to be comfortable wrapped in each other, settling into what I know we both hope will be our new normal. "Thank you," I whisper against him.

He tips my face up with a single finger and presses his lips against mine. There's no hunger this time, just the hope and anticipation of something new.

"Text me when you get close in the morning," I tell him as he breaks away. "I'll meet you at the end of the driveway."

"You got it." He backs down the stairs, holding eye contact. "And Ellie?"

"Yes?"

"This is the start of a whole new adventure. Remember that as you're falling asleep tonight."

"Okay, Mr. Cheesy." I smirk.

"I'm serious," he says, still walking backwards along the sidewalk. "Promise me you'll remember that?"

"I promise," I tell him.

For him, I'll at least try.

CHAPTER 26

EREN

I slept for a grand total of forty-seven minutes.

But I feel like I slept for forty-seven hours as Ellie and I claim our spot in one of the airport parking garages. Every nerve ending in my body has been buzzing since I left her on her porch last night, just trying to hold everything in until I could get in my car to freak out. In a mostly good way, of course.

Kissing Ellie was everything I imagined it would be and more. Each time I would begin to drift off to sleep, another detail of what happened would come to the forefront of my mind and then I would be wide awake, just thinking about it. About the feeling of her straddling my lap, mouths and chests connected. About her fingers threaded into my hair; the gentle scrape of her fingernails against my scalp. About the warmth of her lips and how they matched every single movement of mine.

And, obviously after running through the memory, I had to spend a good deal of time thinking about cold showers and all of those types of things to help myself become less...excited.

Yet, I still let the small fear that she might back out of our trip at the last minute creep into my mind all night long. Typical me. I'm once again waiting for someone to leave me before things even get too serious. Although, this does usually happen later in the relationship. Ellie and I aren't even past the *what are we actually doing* part of our relationship. Friendship. No, relationship?

What do I even call it anymore?

I shut the car off and turn to look at her. We've been chatting all the way to the airport, but she has barely moved an inch the entire ride. She's sitting straight as a board, her back barely touching the seat. Her hands rest on her knees, her fingers occasionally gripping them so tightly that her knuckles turn white. I'm not even sure she has blinked recently.

I've never seen someone trying to fight their nerves so hard. And I don't think it's because of my driving.

"Ellie?"

She snaps her neck in my direction so quickly it gives *me* whiplash. "Yes?"

"Are you in there?" I wave a hand in front of her face and she relaxes slightly.

"Yeah...sorry."

I want to touch her arm, grab her hand, *something* to show her I'm here to support her. But she has made no move to touch me so far this morning, and I don't want to cross a boundary. I have faith we're going to figure everything out, but now, when she's so obviously being eaten alive by other worries, is not the time.

"Let's go." She grabs her backpack from the floorboard and climbs out of the car. We grab our other bags from the trunk and begin walking in the direction of airport security. The wheels of our suitcases echo against the concrete walls of the garage, drowning out every encouraging sentiment I attempt to voice.

Other than helping her through luggage check and security, we barely speak for another forty minutes. We're now standing just on the other side of the security line, where people are already funneling through the terminal to their various gates before the sun is even up. Ellie has her black backpack clutched to her chest. It matches the rest of her outfit—black sneakers, black leggings, black sweatshirt.

"You look like a spy," I had told her when she got into the car earlier.

"Well, I am a *secret* travel agent," she'd replied with a giggle in her voice. The only giggle I got before we casually chatted about the airport breakfast options the whole drive to said airport.

"See, I told you there was coffee just on the other side of TSA." I sweep my arm towards a Starbucks.

"That'll do." She grabs my arm and guides me to the line. "So, I have a confession to make," she tells me over her shoulder, back turned to me.

"What's that?"

"I was more nervous about TSA than the flight itself," she says.

"Don't worry, everyone is!" I laugh, stepping one space up as she moves forward in the line.

"Now that it's over I'm already feeling a million times better." She stops abruptly and I bump into her, drawing a breath at the chills I get from the simple contact.

"Good," I reply, my mouth less than an inch from the back of her head. Finally allowing myself to touch her, I wrap an arm around her shoulders and pull her closer. Lowering my mouth to her ear, I whisper, "I'm here every step of the way."

"Thank you, Eren. Seriously." She turns her head to peck me on the end of my nose. I grin at the sweetness of the gesture, letting her go as the line moves again. If we weren't literally in the middle of a crowded room, I could easily devour her faster than I'm about to devour this latte.

Coffee and pastries in hand, we find seats near our gate to wait for boarding. "What's your plan for the flight?" Ellie asks me. "Reading? Listening to music? Watching a movie?"

"I don't have a plan." I laugh. "I wait until my butt is buckled into that tiny seat and then let my brain tell me what I feel like doing for the next four hours. Let me guess...you have a plan, don't you?"

"Well, I need to keep myself occupied. Keep my mind off the fact that I'm levitating in the air for an extended period of time. That means I can't get bored." She pulls two books, her phone, and an iPad out of her backpack.

"I'd say you're well-prepared." I look at the stack of entertainment in her lap. Her phone sits on top, screen lit up with a notification from United Airlines, advising boarding will be starting soon. Her background is a photo of Brat in a Santa hat, Christmas lights draped around his shoulders like a cape.

"That's my emotional support photo," she jokes.

"If that doesn't make you feel like everything is going to be okay, I don't know what could."

"When you put it that way, I actually have two things that make me feel that way." A blush creeps into her cheeks.

"What's the second?" I ask curiously.

She angles her knees towards me, balancing her things on her lap with one hand and placing the other on my cheek. "You."

Her eyes soften at the corners. For a moment, we just study each other, giving ourselves permission to stare; familiarizing ourselves with each other's features. Her freckle is more apparent on her early-morning makeupless face. I move closer and a tiny crease develops between her brows. Not a crease of worry, but anticipation.

It relaxes right before my mouth finds hers. Yesterday, she tasted of shortbread. Today, she tastes of toothpaste and coffee. I keep it short, not wanting to embarrass her in our public location.

"We're going to have to talk about this at some point." She quirks an eyebrow at me after I pull away. "But, for a while, can we just enjoy how good it feels to explore it?"

"Absolutely, I—"

"Boarding for United flight 4774 to Denver is about to begin. Please stand by." A voice comes over the gate's intercom, interrupting me. Interrupting us.

Immediately becoming frazzled again, Ellie begins shoving things back into her bag with shaking hands. She struggles with the zipper and I reach over to assist, hoping she doesn't mind the help. More than anything, I want her to know I'm here for her. But I also don't want her to feel overwhelmed by me. I don't want her to think that I'm...pushy.

When Ellie first agreed to come on this trip with me, it was mainly about overcoming her fears. Now that there are deepening feelings involved, the need for everything to go smoothly and perfectly seems even more crucial. Ellie is trusting me not only with her deepest worries, but as of yesterday, potentially also her heart.

And I want to be up for both of those challenges more than anything.

We pull our boarding passes up on our phones and join the crowd that is gathering around the gate. Ellie stays close to me, her side pressed against mine. I bend down to kiss the top of her head. She relaxes slightly and reaches for my hand, giving it a squeeze.

"I'm okay, really," she tells me. "Just working through the jitters."

"Now boarding group two," the woman behind the gate's desk announces.

"That's us!" I keep hold of Ellie's hand as we make our way through the line, never letting go until we reach our seats.

"It's time for the most important decision of your life," I say, faking seriousness as I reach up to put my backpack in the overhead bin. "Would you like the window or middle seat?"

"Whichever you don't want."

"Well, I'm impartial, so if you're up for it I have to insist that you take the window."

"Okay..." She scoots to the inner seat, slowly opening the window shade and peering outside. I fall into the spot beside her and fumble with my seatbelt.

"Thoughts so far?" I ask.

"Other than being a bit...compact, it's pretty much what I expected," she says. "But, we're not in the air yet."

"Going up is the fun part. It's like a rollercoaster."

"I've never been on a rollercoaster," she says quietly, almost to herself.

"Let's put that on our list then, shall we?"

"Our list?" she asks, rolling her head onto my shoulder and looking up at me.

"Yes, *our* list," I confirm. "Of things we're going to do. Places we're going to see."

"I didn't realize we had a list." Her voice takes on a flirty tone, and I find myself drowning in the varying shades of green in her eyes.

Ellie Amos is here. Next to me. Going to visit my parents for Thanksgiving. Not as my girlfriend, but now as a... complex friend?

In another version of my life, Kristen would be the one in that window seat. How has this all happened so quickly? Should I be feeling more guilt over the fact that I've barely thought about Kristen since we broke up? Should I be worried about the pace at which Ellie and I are moving? These are the types of questions that always ignite eagerness in me; always lead me away from being happy in the moment, and lead to needing confirmation of what's, and why's, and when's.

But as Ellie said not even 30 minutes ago, we'll talk about it when the time is right.

Live in the present, Eren.

"Do you not want us to have a list?" I ask, pressing my forehead to hers.

"I never said that." She sticks her tongue out at me.

"Ladies and gentlemen, welcome aboard United flight 4774 with nonstop service to Denver." The pilot's voice comes over the intercom. "Boarding is complete and the aircraft door is now closed, which means we are preparing for takeoff. Please make sure all seatbelts are fastened, tray tables are up, and kindly pay attention to the safety demonstration."

Ellie pulls away from me to check her seatbelt and turns her attention to the flight attendant in the aisle, who is showing passengers how to access life vests in the event of an emergency. If I didn't already know Ellie was a first-time flyer, I would be able to tell now, strictly from the intently focused expression on her face.

God, she's perfect, I can't help but think.

The plane shakes with its first movement, backing away from the gate. Ellie finds my hand again and I rub my thumb along her wrist, noting the quick rhythm of her pulse. While her grip is firm and her heartbeat is fast, the rest of her demeanor is brave.

I realize, this is a perfect example of how Ellie lives her life. On the outside, she's organized and put-together. But on the inside, she's sometimes screaming, just trying her hardest to keep all of the uncertainty contained.

I never would have learned this if she hadn't trusted me enough to tell me about her parents. About her past. I would have only continued to know her as private, serious Ellie, who would sometimes break character just long enough to show me the sides of her that make me even more drawn to her.

The sides of her that have me rapidly hurdling over all of

180

our friendship boundaries, hoping we make it through the turbulence of change that is upon us, and into clearer, bluer skies.

The plane speeds up, going faster and faster, until the wheels finally lift off of the ground. Beside me, Ellie takes a deep breath. Then we're in the air, continuing further into the unknown.

CHAPTER 27

ELLIE

A s it turns out, the world isn't entirely made up of flat, Florida-like landscapes. I've always *known* this, of course. But now I can confirm, and I've never been more thankful for it as I stare up at the imposing Rocky Mountains.

The changing elevation makes my ears pop as Eren drives us what feels like further and further into the sky. There's a smudge on the window of the rental car, where I've had my forehead pressed against the glass, fighting for the best possible vantage point of our changing surroundings. While the peaks of the mountains are capped white with snow, all of the trees below create a patchwork of green, orange, and brown.

We go around a corner and I make the mistake of looking down. One wrong move and we could easily slip right over the ledge and tumble down to the bottom to join the many, many rocks that have taken the same path. I shudder and force my gaze forward.

"Don't worry, I've driven here plenty," Eren encourages.

"I'll take your word for it," I say, skipping to the next song on my playlist. Eren has given me DJ responsibilities for the drive. "Wherever You Will Go" by The Calling starts playing over the speakers.

"The Goo Goo Dolls, Counting Crows, Matchbox 20, and now The Calling. Do you have any music produced after 2005?" Eren jokes.

"Hey, nothing compares to this time period for music," I defend myself. "This is the type of stuff Uncle Rob listened to when I was growing up, and nothing else has ever quite been the same for me."

"I suppose I can't argue with the defense of nostalgia. And you're not wrong, it is good." He turns the volume up and sings along with the chorus.

"Maybe you should let them sing it." I reach over to poke him in the arm.

"You think you're funny, huh? Don't forget who's driving us up this mountain." His grin is so big his eyes disappear into his face. I love when he smiles like that. He looks like the happiest man in the world.

Probably because he is one of the happiest men in the world. He feels like it to me, anyway.

"How much further?" I ask.

"Just ten minutes or so," he says. "If you're not into hugging strangers, you should let me know now. Because my mom is very excited to meet you."

A thought hits me. "I'm fine with hugs..." I tell him. "But out of curiosity, do your parents know what's happening here?" I point back and forth between us.

"No," he says simply. "They just know you're my friend."

"Okay, cool." I settle into the seat. "Were they upset about you and Kristen?"

"Not really. Dad is pretty good about staying out of my personal life. Mom was a little bummed, but she also never even met Kristen, so that made it easier on her. My mom is the type of lady who just wants her sons to be happy, so if I'm okay, she's okay."

"She sounds wonderful." I turn to gaze out the window again, thinking about my own mom; fighting to conjure a memory of a time that she ever cared about my happiness for a single second. A cloud forms over my head and I shake it away.

This trip is for me. I won't spend my time thinking about her. About my parents at all. If it wasn't for them, I would have allowed myself to have experiences like this much sooner.

At least I think I would have.

I can't help but wonder though, have Mom and Dad ever traveled along this same, exact road? They've spent a good deal of time in Colorado, so it's very possible. If they have, at least we can be connected to each other in a weird, roundabout way. Maybe some families are meant to be connected solely through means like postcards, and being in the same place, but at very different times.

"Almost there." Eren turns off the main road and begins carefully ascending a steep, uphill curve. I cling to the door handle and close my eyes, refusing to look down again. How do the people who live here simply drive up mountains every day, like it's not one of the most stressful things on the planet?

The wheels give one last spin against the asphalt and the car evens out on flatter terrain, bumping us along a dirt driveway encompassed by thick trees. Bit by bit, a modest ranch-style home appears from the thicket. It's early in the day, but the windows glow warmly. Smoke billows out of the stone chimney, and the front porch is laced in Christmas lights that I can't wait to see at night.

Eren parks next to a red Jeep and shuts the car off before turning to wink at me. "Welcome to The Polat Estate. It's not five stars, but it's close. That's our motto."

"I was immediately drawn in by the mountain charm..." I say, gazing over the top of the house to locate a rocky peak in the distance. "Sorry, just getting a head start on writing my Trip Advisor review."

"Nice," Eren laughs. "Perhaps I can get a head start on giving you one final kiss before we go inside and have to pretend we're strictly friends and co-workers?"

I turn in my seat to get a better look at him. It somehow feels like hours since we last made eye contact—since getting off the plane. I've been so distracted by the drive. By the views, and the dry air, and the way the sky seems to shrink as you get closer and closer to the mountains.

He's wearing a plain blue T-shirt, and while I miss his classic funny button-ups, I like this too. The snug sleeves show off his biceps, which are so nice I have to wonder where they came from since he constantly talks about his hatred for working out. His hair is piled into a messy bun on top of his head and his beard is flattened on one side from the nap he took on my shoulder during the flight.

He'd passed out about an hour in, once he was sure I was feeling okay. He was so heavy my arm fell asleep with him, but I didn't have the heart to move him. So I just looked out the window and happily pondered how I got there while he snoozed away.

Flying isn't so bad, by the way. So far, neither is being thousands of miles from home. Other than the fact that I've never felt more exhausted.

"Of course you can," I tell him, returning my thoughts to his mouth. "But you better make it a good one."

He kisses me like it's something that may never happen again. His hand starts out cupping my cheek, then trails down my neck, accidentally brushing the side of my breast on the route to my hip. I draw a sharp breath at the contact, accidentally pulling his bottom lip between my teeth. He hums contentedly and the vibration tickles my tongue, sending me into a fit of giggles.

"Until we meet again," he jokes as we separate.

The front door to the house flies open as we're climbing out of the car and a short, curvy woman comes jogging across the porch and down the steps toward us. "Hello, hello!" she calls as she runs, clapping her hands together.

"Hi, Mom!" Eren opens the trunk of the car before walking the rest of the way to meet her. He bends and wraps her in a hug, picking her up and giving her a little spin before setting her back on the ground.

My heart does a somersault in my chest, because my god, do I want him to pick me up and spin me around like that.

"And this must be Ellie!" She makes her way over and throws her arms around me. Her long brown hair swirls into my face, glints of gray shining in the sunlight as it moves. It smells just like Eren's. "I'm Yvette, it's so nice to meet you!"

"You too. Thank you for having me!"

Her hug is warm and firm in that way that only hugs from women can be. A lump forms in my throat when she gives me one more squeeze before pulling away. I don't often let myself mourn for things that I've missed out on in life, but some days, when I'm stressed and sad and just trying to figure out how to happily survive on this planet, I wish I had a mom to give me a good, solid "it's all going to be okay" type of hug.

"Couldn't be happier you're here." She gives me a gentle pinch on the cheek. "And look at you! How cute are you!"

"Mom, please don't pinch my guest," Eren chastises, meeting us with our suitcases. I try to grab mine but he pulls it out of my reach and moves around us to carry them inside.

"You're right, I'm sorry hon," she apologizes. "Sometimes I forget everyone doesn't like their personal space encroached upon."

"It's okay." I smile, looking her in the eye so she knows I'm being sincere.

"Please, come in." She links her arm through mine and we follow Eren.

Yvette ushers us into the house and closes the door. We go through the foyer and into the living room, where my eyes are immediately drawn to the floor-to-ceiling windows that run along the back of the house. The ceilings themselves are high with exposed beams.

A live Christmas tree stands in the corner, decorated with white twinkle lights and tons of handmade ornaments that Eren and his brothers must have made throughout their childhoods. Garland is strung across the fireplace mantle, which is home to one of those charming Christmas villages with all of the tiny little people and buildings and ice skating rinks.

The space is homey and warm in the way my uncles' house isn't. Many of the rooms in their home look like they belong in a museum; barely touched and perfectly staged. Yvette's home, going off of the first thought that comes to mind, has been touched by comfort in every single corner.

If I could sink onto the marshmallow-y couch for a nap right now, I would.

Eren sets our luggage near the window and beckons me over. "Ellie, come look. This is my favorite part."

My mouth gapes further and further open as I walk over to join him. A large wooden deck is built off the back of the house; the perfect observation point to view the neverending sea of radiant trees, which begin at eye level and gradually slope higher and higher. A small stream of water separates the deck from the tree line, flowing gracefully over shiny rocks that glint in the sunlight.

Why would anyone want to live anywhere else? I think, brushing off all of my driving-in-the-mountains fears. The beach is cool, but this is something else entirely.

"It's perfect," I murmur, afraid to blink and disrupt what I'm seeing.

"Might I suggest a cup of coffee and a good book on the deck, in your free time this week?" Yvette joins us. "The sound of that water is a white noise that can't be beat."

"Yeah," I say, already imagining myself in one of the Adirondack chairs with my most comfortable pair of fuzzy socks and a sweatshirt.

The faintest tinkling sound fills the space and I turn from the window, looking for the source. At first, I see nothing, but then a tall, gangly man with dark hair strolls slowly into the room, staring at the ground in front of him as he comes.

"Keep it moving, Scrabble. You can do it!" he says to the floor, maneuvering around the furniture.

The tinkling sound grows louder the closer he gets, and I'm almost entirely confused when the oldest dachshund I've ever seen dodders out from behind the couch. At one point it must have been brown, but there's so much gray in its fur that it's difficult to tell. The bells on its collar jingles in rhythm with its clunky gait.

Serotonin shoots through the entire length of my body and I nearly jump up and down. "Eren, you didn't tell me there was going to be a dog!"

"I thought he would be a nice surprise." Bending over, he carefully picks the dog up and brings him to me. "Ellie, this is Scrabble. Scrabble, meet Ellie."

"Aw, Scrabble. Hi!" I hold my hand out for him to sniff and he hurriedly crushes his nose to my knuckles before nonchalantly looking off into the distance, bored with me already.

"Don't take offense," Yvette reassures.

"Yeah," says the still unidentified man. "Not much excites him anymore. But he is friendly."

"Good to see you, Dad." Eren gives him a quick hug with the arm that isn't cradling Scrabble. "This is my friend, Ellie."

"Hey there, Ellie. I'm Emir." He shakes my hand firmly.

He carries an heir of seriousness, but his eyes are warm, like Eren's.

Standing between his parents, it's easy to distinguish all of the physical traits that Eren inherited from them. From his dad's obvious height and dark features, to his mom's sweet smile and long, thick hair.

"You need a haircut, Eren," his dad says, almost as if he's noting my observation.

"I was waiting for that," Eren says and Emir chuckles.

"Leave him alone." Yvette jokingly swats at her husband's arm and takes Scrabble from Eren. "It is quite long, though."

"So is yours." Eren sticks his tongue out at his mom and turns to me. "Come on," he says, grabbing our luggage from the floor. "I'll show you your room."

I follow him out of the living area and up the stairs, which are also lined in Christmas garland with white lights. "Mom and Dad's room is down there." He points to the right before turning left, giving me a quick tour as we go. "This is the bathroom, and this is where the idiots will sleep."

"When will they be here?" I ask, peeking into a bedroom with two twin beds.

"Tomorrow. So we'll all have one night of peace," he jokes. "You get what we call 'the good guest room.' When all three of us are here at the same time we have an arm wrestling competition for it. But you're the guest of honor, so we won't make you go through that. Although, I'm sure you could easily beat Tanner, at least."

"But where will you sleep?" I ask, feeling slightly guilty for having to take up space.

"The couch downstairs pulls out into a bed. It's actually pretty comfortable."

"Are you sure?" I ask him. "I don't mind sleeping on the couch if you want the bed."

"I wouldn't dream of it," he tells me, kicking open the

189

door at the end of the hall. "But I will keep my stuff in here, if that's cool."

"Of course."

The room is an extension of the rest of the house—simple, cozy, and inviting. A large, wooden bed frame takes up the majority of the space. There's one nightstand with a lamp that's shaped like a moose on top, and a small loveseat beneath the window, which has the same perfect view of the backyard.

Eren drops our things and backs toward the hallway. "Make yourself at home. If you'll excuse me for a moment, I'm desperately close to peeing in my pants."

Once he's gone I take a deep breath, relishing in the first moment of alone time I've had all day. It's been nothing but hustle and bustle, and I'm beat. I've always heard that traveling takes it out of you, but I wasn't expecting it to do so at this level. I feel like I need ten gallons of water, and my head hurts a little. I'm also starving.

I start to sit on the edge of the bed, popping back up when my butt meets something other than the comforter. The culprit is a red gift bag. My name is written on the tag in a beautiful cursive script. Did Eren bring this in?

I peek inside, spotting an envelope and plucking it out.

> *Ellie,*
>
> *Welcome to Colorado! We're so happy you and Eren are here for Thanksgiving, and hope you enjoy your visit. Our home is your home. Please let us know if you need anything.*
>
> *Yvette & Emir*

Warmth floods my insides, just like when I found the itinerary Eren made for me. Unexpected generosity always takes me by surprise, but in a good way. It makes me feel wanted—like I deserve to belong somewhere outside of the tiny, contained life I've built for myself.

Not that there's anything wrong with my corner of the world, but maybe I've only kept myself there because I've felt no other world would want to make room for me. Maybe Eren and his family are showing me how wrong I've been in assuming that. Maybe...

It feels too soon to hope for things like that.

I pull the rest of the contents from the bag. There's a dark green sweatshirt with embroidered mountains, a black hand-made scarf, and a bar of locally crafted soap that smells delightful. I run my fingertips over the bumpy threads on the sweatshirt, letting my thoughts wander, more "maybes" coming out of the woods to try and ascertain what I'm feeling.

Before I can catch them, two tears fall from my eyes, absorbing into the sweatshirt just above the tallest mountain peak.

CHAPTER 28

EREN

"How is she feeling?" Tanner asks when I come back downstairs.

"Better," I tell him. "I think she's through the worst of it. More embarrassed than anything."

"No reason to be embarrassed," Dad chimes in. "She can't help it."

"She'll get adjusted," Mom says. "Does she need anything? More ginger ale? Maybe something bland to eat? She must be starving."

"She did say she's starting to feel hungry, but she'll wait until tomorrow to be safe," I tell them.

Ellie threw up not too long after we ate dinner last night. She had been struggling with a headache and dizziness all afternoon, but we had chalked it up to a day of traveling.

"Altitude sickness, probably," Adem said when he arrived today. "Her body isn't used to the elevation. Have her continue to rest and make sure she's getting enough water. She should adjust pretty quickly."

Now we've lost our first full day, and I'm worried her being sick and embarrassed will make her skeptical about the rest of the trip. I've been back and forth to her room all day, bringing water and extra blankets and my laptop so she can watch Netflix, just keeping my fingers crossed that this will pass and she won't be swayed from this trip and beg me to go home.

"She's probably just sick of Eren's face," Tanner says, throwing a pillow at me.

"Shut up, Tanner," Mom, Dad, and Adem all say at the same time.

I roll my eyes at him and check my watch. It's almost 11:00 and I'm itching to go to bed, hoping that the sooner I close my eyes, the sooner I'll wake up to find Ellie and I back on track to the week I have planned. Even though I've seen her throughout the day, I miss her. I miss holding her hand and kissing her and watching her face light up as she experiences new things for the first time.

Seeing her sick has been terrible. I want her to feel better.

"If you don't mind," I say, scooping Scrabble up from his spot on the couch and plopping down between Mom and Dad. "I would love if you would all leave my room so I can go to sleep."

"But I was going to watch *The Mandalorian*," Dad says, holding the television remote up in the air.

"Fine," I sigh. "Dad, you can stay."

I usually fall asleep with the TV on anyway.

The next morning, I'm woken up by a thump on the back deck. I roll over on my couch bed and sit up to look out of the giant windows, which are perfectly framing the sun as it rises above the mountains in the distance. The strengthening rays outline the shapes of two heads peeking over the top of the chairs in front of the window.

Mom, my brain confirms. *And Ellie!*

I excitedly jump out of bed and run to the back door. They look up when I walk out, seeming surprised to see me. Both have blankets and steaming cups of coffee in their laps. Ellie is wearing a green sweatshirt with mountains on it that seems very far from her usual style, but also somehow suits her.

Mountain Ellie, I think. *I like her.*

"Eren! Son, where is your shirt?" Mom yells from across the deck. "You're not in Florida right now."

"Uhhhh, right. Sorry," I say, blushing as I make eye contact with Ellie and crossing my arms over my bare chest. I don't even remember taking my shirt off during the night. "Be right back."

I rush inside and up the stairs to pull a hoodie from my suitcase on the floor of Ellie's room. The bed is made with fresh sheets and all of Ellie's things are neatly piled in a corner. My itinerary sits on top, flipped open to today's activities. I take a deep breath, relieved for a sign that she isn't entirely ready to run back home.

Back downstairs, I stop in the kitchen for a cup of coffee. I step back out onto the porch just as Ellie says, "Last year, I talked to a guy who requested in his words 'somewhere beachy but not too sandy'."

Mom snorts. "How did you pull that one off?"

"Well, I ultimately had to give him a bit of a geography lesson. Then he changed gears and decided he wanted something more along the lines of adventure travel. He ended up here in Colorado actually—did some hiking and mountain biking and such."

"I remember him," I say as I pull up a chair. "He was the same guy who got mad at me because there were no window seats available in premium economy on the flight he wanted."

"Yep, that's him." Ellie laughs, tilting her head at me. "Hi, by the way."

"Hi..." I say, getting lost in how beautiful she looks in the morning light. Yesterday her face had been white as paper, her eyes rimmed red. Today the color is back in her cheeks, her lips pink from the hot coffee she's been sipping.

It would be so easy to lean forward and kiss her good morning, and every fiber of my being is screaming to do so. But Mom is here, and as happy as I think Ellie and I both currently are, things are still complicated. There's much to discuss—much to decipher. For both of us.

"Where's my hello?" Mom jokes, kicking at me with her slippered foot.

"Good morning, Mom." I reach over to pat her hand.

"What do you two have planned today?" she asks Ellie and I.

"Assuming Ellie feels well enough to go out..." I look at her out of the corner of my eye, crossing my fingers.

"Honestly, I feel one hundred percent," she says, crossing her heart. "After yesterday I'm ready to do anything and everything."

"That's exactly what I was hoping you'd say." I grin and turn back to Mom. "We're going to go into town for lunch and perusing. Then for a drive in Rocky Mountain National Park to take in the sights."

"That sounds lovely," Mom says. "Ellie, you'll love the park."

"I do have a favor to ask," I tell Mom. "Well, it's more of a request."

"Hot chocolate?" she asks.

"How'd you know?"

"Eren, I don't think you've ever set foot in that park without a thermos of my hot chocolate with you." She smirks.

"It's a tradition!" I take a sip of my coffee, already imagining the taste of Mom's famous recipe.

"I'll whip some up. *Two* thermoses full, so Ellie can get more than a taste." She winks at Ellie.

We sit on the porch a while longer before I head upstairs to get ready. Adem and Tanner bombard me as I'm coming out of the bathroom, holding me hostage between them in the hallway. Adem has Scrabble in his arms, who is looking like he'd rather be literally anywhere else.

"How's she feeling?" Adem asks.

"Better," I tell him. "We're about to leave to go to town, and then into the park."

"How is everything *else* going?" Tanner asks, wiggling his eyebrows at me.

"Good," I say. "But it's also new and not established. So please don't say anything to Mom and Dad. Or Ellie either, for that matter. I don't want her to think I'm running around telling everyone we're an item."

They pretend to lock their lips closed and throw away the keys, and I squeeze between them to meet Ellie downstairs. She's still wearing the mountain sweatshirt, along with a pair of black leggings and boots. Before the airport a couple of days ago, I had never seen Ellie in leggings. Now she's had them on twice in three days, and each time she wears them it becomes increasingly more difficult to not drool over the way they hug her thighs and the curve of her ass. To make resistance even harder, her sweatshirt is bunched up and sitting on top of her hips.

"What are you looking at, Mr. Polat?" she whispers so my parents can't hear in the next room.

"Just a really cute butt," I whisper back, holding my hands up in apology. "I'm sorry, it's the leggings. They're like magnets for my eyeballs."

"Hm. That's kind of how I felt when a certain someone

came onto the deck shirtless this morning." She quirks an eyebrow at me.

We grab the thermoses of hot chocolate and say our good-byes. The second we make it to the end of the driveway, I put the car in park and we turn to face each other. I take her face between my palms and kiss her on the forehead. "I'm sorry you got sick and I'm happy you're better."

"It's not your fault," she says, placing her hand on my thigh.

"I was afraid you would want to go home."

"Under different circumstances, maybe. But I'm with you. And that's all I need to stay positive."

"I missed you." I use my thumb to brush her hair away from her eyes. Then I kiss her.

She grips my thigh and I move one of my hands to her lower back, toying with the bottom of her sweatshirt. My fingers make contact with her skin and she inhales sharply, the rush of air cool against my lips. She deepens the kiss and I want to melt into her and live there forever. Her hand moves further up my leg, barely an inch from the tent that is forming inside my jeans.

I splay my hand flat against her smooth lower back before sliding it around to her hip and up her side. Making contact with the fabric of her bra, I slip a single finger inside to caress the bottom of her breast. I feel her body tighten beneath my palm, and she gently bites my lower lip before pulling away. We stare at each other for a moment, breathing heavily in the wake of crossing into the new territory of exploring each other's bodies.

"I find it impossible to believe I was ever able to keep my hands off you," I murmur.

"Things were different for most of our friendship," she says. "There were other relationships. Other crushes. Work. Life."

I bristle at the mention of her crush on Rick. The closer Ellie and I get, the more I can't stand the thought of him. Of him with her. It was never more than a mutual attraction, but she still has to sit next to him every day at the office. What if her feelings for him are really still there, just buried beneath what she's currently feeling for me?

Stop it, Eren.

This is jealousy. It's too soon for jealousy. Especially when Ellie has no qualms toward Kristen, or anyone else I've dated. Especially when I can count the number of times Ellie and I have kissed on two hands. We're too new.

But my feelings are growing every second of every day, and if there's one thing I know about myself, it's that big feelings terrify me. When I'm all in, I'm all in. Most people would say that's a positive thing. However, I've been in this spot enough to know that it can also be a downfall.

And I'm already far more "all in" on Ellie than I've ever been on anyone else this early in the relationship.

"Hey, you good?" Ellie reaches out to give my hair a little tug. "Your eyes went all glazey there for a second."

"Yeah, sorry." I force a smile, but it becomes more natural as I bring myself back to Earth and focus on the stunning girl sitting in front of me. "You hungry?"

We grab tacos at a Mexican place that always has the spiciest and strongest jalapeño margaritas I've ever tasted. After that, we meander around town, drifting in and out of all the antique stores, boutiques, and junky gift shops. We go through racks of t-shirts until we find the design that looks most like a tourist would want it, then we buy matching ones. We put them on over our clothes and hop back in the car for a tour of the rest of town.

"It's too beautiful to be haunted," she says as we drive past the Stanley Hotel, which inspired Stephen King to write *The*

Shining. "How much would someone have to pay you to spend a night there?"

"Like ten dollars," I snort. "I would totally stay there."

"I don't believe you," she challenges, gazing up at the red roof that stands out so alarmingly against the white building.

"I swear!" Then I tell her about the time my brothers and I did the ghost tour at the Stanley and Tanner refused to sleep alone for months.

When it's almost time for the sun to set, we drive into the park to head to Forest Canyon Overlook. "You're still feeling okay, right?" I ask her.

"I'm great." She rolls her head across the back of the seat to look at me. The windows are cracked and her hair blows to the other side of her face, blocking her eyes. She's happy and relaxed, and I wish I could take a picture of her at this moment. Gone is Scared Ellie. Carefree Ellie is in her place.

We park and I lead us down the short trail to my favorite place to watch the sun go down. Both of us are now wearing an extra layer to prepare for the dropping temperature. Ellie cradles the thermoses of hot chocolate against her chest, cheeks rosy from the chill in the air.

There's no one else out and about; no sounds other than the rustle of our jackets and the crunch of our shoes against the uneven ground. I sneak a peek at Ellie. She stares straight ahead, mouth slightly agape as she takes in the sights. Mountains surround us on all sides, connecting and tapering down to a vast valley in the middle. The sun sits just above the tallest peak, slowly descending and casting everything in an orange glow.

"I've never understood what people mean when they say a photo doesn't do something justice until now," Ellie says. She stops at the edge of the overlook and peers over cautiously before pulling her phone out of her back pocket to snap a quick picture. "But I'm going to send Uncle Rob one anyway."

I laugh. "It's definitely a postcard-worthy view."

"Mm-hmm..." She goes silent and her face falls a little.

"What's wrong?" I ask.

"Nothing, really." She shrugs, placing the thermoses on the ground and crossing her arms over her chest. "This is breathtaking. Postcards just make me think of my mom and dad. I have a shoebox in my closet, full of them. They're the only bit of consistency I have when it comes to my parents."

I move to stand behind her, wrapping my arms around her and resting my chin on top of her head. She settles into me and we both stare out at the sun, which is now halfway behind the peak. "I'm proud of you," I tell her. "If your parents knew how brave you've been lately, I think they would be proud of you too. And if they weren't, I'd make them be."

"How so?" Ellie laughs.

"I'd simply invite them outside for a little tussle." I sway us back and forth, squeezing her shoulders and she continues to laugh. I kiss her on the neck before releasing her to pour us both some hot chocolate, then sit on the ground and pat the spot next to me.

She snuggles against me, taking her first drink. "Holy shit, that's good."

"I told you."

We drop into a comfortable silence, sipping and cuddling and admiring nature as the world slowly slips into darkness. Ellie's eyes are bright and full of wonder, even in the dim lighting. I think again about how different this week could have been. About how there could be a completely different woman sitting next to me. About how in some roundabout way, Kristen and I's breakup is the only reason this is happening.

Perhaps everything really does happen for a reason.

"It's so...big," Ellie says. "It makes you realize how small you are, but in a good way. Like somehow pressure has been taken off of my shoulders by looking at these mountains, and I can be a little happier with just existing."

"And this is only one very small portion of the world," I say. "Wait until you see the rest."

"Is travel your secret to always being the happiest person in the room?" she asks.

The *happiest*?

"Do you really think I'm the happiest person in the room?" My voice goes low.

"Usually." She smiles. "At least at TST you are."

"So I'm not the loudest? Or the most annoying?"

"Well, you are loud..." she says, jumping when I reach over to tickle her. She lays a hand on my cheek. "But how could you ever be annoying to me?"

"Huh," I say, looking down at my chest to hide my smirk. "I guess I need to try harder."

She laughs deeply, laying back on the ground and immediately shooting up. "It's so cold!"

"Oh, this is mild." I tell her, only a little chilly in the thirty-eight degree weather. "We probably should head back, though."

"Let's do it." She stands, brushing herself off and offering me a hand. She struggles to pull me up, almost losing her balance in the process. I catch her and hold her upright, then pull her closer and kiss her slowly. Her lips still taste of cinnamon from the hot chocolate.

Just like in the car this morning, I immediately feel the need to be closer to her. The want to touch her in new places. The desire for more. But I've already let my mind—and my hands—wander once today. I don't want to cross any lines, or make her feel like I'm moving too quickly.

I want whatever pace is best for her.

So, I kiss her until she pulls away and leads me back to the car.

CHAPTER 29
ELLIE

"YAHTZEE," Adem yells, jumping up from the couch and pumping his fist into the air. "That's three out of three for me, losers."

"He's so humble," Eren mutters out of the corner of his mouth.

"I think you mean 'insufferable.'" Tanner pretends to gag.

"Y'all are just jealous because you haven't won a game of Yahtzee in five years," Adem says.

"To be honest, I kind of think it's weirder that you haven't lost a game in five years," Tanner argues. "Yahtzee freak."

We're all a few hard ciders deep, and every round of the game has gotten progressively more competitive. At the end of the second round, Eren had to separate Tanner and Adem from an intensifying wrestling match on the living room floor. Even I started to feel a little desperate to win halfway through the third game. I got close but Adem managed to roll a third Yahtzee at the very end.

I settle back into the couch and listen to the three brothers argue, smiling sleepily at Eren's waving hands and witty comebacks. Despite the squabbling, the Christmas tree in the corner fills the room with an heir of calm and togetherness, as if a game by the fireplace wasn't already the definition of coziness. I yawn, ready to sleep, but also not ready for the day to end.

Scrabble is next to me and I reach over to pet him. He raises his little doggy eyebrows at me as if to say, "Can you please get them to shut the hell up?" He allows me to continue rubbing his head for a few minutes, then gets up and goes to the other side of the couch to put his face in the corner and ignore all of us.

When we got home from the park, I had spent a couple of hours helping Yvette with Thanksgiving prep in the kitchen before she retired to bed. Then I watched an episode of *The Mandalorian* with the boys and Emir, who is endearingly obsessed with the show. He eventually went to bed as well, although I don't know how they've been sleeping through the downstairs ruckus.

"Anyone else want another?" Tanner asks, waving his cider bottle in the air? "Ellie?"

"I'm fine, thanks. I think I'm going to bed, actually."

"Boooooooooo!" all three of them heckle me.

"Yeah, yeah, yeah..." I stand, walking to the kitchen to toss my empty bottle into the recycling bin. "Goodnight, gentlemen!" I call as I start up the stairs. I look back when I reach the first landing, making eye contact with Eren. My instincts are begging me to give him a kiss goodnight. Or at least a hug.

Yet, I can't argue that there is something that's almost thrilling about keeping the developing side of our relationship a secret.

I take a quick shower and brush my teeth before sliding into bed, enjoying the feel of the cool sheets against my tired body. It's hard to believe I've only been here a couple of days. I was sick for 24 hours, but it felt way longer. And today has been an adventure. Between exploring with Eren, watching the sun set, and hanging out with his family, I feel...fulfilled.

Mine and Eren's matching shirts are draped across the foot of the bed. They're lime green, and have both a Colorado flag and a moose on the front. Across the bottom, in a font not too far off from Comic Sans, they say, "Eat. Sleep. Mountains. Repeat."

On any other day, during any other part of my life, I would have refused to put it on my body. But when Eren begged me with his big brown eyes, how could I say no? It might even be my new favorite shirt now.

Due to the time difference, my uncles have been in bed for hours, but I still grab my phone to send them a goodnight text and give the background photo of Brat a quick kiss. Through the bedroom door, I hear Tanner and Adem come upstairs and into their bedroom. Eren must be going to bed too, so I send him a quick text.

ELLIE

Goodnight! I had fun today.

I roll over to put my phone on the charger, and it buzzes with a reply.

EREN

Me too. I'm so happy you're here with me.
Happy almost Thanksgiving!

My eyes have barely closed when I'm startled awake by yelling from downstairs. "Scrabble, nooooo, Scrabble, wait!" followed by hard footsteps and the sound of the deck's door sliding open.

Inclination catapults me out of bed and to the top of the stairs, where Tanner and Adem are also looking over the railing, but the living room is quiet and empty. Then, Eren bangs inside from the backyard, holding Scrabble away from his body like he might detonate at any second. Eren's hair is falling out of its ponytail and his shirt is soaked on one side. He looks surprised to see us all staring at him. "He pissed on me and the couch bed before we made it outside!"

Tanner and Adem burst into hysterical laughter, and I can't help but do the same. Between Eren's wet shirt, the soaked sheets on the pullout couch that he just worked so diligently to set up, and an unbothered Scrabble suspended in the air like a newborn baby, the scene is something straight out of a sitcom.

"Can one of you take him, please?" Eren asks his brothers, unphased by our laughter. Tanner trots down the stairs to grab the dog.

"Good job," he whispers in Scrabble's ear on the way back up.

"I'll help you," I tell Eren. I walk down and begin stripping the sheets off the bed. He pulls his t-shirt over his head and adds it to the soiled pile of fabric.

My eyes go to his chest, which is broad and covered in dark hair. He's solid—not overweight but filled out to suit his height. His tan skin is smooth and glowy. I'm used to Eren with all of his kitschy shirts and teddy bear demeanor, which are cute. But here he is, standing in the light of the fireplace with free-flowing hair, a half-naked body, and eyes that are slightly wild from the Scrabble shenanigans.

God, I want him, my brain says so naturally.

"Thanks, El." He takes the pile of sheets from me and checks to make sure his brothers are gone before giving me a kiss on the forehead. "Sorry about that. Go back to sleep. I'm going to put these in the wash and find some clean blankets."

I force myself back to bed, even though I'd rather stay with newly-unlocked sexy Eren. My thoughts roam to our kiss in the car this morning, and my lower abdomen tightens at the memory of Eren's hand on my skin, of his finger dipping inside my bra, of my hand on his thigh, so close to parts of him I've yet to explore. Parts of him that I'm dying to acquaint myself with.

There's a knock on the door. "Ellie, it's me. I need to grab a shirt from my suitcase," Eren's voice whispers.

"Sure, come in." I sit up and clutch the covers to my chest. Eren grins at me and goes to rummage through his things, bending over so his pajama pants cling tighter to his ass and flustering me further.

"Sorry to keep distracting you from rest," he says over his shoulder.

"It's okay. I'm kind of awake now anyway," I say truthfully.

Finding what he's looking for, he stands and puts a new shirt on. "Is there anything I can do to help?"

"Maybe you can hang out for a bit?" I ask, suddenly nervous he might say no.

"Of course." He eyes the spot next to me on the bed. "Do you mind if I sit by you?"

I wouldn't want you to be anywhere else.

"Not at all." I scoot to one side of the bed and put one of the extra pillows against the headboard for him.

The mattress groans under his weight as he climbs up next to me and sticks his bare feet beneath the comforter. Even sitting up, his long legs aren't far from the edge of the bed. I prop myself up on my elbow and turn onto my side to face him, feeling shy in the intimacy of the moment. He smiles and reaches out to ruffle my hair.

"That's something you've always done to me," I say. "Since we've been friends. You like to mess up my hair."

"It's because you do this scrunchy thing with your nose when I do it. Like you're annoyed but you also secretly love it," he tells me.

"Do I?"

"Yes, and it's adorable. I think I might be fully addicted to the nose scrunch now. So please never stop."

"No promises," I joke.

He slides down and rolls to his side, matching my position. We stare at each other for several seconds. I watch his facial expression change slightly, from happy, to content, to contemplative. I want to ask him what he's thinking—to have the conversation we've been dancing around but ultimately avoiding. Serious conversations lead to decision-making though, and that's where it gets scary for me.

I think I want to be with Eren. And I think Eren wants to be with me. With the timing of everything, with him freshly broken up with Kristen, and me trying to direct my life onto a new, more adventurous path, I'm afraid we could be setting ourselves up for failure. What if we've mistaken our mutual support of each other for something else? What if Eren only thinks he's into me because he's searching for comfort after ending his relationship?

What if I'm putting too much pressure on myself by falling into too many new things at once?

What if we ruin our friendship and have to avoid each other at TST for the rest of our careers?

"You look like you're deep in thought," he says, his voice gravelly and tired.

"I could say the same about you." I try not to sound defensive.

"Probably because I am."

"What are you thinking about?" I ask tentatively.

"You," he says. "Us."

"What about us?"

"About how this all seems like it shouldn't be working out, but it strangely is. About how I've never felt more sure about someone in my life, but simultaneously I'm worried about jumping in too quickly and ruining everything once again." He stares at the wall behind me.

"Is this about your 'curse?'" I make quotation marks with one of my hands. "Don't let your brothers control your life like that, Eren."

"It's really not them," he tells me. "I mean, obviously they give me shit about it, and that stays in my head. But I *have* also been in a lot of failed relationships. The proof is in the pudding. I'm surprised you're not running away from me screaming."

"Everyone has different experiences in life, Eren." I reach for his hand. "I know you. I see you for who you are every day. There's no way that some failed relationships or stupid curse could outweigh that for me."

"Promise?"

I offer him my pinky and he locks it in his. "I promise."

I move closer and he pulls me against him, pressing my head into his chest. I rub my cheek against the soft cotton of his shirt. "I do have to ask you one thing, though. And I swear it doesn't come from a place of jealousy or malice. It's just something I need to know for my own peace of mind," I say.

"Ask away." His face is buried in my neck, his breath hot against my skin.

"This isn't a...rebound situation for you? Right?"

He shifts back to look me in the eyes, brow furrowed, concern masking his features. "Ellie, *no*. It's not like that at all. You have every right to ask, but it's not like that. If you ever start to feel that way, let me know immediately. I'll do everything in my power to convince you that I want you for you. Not for a distraction."

His reassurance is all I need to muster up the courage and kiss him. I wrap my arms around his neck and pull him onto the pillow with me, desperate to feel his mouth and body on mine. He plants a hand behind my back, caging me in, our chests pressed together. I put a hand under his shirt, needing to feel the bare skin I've been subjected to twice today. He tenses, laughing against my lips. "Your hands are freezing."

I go to remove my palm and he pins my arm with his elbow. "Don't do that. I'll warm it up."

Following suit, he slips a hand beneath my own shirt, tentatively splaying his palm on my stomach. "Is this okay?" he murmurs in my ear.

"Yes," I whisper, squirming beneath him, dying for more. "Since we're being honest, can I tell you something else?"

"Anything."

"Okay then." I take a deep breath, placing my other hand on top of his and guiding it up to my bra-less chest. "I've wanted you since you came outside shirtless this morning."

"I've wanted you since we made out on the couch at your uncle's house," he says, gently squeezing my right breast. My hips lift unwillingly off the bed.

"Now that that's settled…" I grab the hem of his shirt and push it up his back. He laughs and helps me take it off, throwing it to the floor. I plant a kiss against his chest and he surprises me by wrapping his arms around me, rolling onto his back and pulling me on top of him. He undoes the buttons of my pajama shirt one at a time, then slips it off of my shoulders.

"Oh my god, Ellie." He leans up to kiss the space between my breasts before swirling his tongue around each of my nipples. Then he pulls me on top of him, chest to chest, and kisses me with newfound roughness. His hands slide down my back and into my shorts to cup my ass. I can feel him hard against me through the thin layers of our pajama bottoms.

Breaking the kiss, I sit up and scoot further down his legs, trailing kisses from his neck down to his groin. He threads his fingers in my hair when I reach the skin just above his draw-string, using his other hand to untie the knot. I take the invitation and hook my fingers in his waistband, guiding his pants and boxers down over his hips. He laughs as I move off of his legs to pull the pants off of his ankles.

He's long and thick, and the sight ignites every bit of adrenaline in my body. I lay beside him, wrapping my fingers around him and searching for his mouth in the dark. His breaths come more and more quickly as I touch him, moving up and down and feeling him continue to harden. He slides one of his hands into my shorts, tentatively at first, then with more confidence when he feels how wet I am.

"Now," I pant into his ear. "Please, Eren."

He detaches from me long enough to get a condom from his suitcase. I sit up and watch, buzzing with the need for him to be inside of me. For us to be connected.

He rips the foil open and slides the condom on. Coming back to the bed, he grabs my ankles and pulls me to the edge, yanking my pajama shorts and panties off in one swift movement. He parts my thighs, standing between them and planting a hand on either side of my head long enough to kiss me. Then he inserts his tip and grabs my hips, slowly pushing into me until he fills every corner.

"We have to be so quiet," he whispers shakily, lowering further to press his forearms into the bed on either side of my head. "Are you up for the challenge?"

Staring him in the eye, I bring my hand to my mouth and pretend to zip my lips, then reach up to zip his as well. His eyes crinkle at the corners in amusement.

We move together, slowly at first, then faster as our hands and mouths continue to explore all other available inches of skin. Staying true to our promise, we don't speak, too caught up in the need to be as close as possible. His hair falls out of its ponytail and into my face, and I push it back so I can see the desire and concentration in his eyes.

He finds just the right spot and my breathing intensifies. Smiling knowingly, he picks up the pace. I wrap my arms around his back, holding him close to me as we both come undone, sweat slicking our bodies. He collapses against me and groans.

"You're perfect," he pants, the full weight of him comforting. I run my fingers through his hair aimlessly.

"Far from it," I say. "But you make me feel like I am."

"Good." He kisses me one more time before getting up to make his way to the bathroom. I find my pajamas and re-dress, fighting the urge to jump on the bed and squeal at the top of my lungs.

Eren Polat, I think. *I never could have imagined...*

"Can I sleep in here tonight?" Eren asks when he returns. "I'll set an alarm and be back downstairs before my parents wake up."

"Of course. Please, please sleep here."

He crawls beneath the covers and turns me into the small spoon, placing a kiss on my earlobe. I stay awake as he slowly drifts off. I realize, I don't really care if his parents know.

In fact, I'm so far in, I don't really care if anyone knows.

CHAPTER 30

EREN

Dim sunlight peeks through the blinds when I slip out of bed the next morning.

I move quietly, being careful not to wake Ellie. After last night, she deserves to sleep as late as she would like. If it were up to me, both of us would stay in bed all day. But it's Thanksgiving, and the Polat household will be bustling.

The door creaks as I step out and close it gently behind me. I turn to tiptoe to the bathroom, stopping in my tracks when I notice a pair of eyes watching me from the other end of the hall. Scrabble sits stoically, an expression of judgment so apparent on his gray face that I forget he's a dog and begin to feel uncomfortable.

"In a weird way, I should thank you for peeing on me," I whisper. He tilts his head to the side.

I'm almost to the bathroom when the door to the other room opens and Tanner comes out, blocking my path. He jumps, startled by my presence in the dark hallway. Then he narrows his eyes at me, looking back and forth between me and Ellie's room. "Where are you coming from?" he asks, voice full of the same judgment Scrabble is exuding.

"You're an adult," I tell him. "Figure it out."

He blocks me when I try to step around, bolting into the bathroom and locking it behind him. "First come, first serve!" he says through the door.

"Asshole," I whisper loudly.

I rush to the downstairs bathroom, crossing my fingers that no one is in there. The time on the microwave shows 6:30 a.m., but Mom is already in the kitchen, working on the turkey and dressing. "Good morning," she says as I rush by. "Happy Thanksgiving!"

"Oh, uh...morning."

Shit, I think. *Shit, shit, shit*. Why is everyone in this family a morning person?

You're an adult, Eren, I remind myself. *You don't owe anyone an explanation.*

In the bathroom, I take a few deep breaths, reflecting on the events of last night. The smell of Ellie lingers on my skin, and I wish I could keep it there forever. Thoughts of how she looked flicker through my mind like an old reel of film. My fingertips still burn with the feeling of her bare skin as I unbuttoned her shirt, revealing her beautiful body bit by bit.

Her touch. Her smell. Her sounds. All so *beautiful*. She has invigorated me, and I can't wait for it to happen again. Again, and again, and again.

After showering downstairs, I walk back to Ellie's room (our room?) for clean clothes. She's sitting on the edge of the bed, applying makeup in a tiny hand mirror. She blushes when she looks at me, and I want to ruin the makeup she's just worked so hard on.

"If there's someone in the bathroom, I can kick them out so you have a bigger mirror to work with," I tell her.

"That's okay, I do this all the time. Even at home." She zips her cosmetics bag and tosses it onto her pile of stuff in the corner. "Happy Thanksgiving."

I pull her up from the bed and crush my mouth to hers. "Wanna know what I'm thankful for?"

"Scrabble?" she jokes, provoking an embarrassing high-pitched laugh from my throat.

"Yes, actually," I answer. "But also you. Just a little."

"*A little*, huh?" She playfully pushes me away and rolls her eyes. "You can sleep downstairs tonight then."

Unable to help it any longer, I tackle her onto the bed. She scrunches her nose at me in the same way she does when I ruffle her hair. "Speaking of that, we might have a little problem," I tell her.

"Problem?"

"A couple of problems." I trace my thumb across her bottom lip. "First, Tanner assumes I came out of your room earlier."

"Okay, not a huge deal," she says. "And the second problem?"

"Mom is already downstairs in the kitchen, so she knows I wasn't on the couch this morning."

She bites my thumb playfully, which sends my downstairs friend into over-excitement. "I have to be real with you, Eren," she says huskily. "I don't really care if your family knows. If you're cool with it, I'm cool with it."

"Yeah?"

"Yeah," she reassures me. "I'm not saying we have to go downstairs and make a big public announcement, but let's just see how things play out."

"Damn, Ellie. Travel has changed you," I jest.

"What do you mean?"

"The Ellie I've always known, TST Ellie, would never want to go into unknown territory without a plan," I point out.

"I guess I had to go into unknown territory..." She motions to our surroundings with her hand. "To be okay with learning how to navigate the unknown territories of life."

She means it as a joke, but it makes me want to hold onto her forever and never let her go. She pulls my ponytail over one shoulder and gives it a light tug. The freckle on her cheek jumps out at me, and I make a mental note to search her body for others later.

Pecking me on the lips, she rolls off the bed and stands. "I'm going to go help your mom in the kitchen."

"Okay. I'll be down soon."

When I make it to the kitchen a few minutes later, it isn't Mom who Ellie is helping.

"I was fifteen when I came with my parents to the U.S. from Turkey," Dad is telling her while dumping coriander into a bowl of ground lamb. "This is my mom's kebab recipe, and I made it for Yvette and I on the first Thanksgiving we spent together, in lieu of a traditional American meal. Since the boys were born, we've had both."

"Do you always use lamb?" Ellie props her elbows on the counter, watching Dad concoct the mixture of meat, spices, and egg.

"Sometimes beef," he answers. "Traditionally it's cooked on a rotating spit, but I improvise and make it in the oven, then give it a little pan fry after slicing it. We will eat it in pita with veggies."

"You're going to love it," I tell Ellie, joining them.

"I'm surprised you've never had it," Dad says. "It's a popular street food in Europe."

"Oh, I've never been to Europe," Ellie says before she can catch herself.

"You're a travel agent and you've never been to Europe?" Dad asks, surprised.

"It's kind of a long story," she says sheepishly.

"But she might be going soon," I chime in, turning to

Dad. "TST brought back travel stipends, and Ellie is our top agent so she gets to go first!"

"How exciting." Dad's naturally monotone voice doesn't make him sound excited at all, but I know he means it. He sticks his hands directly into the raw meat and begins to combine everything.

A few hours later, Ellie and I set the table on the deck with Mom's special Thanksgiving dishes. The plates have turkeys in the middle of them, and the napkin rings are shaped like tail feathers. Tanner and Adem bring the food out, setting all of the kebab ingredients on one end, and the turkey, dressing, and sides on the other. Even Scrabble gets a special turkey plate, on the ground next to Mom.

Thanksgiving is one of the only times of year that Scrabble actually wags his tail. He's a crotchety old dude, unless there's some type of exceptional food involved.

Dad makes Ellie's kebab for her, expertly packing the meat, veggies, and sauce into her pita. Her eyes light up when she takes a bite. "I think I need this on Thanksgiving every year," she says. Dad preens at the compliment.

"It's been so lovely having you this week, Ellie," Mom says. "Eren has always been good at picking friends."

"Yeah, Eren," Tanner says, elbowing me in the side. "You do know how to pick friends." I kick him beneath the table and Ellie laughs into her hand.

"I bet you wish you had a friend like me, Tanner," Ellie leans around me to tell him. Adem and I snort into our mashed potatoes.

I love when Ellie gives back what my brothers dish out.

"Am I missing something?" Mom asks, looking between all of us, her fork suspended in the air halfway to her mouth. Dad continues to shove alternating bites of turkey and kebab into his mouth.

"Tanner is just being a butthead," I say, taking special care not to curse at the table on Thanksgiving. "Because he thinks Ellie and I are more than friends..."

I look at Ellie out of the corner of my eye, gauging her reaction. She places her hand on my leg. Tanner notices immediately and whispers "I told you" to Adem.

"Well, honey, I already figured that out," Mom says bluntly.

"Yeah, tell us something we don't know," Dad chimes in.

"Seriously?" I ask, thinking back over the past few days. Other than sleeping in Ellie's room last night, I thought we have been pulling off the whole "work friends" dynamic.

"I wasn't going to say anything, but when you first arrived I looked out the window and saw you two kissing in the car." She takes a bite of her roll. "I approve, by the way."

Ellie and I both shrink into our chairs with matching red cheeks. "I'm so glad this can be a family dinner conversation," I say.

"You know it's always been hard to keep a secret in the Polat household," Adem points out.

The conversation fizzles out and we move into safer territory for the rest of dinner. Ellie and I quickly grow comfortable with showing displays of affection in front of everyone. I wrap my arm around her and she settles into the crook like she's been doing it her whole life. The sun goes down and the Christmas lights automatically click on, twinkling like the stars in the black sky above us.

Dad starts a fire in the pit and finds a Christmas playlist, syncing it to the bluetooth speaker Adem got him for his birthday. I go upstairs and grab jackets for Ellie and I, then help Mom carry an assortment of pies and mugs of hot chocolate outside. With a plate of pumpkin pie in hand, I settle into my chair and look around at my family.

We do almost the same thing every year. And it's always special, but something about this year in particular feels even more so. That something is the woman sitting next to me. There's no doubt in my mind.

Ellie's legs are crossed, and she's wearing one of my sweat-shirts. Scrabble is in a turkey-induced coma in her lap. I offer her a bite of my pie and she accepts it, then asks for another and gives me a kiss to say thank you. She rests her head on the back of her chair and stares up at the Christmas lights, relaxed and content.

I wish we could stay here forever, I think.

Then I realize—I'm excited to go home too. To go back to my routine with Ellie added in. To make her a part of my everyday life, and also plan more adventures for us.

To kiss her every single day, and grow with her, and become the best possible versions of ourselves...together.

"Can I tell you something?" she asks quietly, her voice barely audible over the buzz and laughter of my family.

"Always." I give her my full attention.

"I wish you could come with me on my stipend trip," she says.

"Me too," I say honestly. "But it's not my turn yet. And a big Christmas trip unfortunately isn't in the cards for me this year."

"Yeah..." Her eyes go glassy and I grab the arm of her chair to pull her closer.

"Plus, this sounds really hard to believe, but a solo trip will be so good for you. This week has been a good start, but doing something bigger, by yourself...it will change your life. I promise."

"It is hard to believe." She swallows and pulls the neck of my sweatshirt over her face, muffling her voice. "I don't think I'm brave enough."

I reach over and tug the sweatshirt down. "You're always braver than you think," I tell her. "I have an idea."

"Hm?" She yanks the sweatshirt back up.

"Let's talk about where you're going to go." I pull my phone out and open the notes app. "When you've made a decision on your destination, it'll seem less overwhelming because you won't be contemplating the entire world."

"Okay," she says tentatively, coming out of her makeshift hiding place once more.

"First, let's start with a region."

"Europe," she answers without hesitation.

"See?" I sit up straighter in my seat. "You already have more decided than you thought."

"Except Europe is still huge," she says, pouting.

Another idea strikes and I stand up. "Hey, everyone," I yell, getting my family's attention. "Do me a favor. Call out names of all the European cities you can think of."

"Paris," Mom starts. I add it to my list.

"Krakow," Adem says.

"Budapest, Vienna, Berlin," Dad adds.

"London," Tanner yells in a British accent.

They complete two more rounds, and before I know it I have thirty on my list. "Thanks, everyone." I bow and sit down, turning my phone screen to Ellie.

"Maybe I could even do a couple," she considers, her uncertainty dissipating. The sparkle of excitement has returned to her eyes and I internally breathe a sigh of relief.

"Great idea." I kiss her on the cheek. "Do any of them stand out to you?"

"You know that photo of Big Ben that's on the refrigerator at the office?" she asks.

"Yep."

"Well, I look at it every single day and try to imagine seeing it in person," she tells me. "I've been doing that since I started working at TST."

"Really?"

"Really, really. So I think it's only fair that London be my first stop, right?" She clasps her hands together as if locking in the decision.

"Next stop, London!" I say, squeezing her thigh. "Perfect, Ellie. Now, you need city number two."

"How about this?" she says. "You pick three from the list, and I'll pick from that three."

"Spontaneous! I love it."

I take a few minutes to pick my three. "Are you ready?"

She scoots to the edge of her chair and closes her eyes, relaxing her shoulders and releasing a breath through her mouth. Scrabble starts slipping from her lap and she fumbles to keep him in place. Opening her eyes, she holds her hand out for my phone. I place it in her palm and she briefly looks up at the sky before gazing down at the list.

Amsterdam. Prague. Rome.

Hiding the screen from me, she taps it a couple of times and hits the backspace button before passing it back. "Destination two, confirmed."

I smile at the screen and stand up, once more calling my family to attention. "Ladies and gentlemen, I'm pleased to announce that Ellie Amos, #1 Secret Travel Agent at Top Secret Travel, will be doing a bit of travel herself in a few weeks. To, drumroll please..."

My family slaps their thighs. Mom verbally makes a noise that couldn't sound less like a drumroll.

"London! Andddddddddd Prague!"

Everyone claps, even Ellie. Bending to place Scrabble on the ground, I pull her up from the chair and give her a hug. "You surprise me every day," I whisper in her ear.

"Thank you," she says. "For always pushing me in exactly the right way."

"I'm always here," I tell her. "Now, let's go to bed."

December 2, 2019 9:17 AM
FROM: y.tanaka@topsecrettravel.com
TO: TST OFFICE – ALL
SUBJECT: TST Holiday Party

Welcome back, TST-ers!

I hope you all had a great week off with your friends and families!

We have a date for this year's annual holiday party. Details are below, so mark your calendars! There will be a catered dinner, and, of course, an open bar.

When: Saturday, December 21st @ 7:00 p.m.
Where: Miller's Event Hall
Dress Code: Cocktail

Please RSVP to Petra by the end of the week, and let her know if you'll be bringing a plus-one.

Looking forward to it!

Best wishes,
Yuke Tanaka
President
Top Secret Travel

CHAPTER 31

ELLIE

We've been back in the office for a week, and it feels like a different world.

Eren and I have spent most of the time trying to figure out how to interact without drawing unwanted attention. We've been having lunch and hanging out like always, but it's getting progressively more difficult to not touch, kiss, or do something else that will completely give us away to the masses. Focusing on actual work has also been difficult, because all I can think about for the majority of the day is 5:00 rolling around so I can be with Eren away from prying eyes.

On Monday, I met with Yuke to give her the decision on my trip. In return, she gave me the company credit card. Now I have an inbox full of confirmation emails for hotels and tours in both London and Prague. Eren is working on my flights, and Petra is cutting me a check for the money I didn't use on accommodations and activities. I leave December 22nd, the day after the holiday party.

I can't believe this is all happening.

It's Friday, and the sales room is buzzing with talk of the weekend and deadline for the sales manager position. On the flight home from Colorado, I made the final decision not to apply. I've been lying about my experience for so long that it doesn't feel right. And it doesn't matter that I've technically traveled now, and will be traveling more. The world is big. Someone else still deserves the job more than me. Secretly, I hope Sherry gets it.

Anyone but Rick, because he's still giving me the cold shoulder. He even stole a sale from me on Wednesday.

"Is Wales in England?" Lucia asks.

"No," the rest of us say in unison.

"Well, what's the difference then?" she presses.

"They're both countries in the United Kingdom," I explain.

"What Ellie said," Lamar agrees.

"Yeah, because Ellie is *always* right," Rick grumbles quietly.

I glare at him through the wall, clearing my throat so he knows I heard him. "Thank you, Rick."

He responds by ferociously slamming away on his keyboard. Probably creating a new plan to steal more of my leads and make me feel like an idiot. He's really been ruining the new, more carefree attitude I've been trying on.

My computer pings with a new instant message.

Eren Polat:
I'll miss you tonight.

It fixes the mood Rick put me in.

Ellie Amos:
I'll miss you too. But we'll still have the whole weekend :)

Uncle Rob and I have our monthly date tonight. It's something we've been doing since I was a little girl. I have dinner with him and Sai most nights, but our date remains a must-have. It's our time to catch up and check in one-on-one. It keeps our communication open and honest, which Uncle Rob has learned to value over the years of being a father figure.

Eren Polat:
I can't wait.

Ellie Amos:
What time should I come over tomorrow?

Eren Polat:
Whenever you want. Should I come pick you up?

Ellie Amos:
Yes please! Both uncles need their cars this weekend. I'm excited to see your apartment.

Eren Polat:
I'm excited to see you in my apartment.

Tonight, I'm telling Uncle Rob about Eren. And my London/Prague trip. I wouldn't say I've been avoiding my uncles this week, but if I haven't been with Eren, I've been spending time alone, processing all of the change. My life is currently the awkward combination of wonderful, yet overwhelming.

Another good reason not to apply for a promotion right now. Others will come.

The tiny hairs on the back of my neck start to prickle and I spin around in my chair. Rick is standing there, arms crossed, leaning against the wall in that way that used to make me crazy. Now, it makes me crazy in a completely different way. "Can I help you?" I ask.

"I just wanted to apologize," he says. "For getting grumpy and talking about you like you weren't here a few minutes ago. It was out of line."

I lift my eyebrows, caught off guard. "It's okay."

"I've kinda been an ass all week," he continues. "I'm sorry. I don't want us to keep going further and further down the 'office enemy' road. Especially when one of us might be the other's boss soon."

It's impossible to tell whether he's being truthful, or fishing for information on my job application status. I want to believe it's the former, to believe that he and I can be friends and colleagues without our history of competition and fleeing attraction getting in the way. My inability to fully trust makes it difficult to read situations like this.

"I forgive you," I say, choosing to be positive. "I can be condescending toward you, too, and I need to own up to that. Truce?"

Holding my hand out, I look at him in a way that hopefully conveys I'm sorry about more than our daily quarrels. Whether he was more into me than I thought, or it's a blow to his ego...it doesn't matter. We have to move forward for the sake of our jobs. For the sake of the fact that he's eventually going to find out about Eren and I. For the sake that he really could be my superior soon.

God, I'm going to hate that.

I chastise myself for letting negativity creep in so quickly. He shakes my hand with a smile and goes back to his desk.

"Look at you two," Sherry says. "Communicating and stuff. Thanks for making my job easier when *I'm* your boss," she cackles.

"Anytime, Sher," Rick says.

"Don't call me that," she retorts.

At five fifteen, I meet Eren at his car and he drives me home, pulling over two blocks from the office to kiss me, making up for all of the affection we've missed out on over the past eight hours. "I think one of the 'T's' in TST now stands for torture," he says, kissing my neck. "Because it's absolute torture knowing you're downstairs from me all day and I can't do this whenever I want."

"Drama king," I joke. "I know, though. Sometimes I want to run up to your office, close the door, wipe everything off your desk, and push you on top of it."

"New fantasy unlocked." He grins. "One day, perhaps..."

He drops me off at home and I run up to my apartment to change clothes before going down to the main house. Per usual, Brat meets me at the door and attacks me, getting black and white dog hair all over my fresh outfit. Uncle Sai isn't home yet, but Uncle Rob is waiting for me in the kitchen.

"Happy uncle-niece date night," he says. "I was thinking we could grab a coffee and walk around that neighborhood you like with all of the Christmas lights."

"That sounds perfect!"

There are few things from my childhood that I still enjoy as an adult. Christmas lights are one of them.

"I feel like we've barely spoken this week," Uncle Rob says when we reach our destination. It's one of those unseasonably warm, balmy Florida nights, and the Christmas lights seem out of place compared to the ones on Eren's parent's house in Colorado. It doesn't make me love them any less, it's just...different.

I'm viewing more and more things differently lately.

"Going back to work has never been so hard," I tell him. "I've been in a readjustment period."

"You were exhausted, I'm sure. Fill me in on the trip! I want to know everything."

Starting at the beginning, I tell him about flying, and my altitude sickness. I tell him about Eren and I driving around Estes Park, our silly matching t-shirts, and the views from

Rocky Mountain National Park. I tell him about Thanksgiving, Eren's mom's hot chocolate, and Scrabble the grumpy dachshund. He listens intently, asking animated questions and wondering why Scrabble didn't come home in my suitcase.

"Which all leads me to a couple of pieces of bigger news," I say, finishing off my coffee. We're walking along a row of homes decorated like gingerbread houses. Giant lollipops are staked in grass along the sidewalk, glowing red and white against the still-green Florida grass.

"Don't leave me waiting! Spill." Uncle Rob links his arm in mine.

"Okay," I begin. "First and foremost, Eren and I are kind of a thing now."

Excited, he does something that looks like a combination of a skip and a hop. "I don't want to say I knew it." He attempts to be humble. "But, I *knew* it! Ellie, I'm so happy for you. Eren is awesome. You have your very own tall, dark, and handsome cuddly vampire! How long has this been going on?"

"Really only since he came over that night before we left," I explain. "But weird tensions were building for a few weeks before that."

"Is it official?" Uncle Rob asks.

"Not in the boyfriend-girlfriend sense. Not yet," I say. "But I'm confident we're on the same page. I'm confident we'll get there. Soon."

"I for one am thrilled, Ellie Smellie." He kisses me on top of my head. "What's your other news?"

"It's big. Are you ready?"

"Spit it out!"

"I'm going to London in two weeks," I tell him. "And Prague. By myself."

He halts in the middle of the sidewalk, unintentionally yanking me with him. I look at him questioningly, but he doesn't say anything. He only pulls me into a hug, crushing me so tightly to his chest I can barely breathe. There are tears on his face when we break apart and my heart sinks.

"Is this because I already missed Thanksgiving and now I'll be missing Christmas?" I ask, a lump building in my throat at the sight of his wet cheeks. Uncle Rob never really cries in front of me. "I could probably wait until next year…"

"Don't you dare!" He wipes his face, maneuvering us to the edge of the sidewalk to let a group of people pass. "El, I've never said this to you, but I worry about you. A lot. Not because you aren't amazing and smart and successful, but you tend to put up these walls and block out the most important parts of life. I know you do these things to make yourself feel safe, but you have so much potential that you don't let yourself see. Or, rather, you haven't let yourself see until recently."

If Uncle Rob said these things to me a few weeks ago, my gut reaction would have been to get defensive, and probably even a little mad. Now, it's not easy to hear, but I know it's the truth. It's what I've been trying to accept, so I can change it. So I can move forward with my life without fear. At least the irrational kind.

I don't know how to respond, so I let Uncle Rob continue.

"What I'm trying to say is, I see your bravery. I see your resilience. You've been dealt a shitty hand in a lot of ways. And I don't know what sparked the change in you, but I see it. Dammit, I'm so fucking proud of you."

Sniffling, he wraps me in another hug. "Thank you," I say, so quietly I'm not sure he hears.

We continue along our path, once again arm in arm. "I really needed some good news," Uncle Rob says, more to himself than me.

"Have you been that worried about me?" I ask, guilt creeping in.

"Not just about you," he says. "There's been a lot going on that I haven't talked to you about."

"Why can't you talk to me about it?"

"I haven't wanted to add any additional stress to your life," he admits. "You've had so many great things going."

"Well, now I'm worried. And I would really like to know. Is this about Uncle Sai? You two are okay, right?" My sixth sense kicks in, sending a reminder signal of all the ways Sai has been off lately to my brain. His sick days. His tired eyes. His constant napping.

Oh, god. Why haven't I been more concerned? I've been so self-absorbed.

"We're fine," he clarifies, easing some of the nausea clawing its way up my throat. "He's fine. Physically. But he's depressed. It's something he's struggled with since we've been together, but we've never wanted you to know."

"Why not?"

"Again, Sai didn't want to concern you," he says.

"And your reason?" I ask, trying to wrap my head around this rollercoaster of a conversation.

"You're well into adulthood now, so I'm going to be honest with you—you and Sai are more similar than you might think. He had a tough childhood. And I've always had this fear that you'll eventually struggle in the same ways he does."

We're almost to the end of the street, and I spend the next several steps in silence. Thinking. About myself. About Uncle Sai. About Uncle Rob.

"I didn't mean to drag you down after your good news," Uncle Rob says. "I guess I needed to get it off my chest."

"You didn't drag me down," I tell him, honing in on the final house of lights. "I'm glad you told me. It helps me understand things a little more clearly. About Uncle Sai, and myself. I needed to know."

"He's been seeing a therapist. I feel like things are improving." One corner of his mouth quirks hopefully.

"What can I do to help?" I ask.

"Everything you're currently doing," he answers quickly. "You might be our Ellie Smellie, but you can still be a role model. You can still help him realize it's okay to exist outside of the boxes you build around yourselves."

Outside of the small spaces our minds convince us we belong in, I think.

It's not the direction I expected our date to take. But maybe it's the direction I needed to keep me on the road I've been traveling.

CHAPTER 32

EREN

Saturday turns into Sunday, and Ellie is still at my apartment.

"So where is that in proximity to Charles Bridge?" she asks.

I open Google maps on my laptop, putting in the address of Ellie's Prague hotel and showing her the walking distance to the bridge. Watching intently, she makes a small note in the margin of her itinerary. We've been sitting on the floor for over an hour, leaning against the couch and planning all the smaller specifics of Ellie's trip. She's focused and interested, her eyes luminous with the new knowledge of new places.

I always love catching an in-person glimpse of the passion she puts into her work. Trip planning takes a lot of attention to detail, and she's obviously good at it. Combined with the excitement and nervousness of preparing for her first solo trip, she's absolutely glowing.

"You're going to have a leg up on me after this trip," I tell her. "I've never been to Czechia."

"Oh, really?" she asks, surprised. "Haven't you been to like one hundred countries?"

"Fifty," I correct, casting my laptop aside and pulling her close to me. She rests her head on my shoulder.

"Do you want to know where I've never been?" she asks.

"Everywhere?" I snort.

"Touché," she laughs. "But I was going to say, I've never been...here." She lifts my hair and kisses the back of my neck, sending chills down my spine.

"Where else?" I ask, liking where this game is leading.

Walking her fingers down my arm, she gently grabs my wrist and brushes her lips against my bicep. "Perhaps here."

A ball of fire forms in my stomach and I push myself up to my knees. "My turn," I tell her.

Before she can expect it, I scoop her up, placing her on the couch. "What are you doing?" she giggles.

"Lie flat on your back," I instruct, helping her stretch out. Her black cotton dress rides up, revealing her strong, smooth legs. She reaches to pull it down but I stop her by placing a hand between her thighs. She stays silent, watching me curiously.

"When it comes to the country of Ellie," I continue. "I can think of several places my lips haven't been. Here, for example." I kiss her temple and she closes her eyes, smiling.

"Next stop?" she asks.

"Here, of course." I barely touch my lips to the sensitive skin of her inner elbow.

She flinches. "That tickles!"

"And last but not least—here." I take my attention back to her lower body, gently parting her thighs and kissing the insides of both of them.

Her body writhes beneath me. I push her dress up over her black lacy panties, exposing her body inch by inch. I trail kisses up her thighs, over her left hip, and across her stomach, eventually making my way back to her mouth.

She pulls me on top of her, widening her legs to make

space for me to lie between them. She pushes her hands into the back of my jeans, cupping my ass, somehow kissing me deeper than ever before. Each time we're together, I find myself wanting to take every step slower. Wanting to savor her as much as humanly possible.

There's no way it gets any better than this.

Suddenly distracted, Ellie stops our kiss. "Fifty countries?" She asks, holding my face between her hands. "I'm having a hard time wrapping my head around visiting two countries, let alone fifty."

I press my forehead to hers. "You'll make it there. We will make it there. We're going to go everywhere we've never been. Together."

"Except for Prague."

"Except for Prague," I laugh.

On Monday morning, we make our first official drive of shame to TST. Except there's nothing shameful about the feelings I'm having for Ellie.

"If you're worried about someone seeing us, we'll park a block over," I tell her.

"It's not that I'm worried," she says. "I just want to go about this in the right way."

I sneak a peek at her in the passenger seat. Her hair is still wet because we got carried away in the shower this morning and she didn't have time to dry it. She's wearing the same black dress she's had on all weekend, which I washed and dried for her last night. It was the perfect excuse to get her into one of my t-shirts for bed. Her face is makeup free, and I can tell she's feeling self-conscious over not being her usual put together self.

To me, though, she's still perfect. I park at the far end of the street, hoping it will be enough to ease her nerves.

Since our first kiss only a couple of weeks ago, we've spent almost every waking (and sleeping) moment together. It's the most natural relationship progression I've ever been one half of, and I'm dying to ask her to be my girlfriend. Each conversation we've had about being together is full of green flags. Any worries we've had have been addressed along the way, with maybe my bitterness towards Rick being the only exception.

That bitterness has only grown after hearing about Ellie's week with him. About his back and forth between ignoring her, challenging her, and eventually apologizing. Initially, I thought the worst of my worries about Rick would be in regard to his feelings for Ellie. Now, I'm concerned his ego and potential new position of power will be the actual problem.

But Ellie still refuses to apply for the sales manager job, and I will always respect her wishes.

As if summoned from thin air, Rick's big blue truck whips into the spot behind us as we're climbing out of the car. "*Fuck*," Ellie whispers. "Happy Monday to me."

"Good morning, Ellie," he says, meeting us on the sidewalk. He looks at me coolly, all signs of the office bro connection we used to have are gone. "Eren. The two E's are carpooling now?"

"You know I usually walk," she tells him. "But Eren was kind enough to pick me up this morning."

"I'm sure he was..." His expression stays blank. "See y'all inside."

Ellie hoists her bag further up her shoulder and gives me a what the fuck look. Once his back is turned, I grab her hand and give it a squeeze. "Don't worry about him. This will pass."

It's going to be a long day.

Rick is at reception with Jade when we step inside. "Hey

you two!" she calls. Rick doesn't even look in our direction, roping Jade back into whatever conversation they were having.

"I'll see you later," I tell Ellie at the bottom of the stairs.

"Can't we just both pretend to be sick?" she asks, only partially joking.

"I wish." I ruffle her hair and head up to my office.

In true Monday fashion, shit continues to hit the fan. A client's connecting flight from London to Tokyo gets canceled, and there's nothing else available for two days so I have to work with Lucia to book him a hotel and rearrange his itinerary. Business class prices from Miami to Buenos Aires skyrocket, and a client who has been dragging their feet on purchasing gets angry and blames me. Walt finds a mistake I made on a schedule change, and I have to spend two hours on hold with American Airlines to get it corrected.

Throughout it all, I hold on to thoughts of my weekend with Ellie, and the reassurance that I'll be back in her arms tonight.

Around three thirty, Yuke calls me into her office to go over schedules for a New Zealand trip she's planning for a VIP group. "They'll need the best seats on every flight," she tells me. "One of them will also need a wheelchair at the gate at each airport."

I ferociously take notes, internally crossing my fingers that everything she needs will be available and as easy to book as possible. I'm getting behind on all of my tasks, and there are only a couple of weeks left before we're off for Christmas. It's nice that Yuke gives us so much time off during the holidays, but it also makes this period the most stressful part of my year.

"Thank you Eren, if you have any questions let me know," she says when we finish. "How was your trip to Colorado? I haven't gotten a chance to ask. Ellie joined you, right?"

"She did, I hope that's okay." I smile sheepishly.

"Of course. I've loved watching your friendship grow over

the past couple of years," she says. "Plus, you know my policy —if it's not hindering your work, I'm a-okay with taking relationships outside the workplace."

She knows, I think.

I don't know how she knows, but I feel it in my gut.

"Ellie is great," I say. "Kind, and talented, and really great."

"Did you have fun?" she asks. "Smooth flights, I hope?"

"It was a perfect trip," I say candidly, getting into the conversation. "The weather was nice—cool but not freezing. No hitches with the flights. And Ellie did great. You would have never guessed it was her first time fly—"

The words slip out of my mouth before I can stop them. I immediately want to cry. It takes my body's entire supply of poise not to slap my hand over my mouth and run out of the room.

"First time flying?" Yuke asks, frowning.

"S-sorry, I misspoke!" My voice is a million octaves too high. "I meant to say, it was her first time flying United. She's a Southwest fan."

It's the stupidest save I've ever heard, but it's also the best I've got at the moment.

Oh my god. Oh my god.

I'm going to throw up.

"Oh, okay," Yuke says, skeptically. "I'm glad you had fun. Thanks for meeting with me."

"I'll have this schedule over to you shortly," I say with too much gusto, standing on shaky legs.

Once I'm out of her office, I start running, sharply turning into my office and slamming the door behind me. I lean against it, breathing hard. My ears are ringing, and my hands won't stop shaking. I throw my notebook and pen across the room and press my palms into my eyes.

What the fuck have I done?

CHAPTER 33

ELLIE

E ren has been acting bizarrely since last Monday.

For the life of me, I can't figure out why. Despite that morning starting strangely, and his I.M.'s growing continuously more stressed throughout the day, I expected him to be his normal self when we stepped outside at 5:00 p.m.

Now it's over a week later, and he's only gotten farther and farther away from the Eren I know. The Eren I'm starting to love. The Eren I think I already love.

I love him. I know I do.

And I want to tell him. But now I feel like I can't, because I don't know what's happening. We spent most nights last week apart, due to him not feeling well. Then we were together over the weekend, but he was quiet and distracted. Distant, even. He's told me several times that he's fine, but I'm drowning in suspicion, fighting hard to keep my overthinking at bay.

He's over me, says my brain.

I'm not ready to believe that yet, though. After what we've shared, in both our friendship and our new relationship, I *refuse* to believe that. It couldn't have happened that quickly.

The holiday party is only two days away, which means I leave for London in three. I can't handle the stress of an international solo trip without knowing he's going to be waiting for me when I get back. I would rather cancel the whole thing.

As much as I've tried not to, the rest of the sales team has been getting the brunt of my bad mood. As a result, Rick is back to being a total ass toward me, questioning my work and giving his unwanted opinion on everything I touch. There's no doubt he's threatened by me and this new management position. But because he's being overbearing, I don't bother telling him that I'm not even applying for it.

Around eleven, I go to the kitchen for a cup of coffee, hoping to run into Eren. I haven't seen him since we left work yesterday, and the only correspondence we've had since is the "sweet dreams" text he sent me last night. Maybe today will be the day he comes back with that familiar love for life written all over his face.

The kitchen is empty. I pour coffee into my mug and put it in the microwave to get it to my preferred temperature. Someone enters the room and I turn eagerly, only to direct my attention back to the spinning coffee cup in front of me when I see it's Rick.

"Hey," he says, opening the cabinet to grab a mug.

"Hi."

"How's your morning?" he asks.

I let him suffer in silence for a few moments, frustration building and building and building in my chest. Between Eren, and Rick, and this trip, I could easily explode at any moment. If anyone deserves the explosion, I think it's Rick.

"So you can be nice to me outside the sales room, huh?" I say bluntly.

He steps next to me, filling his cup and waiting for the microwave. "Sorry for breathing," he retorts.

"You're so immature, Rick."

"*I'm* immature?" He leans his hip against the counter and crosses his arms, staring at me wide-eyed. "I'm not the one who led you on."

"You think I led you on?" The microwave beeps but I ignore it, directing my full wrath upon him. "I was honest with you! About everything."

"Yeah, super honest. About *everything* other than the fact that you didn't want to get to know me because you wanted to be with Eren instead. Eren, who has a girlfriend."

"You don't know anything," I spit at him. "He doesn't have a girlfriend anymore. And when I shut things down between us, I was trying to figure everything out. Figure myself out. I was trying to do the right thing."

We glare at each other, his coffee cup the only barrier to keep us from clawing each other's eyes out. I end the stare-down, looking nervously at the door. We haven't bothered using our inside voices and someone could walk in any minute.

Mental exhaustion replaces the anger within me. What the hell am I doing? Lying to my employer, falling for my best friend, unintentionally creating an office love triangle that has now turned one member sour towards me...

How have things gone from fine to great to terrible so quickly?

"I've been out of line again, haven't I?" Rick asks, backing off when he sees the tears spring into my eyes.

I nod, swallowing. "Yeah, but I haven't exactly kept myself on the straight and narrow either."

"I'll be real with you, Ellie," he says. "I'm not used to being told no. It's a problem I'm working on, but as you can see, the results aren't super great yet."

"We all have things we need to work on. Trust me, you don't know half of it." I laugh nervously.

"And..." he continues. "I'd be lying if I said I didn't want this promotion. And that's hard for me because I know you or Sherry deserve it more."

"I don't deserve it." I open the microwave to grab my coffee. "I didn't even apply for it."

"What?" He spills a little coffee over the side of his mug and it splats on the floor by my foot. "Ellie, why? You know Yuke wants you to have that job."

"I don't deserve it." I reiterate, shrugging. "You, or Sherry, or even Lamar, do though."

"I'm really confused..." He grabs a paper towel to wipe up his mess. "This makes no sense."

"All I can say is, I don't have the experience." I glance at the Big Ben photo on the fridge. "Not yet, anyway. Take that for what you will."

I make my exit, leaving him to decipher my riddle. A week ago, I would have been worried. Now, there is no room for more worries in my head. I'm at capacity.

When I get back to my desk, there's an I.M. from Eren on the screen.

Eren Polat:
I can't come over for dinner tonight. I'll be here late.

It does nothing to improve my mood. Making myself comfortable in my pessimism, I respond with a thumbs up emoji. He doesn't send anything else.

Later, I walk home without telling him goodbye. Fresh air is normally my favorite form of stress relief, but all I can focus on are the exhaust fumes of the passing cars, which add to the pressure in my head. I finally succumb to the tears, letting them fall freely, ignoring the stains they make on my favorite top.

When I make it home, I decide to take Brat for a walk.

With everything else going on, we've fallen out of our routine, and if anything is going to help my mindset, it will be a dog. He shoots into the kitchen, stopping in his tracks when he sees me. I drop to my knees to pet him, and he approaches slowly, then begins licking the tears from my face. It only makes me cry harder.

That's how Uncle Sai finds me when he gets home—in a crumpled mess on the floor, Brat attached to my side.

"Oh my god, Ellie!" He sits his keys and briefcase on the counter and falls down next to us. "What's the matter?"

"Nothing," I lie, thinking back to my conversation with Uncle Rob, not wanting to add to Sai's stress. "Just a long day at work."

He exchanges a glance with Brat. "I don't believe you."

"Traitor," I say to Brat, who thumps his tail on the floor once.

"If you don't tell me what's wrong, I'll have to bring in reinforcement," Sai says, grabbing his phone from his pocket and finding Uncle Rob's number.

"No!" I reach over to lock the phone. "Don't bother him. I'll talk."

He removes his suit jacket and tosses it aside, crossing his legs to make himself more comfortable.

"We can sit at the table like civilized humans," I tell him, knowing he's dying inside over the dust, dirt, and dog hair that are slowly covering his dress pants.

"I'm fine here," he says, unconvincingly. "Now, spill."

It takes a while, but I fill him in on everything that has happened since Eren and I returned from Colorado. Keeping our relationship a secret at work. Rick, and the tension around the sales job. The preparation for Europe. Eren's strange behavior and decreasing interest in me.

"He's finished with me." More tears spill when I say it out loud. "I thought I knew him, but maybe I never really did."

"That can't be it," Uncle Sai looks just as confused as I feel. "El, I've seen the way he looks at you. I've seen the way he acts around you. I can sniff a dog—sorry, Brat—out from a hundred miles away. And Eren? He's one of the good ones."

"So what do I do? How do I get to the bottom of this without seeming, I don't know...clingy?"

"There is a huge difference between communication, and clinginess, love," he says. "Telling someone what you need isn't clinginess. It's what you deserve. Not every person you let yourself depend on is going to disappear."

Stroking Brat's head, I consider Uncle Sai's advice. Is that really what I think? That everyone I let into my life is going to take the same path out that my parents did? That every person I love is going to decide I'm not worth it?

My walls, I think.

Having the courage to tear them down was only half the battle. Now, I have to learn how to exist outside of them and accept both the good and the bad. I have to learn how to live, and find the courage to live fully.

Uncle Sai reaches for my hand. "I love you, Ellie Smellie. You and Rob, you're everything to me. Even through the hard times, I wouldn't want to be a part of any other family."

Next to me, Brat huffs and lets out a bark.

"You're part of the family, obviously!" Sai leans over to kiss him on the nose.

"I love you too," I tell him. "Thank you."

He retrieves his suit jacket and pushes himself up from the floor. "Isn't your work party this weekend?" he asks.

"Yeah, on Saturday." I stand up and walk to the mirror on the dining room wall to check my makeup.

"Do you have a dress?" he asks.

"I'm wearing one I already have," I tell him.

"That just won't do." He grabs his keys from the counter. "Come on. We're going shopping."

CHAPTER 34

EREN

On Friday, I take a sick day.

It's a dumb move, considering it's the last day before we're off for the week of Christmas, and I still have a to-do list a mile long. But I'm so riddled with the guilt I've been carrying for two weeks that I can't function. I might not be sick in the literal sense of the word, but I'm certainly sick with wrongdoing.

And I'm not even brave enough to talk to Ellie about it. Me and my big fucking mouth—sometimes we absolutely suck. I really am too much.

She texted me last night.

ELLIE

> I know something is wrong. When you want to talk about it, I'm here. Please don't string me along, Eren.

I love you. Please stick with me until I figure this out, is what I wanted to say. Instead I sent:

EREN

I'm fine. I promise we'll talk soon.

Yesterday, things went from bad to worse when Yuke called me into her office.

"I'm not trying to get anyone in trouble," she'd said. "But there's a rumor going around the sales team that I need to talk to Ellie about, and it would help if you could clarify something for me."

Rumor? Ellie? Sales team?

Did she tell someone?

"Okay," I'd agreed, wiping my palms on my jeans.

"When you said Colorado was Ellie's first time flying, did you mean it?"

"Yes," I'd said honestly, far past the point of being able to fix the situation with a lie.

"Thank you for being truthful, Eren," was the last thing she said before dismissing me.

Last night, I wrote Yuke a long email, begging her to talk to Ellie about the situation. Begging her to let Ellie explain. Yuke replied to me early this morning, telling me not to worry, that she just wanted to clear some things up. It settled my nerves for a few minutes, but now, as I'm sitting on my couch in my lime green Colorado t-shirt, my mind is reeling with new worries.

What if Yuke talks to Ellie today?

What if Ellie is completely caught off guard?

What if Yuke revokes Ellie's trip?

I should have told Ellie the second I let her secret slip. This could have been cleared up days ago. But instead, I was a coward, choosing instead to live with the guilt and hoping my lie was enough to save the conversation. While I can't be responsible for whatever information the sales team has gotten wind of, I can still take accountability for my portion of the stupidity. I can still try to soften whatever blow is coming Ellie's way.

Checking the time, I propel myself from the couch and go to my room to search for a pair of jeans. I yank them on and grab my keys, typing a text to Ellie as I jog to my car.

I'm on my way to the office, I type. *Is there any way you can meet me outside in 20 minutes?*

She doesn't respond, but I make the drive anyway. I'm done being stupid. I'm committed—to Ellie, and to admitting my mistake. If I have to go inside and carry her out of her cubicle to make her see that, I will. I don't care what anyone else at TST thinks. I only care about her. About us.

I turn onto TST's street, checking my phone one last time. She still hasn't replied, so I find the closest parking spot and throw my seatbelt off. I jump out of the car, heading for the front door.

Ellie is on the steps, waiting for me. I slow my pace, pushing my hair behind my ears and trying to decipher her facial expression. She stands and meets me halfway down the sidewalk.

"Hey," she says, stopping a foot away. She makes no move to touch me. I want to pull her to my chest and never let go, but I respect her body language.

"I need to tell you something," I pant. "Something I should have told you days ago."

"Okay." She puts her hands in her pockets.

"I was in Yuke's office last Monday, meeting about a VIP group," I start. "She asked me about our trip, and somewhere along the way, I made the remark that it was your first time flying..."

She frowns, looking away from me to share over my shoulder. "Eren, how?"

"It slipped out. I'm so sorry, and I immediately tried to cover it up. I thought Yuke had accepted it. But yesterday she called me into her office and asked about a rumor the sales team started. I don't know anything about that, I swear. But Yuke is going to talk to you, and you deserve to know."

"She already talked to me," Ellie says stoically. "This morning."

"She did? And you're still here?"

"Yes, everything is fine. As fine as it can be."

I'm so relieved I could melt into the sidewalk. The worries I've let grow to astronomical levels shrink to a more manageable size. I step forward and try to reach for her, but she shrinks away, shaking her head at me. New worries take the place of the old ones.

"Did you tell someone?" I ask. "How did the rumor start?"

"I made a remark to Rick," she says. "I told him I wasn't applying to be sales manager because I don't have the experience. He mentioned it to Lamar, who mentioned it to Lucia, who mentioned it to Sherry. Before the day was over they were joking about how I've probably never traveled. And it's not a rumor if it's true, is it?"

"I guess not," I agree. "Still, I'm sorry this happened."

"It's how it should be," she says. "The truth is always best, wouldn't you agree?"

Her eyes bore into me, making me feel the consequences of my actions more deeply. "Always," I tell her. "I fucked up, El. I promise you, this will never happen again. You mean more to me than anyone or anything, and I'll do whatever I have to do to make you trust me again."

"It's not the telling Yuke that hurts, Eren." Her voice cracks. "It's the not telling me. The avoiding me. The fact that you let it get to this point before you said anything."

"I know." There's nothing else I can say. No defense I can make for myself, because I'm not the one who needs reassurance. She is. I stand rooted to my spot on the sidewalk, helpless and hoping no one inside can hear as I beg Ellie not to break my heart.

Which I don't deserve, because I've already broken hers.

She finally steps closer to me, taking my hands in hers and looking up at me. "Give me some time to think," she says. "I just have to make sure us being together is the best thing. For you and me."

"How much time?" I ask, because I don't know If I can make it without knowing how long I have to wait to get back to the place we were at before this all happened.

"We'll talk when I get back from Europe." All too soon, she lets go of my hands. "Go home and enjoy the rest of your day off. I'll see you at the party tomorrow."

She goes back inside, leaving me more alone than I've ever felt before.

CHAPTER 35

ELLIE

E mpowered by the confidence that only my favorite heels can provide, I grab my clutch and tuck it under my arm. *Let's do this, Ellie*, I tell myself.

On the way out the door, I pass my suitcase, which I've spent all day packing, checking items off my list one by one. My brand new passport is in the front pocket of my backpack, full of fresh pages ready to be stamped. When we went shopping the other night, Uncle Sai bought me a protective case for it. Everything is prepped and ready to go, including two copies of my Europe itinerary, and even the Colorado itinerary Eren made for me.

Of course I won't need that one, but knowing it's with me is comforting.

While I'm still nervous, the events of the past couple of weeks have me more conflicted than anything. Part of me is itching to get away—to be in a place where no one knows me. To truly have the time to get to know myself, and reflect on how I want to move forward. To learn how to be comfortable exploring on my own.

The other part of me wants to nix the trip, make things

right with Eren, and spend our whole week off wrapped in each other.

Our conversation played in my head for hours after work yesterday. Funnily enough, thanks to Rick's big mouth, I never would have found out Eren was the one who initially spilled the beans to Yuke if he hadn't told me. Eren's part in it could have easily been swept under the rug. But, his conscience could have never handled that.

If only he had told me sooner. If only he hadn't spent nearly two weeks putting more and more distance between us. If only he had handled it differently.

Those are the things that keep tripping me up.

I stop inside to get Uncle Rob's keys and show off my dress. It's long-sleeved, covered in dark green sequins, and it stops right above my knees. It hugs my body perfectly. In Uncle Sai's words, it looks like it was made for me.

"Ow, ow," Uncle Rob catcalls, grabbing my hand to give me a twirl. "You're gonna give every single one of your male colleagues a heart attack."

"Don't joke about that," I laugh. "What if it actually happens?"

"Okay, okay," he digresses. "But it will make Eren lose his mind."

Good, I think. Then I take it back, because I genuinely wish things were normal so he can peel it off of me later.

I dreamed about him all night. When I woke up this morning, I was already itching to text him and tell him I forgive him. But, as Uncle Sai told me last night when I filled him in on everything, that would be doing myself a disservice. "Make sure you give yourself at least a few days," he'd said. "You have to make sure your want to forgive stays consistent."

So, after Europe it remains, I suppose.

"If you drink too much and can't drive home, call us," Uncle Sai says. "We'll come get you and the car."

"Okay," I laugh. "But I have to be up early, so I doubt I'll have more than a drink or two."

"Have fun!" Uncle Rob pinches my cheek. "And don't forget, you deserve to be there just as much as anyone else. Your boss obviously sees real potential in you. This is your chance to do it all the right way."

If there's anything good that has come from me being outed, it's that I can at least have a clear conscience. Everyone knows the truth. I don't have to lie anymore. I'll have the opportunity to grow, and improve, and re-earn my team's trust along the way.

The event hall is across town in Jacksonville Beach. When I get out of the car, the coastal wind is whipping so hard I think I might blow away before I get inside. The door opens as I approach, and Jade steps out, holding it for me.

"Evening, Ellie," she says. "You look hot."

"So do you." I admire her red, backless dress.

"Sorry I have to ruin your dress with this." She passes me a name tag. "For the benefit of everyone's guests."

"No worries," I laugh, forcing it to stick to my sequins.

I wander into the ballroom, which is full of round tables decked out in holly and white candles, trying to convince myself I'm looking for familiar faces when I'm really searching for one face in particular. It's nowhere to be found, but I do find Rick, Sherry, and her husband hanging out by the bar. Taking a deep breath, I walk over to them.

"Hi everyone," I say. "You all look nice."

"Hey, Ellie," Rick says with feigned enthusiasm. "Any big secrets to share with us?"

After my meeting with Yuke, I went back to the sales room and told everyone the rumor was true. I didn't go into my initial reasoning for telling the lie, but I did apologize. Everyone was receptive and understanding, but it made things awkward for the rest of the afternoon.

Considering I still get to go on my trip, they'll probably be salty for a while. But like Uncle Rob said, things will get better as time goes on.

"Shut up, Rick. Be an adult," Sherry chastises before turning to me. "Hi, Ellie. This is my husband Brad. I think you met him at the party last year."

"Yes, I remember. Good to see you, Brad." I shake his hand.

"Just so you know," Sherry says, stepping closer to me. "I do think it's admirable that you chose not to apply for the management position. I've always liked you, and your mistake doesn't make me think any less of you."

"Thank you," I tell her. "I appreciate that."

Excusing myself, I go to the bar for a glass of wine. A hand lands on my shoulder and I turn to find Lamar. "Looking sharp!" I tell him, checking out his black suit and leaning in for a hug.

"Really?" He straightens his tie, looking unsure. "I hate dressing up. It makes me feel like I'm pretending to be someone else."

"Don't overthink it," I tell him. "Sometimes it's nice to be someone else for a while."

"Hm, maybe you're right."

The bartender brings my wine and Lamar orders an old fashioned before turning his attention back to me. "Just so you know, no hard feelings about anything. Honestly, everyone else was blowing it out of proportion."

"I'm actually glad everyone knows," I tell him. "Keeping it up was too much press—"

I spot Eren over Lamar's shoulder and completely lose my train of thought. Lamar collects his drink from the bar and follows my gaze, grinning. "See something you like?" he jokes. I elbow him gently in the chest.

Eren locks eyes with me across the room and lifts a hand. I

wave back, struggling to keep composure at the sight of him. He's wearing khaki dress pants with a plum-colored button-down. His hair is loose, and I can tell he trimmed his beard for the occasion. He starts weaving his way through the room, stopping to talk to people but never looking away from me.

"I'll catch up with you later," I tell Lamar. "Have fun, and enjoy your alter ego."

He winks at me and I grab my wine from the bar, on a mission to find the man I can't stay away from, even though I should.

"Ellie, hi!" Yuke bumps into me halfway to my destination. "Happy holidays."

"Happy holidays," I tell her, unsure of how to react after yesterday. I really could use another glass of wine.

"All packed and ready to go?" she asks.

"I am. It took me all day, but I'm ready."

"You'll love Prague," she says. "And London."

Her demeanor towards me is the same as it has always been. Even in our meeting yesterday, she made sure to let me say my part. She didn't speak over me, or accuse me of anything I didn't admit to. Yuke is a great boss, and all of us at TST are really lucky.

"I'm excited," I tell her. "And...thank you again, Yuke. I'm truly sorry for everything and I promise nothing like that will ever happen again."

"No more apologies." She lays her hand on my forearm. "In a lot of ways, travel is similar to life. You learn from your experiences. Every now and then you make a wrong turn, but if your intentions are good everything works out in the end."

She clinks her wine glass to mine.

"Have fun tonight," she tells me. "I have to go announce dinner."

Eren is no longer in the same place when Yuke walks away. I look around, seeking out the man who towers above almost everyone else in the room. I finally spot him at the bar with Walt, and try once again to get to him. I'm a few steps away when the high-pitched squeal of a microphone echoes through the room.

"Welcome, TST-ers," Yuke says. "Thank you all for being here tonight! There isn't a better team out there, and I'm glad we can all be together to loosen up and hang out outside of the office. Dinner will be served in five minutes, so please find your assigned seat!"

The crowd shifts, sweeping me along with them. Each table setting has a name card, and it takes me a couple of minutes to find my seat at a table with Jade and the rest of the sales team. I sit down and place my napkin over my lap, once again looking for Eren, discouragement setting in. Just when I think he's disappeared, he takes his seat at the table next to me.

"Hi," he mouths, his brown eyes still soft with apology.

"Hi," I mouth back, wondering why I have the sudden urge to cry.

Forgive him immediately, one side of my brain says.

Go on your trip and keep thinking about things, the other says.

I love him, both say.

Dinner is served, but I have very little appetite. Everyone at the table makes small talk, which turns to more discussion of my secret, and eventually into jokes about it. Even Rick laughs along with everyone, making me hopeful that I'm already on the path to a new normal with my team.

I look over at Eren's table, but his seat is empty. Standing, I excuse myself to the bathroom, searching for him as I go. Just as I'm about to give up, he comes out of the men's room, head down as he ties his hair into a ponytail.

"Eren," I call, getting his attention. He rushes over and goes in for a hug, stopping at the last second. Disappointment fills the air between us. I know he's only respecting my wishes, but I wish he had done it anyway.

"I was worried I would keep missing you all night," he says.

"Me too."

"You look fantastic," he tells me. "That dress is killer."

"Thanks." My hands twitch at my sides, begging to touch him. My brain is at war.

"So, tomorrow? You ready?" he asks.

"As I'll ever be," I tell him.

He puts his hands in his pockets, rocking back and forth on his heels. "I need you to know something."

"Yes?' I ask.

"I'll be here when you get back," he says. "Whether you're ready for me or not, I'll be here. And if you're not ready then, I'll keep waiting until you tell me not to."

"Promise?" I ask.

He grabs my hand, leading me out of the ballroom and into the foyer. The sudden silence feels deafening, our breath and the rustling of our clothing the only noise in the small space. He releases my hand and leans against the wall.

"You're it for me, Ellie," he confesses. "There's no way you're not supposed to be my forever. So yes, I promise. I'll promise you over and over again if that's what it takes."

"You're making this hard for me." I run a hand through my hair.

"That's not my intention. I just needed you to know."

I consider telling him that I came into tonight knowing I was no longer mad at him. Knowing that I dreamed about him all night, and have been waffling back and forth between telling him I love him and sticking to my guns. Feeling like he's it for me too, but still giving the tiny voice in my head that says he's not way too much credit.

The voice is tiny, but it's still enough to keep a seed of doubt rooted. A seed of fear.

I step forward, wrapping my arms around his waist. He clings to me for a few moments, then lets go and holds me at arm's distance. "Have fun and be safe. I'll see you in a week."

Then he leads me back to the ballroom, where I stay for a while longer before saying my goodbyes.

The second I get home, I realize I've made a big mistake.

CHAPTER 36

EREN

ELLIE

I love you.

T his morning I woke up to a text from Ellie, and that's
what it said.

EREN

I love you too!

I'd responded right away, but the message came back as
undeliverable, and that's when I remembered she's somewhere
over the Atlantic Ocean.

After pacing my apartment for an hour, trying and failing
to make plans with my brothers, and attempting to start three
different movies, I finally decide to go to the office to catch up
on work. On a Sunday. We're closed all week for Christmas,
and even though I'm just hanging around Jacksonville, it
would be nice to not stress about what I have to go back to
next week.

Plus, it will be a nice distraction while I wait for Ellie to
land.

She loves me?

Why didn't she tell me that last night? Does this mean she's forgiven me?

I filter through my schedule changes and reply to emails I missed on Friday. I finish the schedule for Yuke's VIP group and put it on her desk. When I get bored of being productive, I open the copy of Ellie's itinerary that she sent me last week.

Today, she lands in London. Wednesday—Christmas Day —she flies to Prague. Saturday night, she'll be back in Jacksonville.

It's only a week, but it might as well be a year.

A few hours later, I'm getting ready to leave when I hear the chime of the front door's alarm. "Hello?" I call, turning my light off and trotting down the stairs.

"Hello!" A man's voice comes from the sales room. "In here!"

I walk down the hall to investigate and find Rick settling into his cube.

"Oh, hey," I say. He doesn't look too pleased to see me either.

"Why are you working on a Sunday?" he asks.

"I could ask you the same thing."

"I'm behind and leaving town tomorrow," he tells me. "Trying to catch up."

"I'm also behind." I lean against the door frame. "And trying to distract myself."

"From Ellie?" He comes to stand across from me, matching my stance.

My defenses rise and I narrow my eyes at him. The energy between us has been off lately, but a quick scan of his face doesn't reveal any of the malice or competitiveness that I've learned to expect from him. Relaxing, I uncross my arms.

"Why would you say that?" I ask.

"Come on, Eren, it's obvious you two are in love." He purses his lips. "Much to my chagrin."

"I know you liked her," I tell him. "Everything happened so quickly, and we didn't mean for you to get caught in the middle of it."

"It's okay." He smiles. "It would have never worked with Ellie and I anyway. You two on the other hand—a pretty perfect match."

"'Perfect' isn't' the word I'd use to describe things right now," I admit.

"Can I ask why?"

"Things *were* perfect," I begin. "Without going into too much detail, I mishandled information she trusted me with, and now she's trying to trust me again."

"Classic relationship issue," Rick says, shaking his head. "Did you resolve anything before she left?"

"Not really," I tell him. "But I did wake up to this. And now I don't know how I'm supposed to stay sane until she gets home."

I pull my phone out of my pocket and show him the text.

"Damn, dude. That's huge!" He gives the phone back to me. "I gotta ask though, why wait until she's back when you could just...go to her?"

"She's on a different continent, not just down the street." I roll my eyes.

"And?" he presses. "You know how to book a plane ticket, right? It's kind of your profession."

"I can't follow her to Europe," I say, despite the cogs that are beginning to turn in my head.

"Can't? Or won't?" Rick asks. "She loves you, man."

"But...what if...she said...she doesn't..." Every excuse I try to throw out disappears on my tongue.

What if Rick is right?

My phone buzzes in my hand, Ellie's name once again

filling the screen. "It's her!" I tell him, opening the text with trembling fingers.

ELLIE

> Just landed. It was a mistake not to tell you last night. I'm going to enjoy my trip, but I'll also be counting the moments until I see you.

Rick comes to stand beside me, reading the message over my shoulder and clapping me on the back. "Go get her."

I race back to the stairs, stopping at the bottom to look at him one more time. "Thank you."

He smiles, nodding at me. I take the stairs two at a time and fall into my chair so hard I roll into the wall.

I text her back.

EREN

> I love you too!!

Then I log back into the booking system, tapping my fingers on the desk while I wait for it to load. There's no space from Jacksonville to London for the next couple of days, but there is space on a Christmas Eve night flight to Prague.

I pull my credit card out and secure the ticket before I can talk myself out of it.

CHAPTER 37

ELLIE

My two days in London pass with a quickness I didn't know was possible.

Despite the jet lag, I push through, completing every activity on my itinerary and more. London is the perfect introduction to international travel. It's different enough that I've felt like I'm in a foreign country, but also comes with the comfortability of the English language and similar culture.

I've drank copious pints of beer and cups of hot tea. I've consumed fish and chips, full English breakfasts, and at least five meat pies. Each time I've walked past a bakery or coffee shop, I've had to stop in for a tart, scone, or some other irresistible flaky pastry. My blood sugar levels are probably out of this world, but I'm okay with it.

On Christmas Eve evening, my final evening in the city, I take The Tube to Westminster to see Big Ben one last time. On the ride, I scroll through all of the photos I've taken over the past couple of days, smiling at all of the new memories.

A selfie in front of Buckingham Palace. A panoramic photo of the city taken from the London Eye. A touristy snap of me inside one of the famous red phone booths, that I only had the courage to ask a stranger to take because Eren was hyping me up via text message.

EREN

They won't mind! They live in London. They do it all the time.

We've been talking nonstop. Our text thread is full of the photos I've sent him, along with various last-minute restaurant, bar, and bookstore recommendations he's sent me. Weaved throughout are the occasional "I can't wait to see you's" and "I love you's." The latter of the two still make my stomach do cartwheels each time they appear.

The Tube comes to a stop and the doors open. I join the holiday crowd, shuffling off the train and up the nearest set of stairs, apologizing to every person I accidentally bump into along the way. At the top of the stairs I round the corner of the building, and there it is—Big Ben in all its glory. I duck into a nearby cafe for a hot chocolate, then meander about until I find a free bench to settle on.

It's freezing, but I want to take everything in one last time. I pull the scarf Eren's mom made for me tighter around my neck and carefully sip my scalding drink. People mill about, abuzz with the joy of the holiday. A group of carolers pass by, singing a melancholy version of *Silent Night*. Christmas lights flick on as it grows darker, bringing the night to life.

A double-decker bus passes by and some of the people on board wave at me. I smile and wave back. I'm alone, but I'm not lonely. It's difficult to feel lonely when you're surrounded by so much newness—when your senses are alight with the unfamiliar.

Eren was right. Even though I still wish he was here more than anything, I needed to do this on my own. I needed to prove to myself that I can.

I gaze up at Big Ben's face, now a glowing orb above the

city. My mind flashes to the picture on TST's refrigerator. I don't know when it was taken, or who took it, but the angle it was taken from is almost identical to the view I have of it now. I pull my phone out of my coat pocket and take another photo. I probably have ten more of it in my camera roll already, but this one feels special.

When I get home, I'll hang it on my own refrigerator. Not as a reminder of what I wish I could see, but as a souvenir to remind myself that I finally made it, and it was everything I hoped it would be.

I'm proud of you, Ellie, I think to myself.

Tears spring into my eyes. Giving myself permission to be happy and content isn't something I've done very often in my life. Just like most other events of the past couple of months, it's new territory. But it's a new territory that I definitely plan to explore deeper.

I dab at the corners of my eyes with my scarf, worried the tears will freeze to my cheeks if I allow them to flow. It's not nearly cold enough for that, but I'm still learning how to function in non-Florida weather. My phone buzzes with a text from Eren and I read it through blurry eyes. I had sent him a photo of me in my coat and boots before I left the hotel.

EREN

You're so fucking beautiful, London Ellie is a babe.

I laugh out loud, sniffling the remaining tears away and sitting my hot chocolate on the bench beside me. *Your turn to send me a photo*, I reply, adding a winking face emoji to the end.

A couple of minutes later, a photo of him and his brothers appears. He's in the forefront, giving one of those big, eye-consuming grins that I love so much. Tanner stands behind him, shooting his middle finger at the camera. Off to the side,

Adem is pushing his glasses further up his nose, obviously not prepared for the photo.

EREN

Christmas Eve shenanigans.

ELLIE

Don't do anything I wouldn't do.

EREN

You're not giving me much to work with.

I throw my head back, laughing even harder, not caring that someone passing by might wonder what the woman sitting alone on a random London bench could possibly think is so funny. I put my phone away and finish my hot chocolate, then head off to make the most of my final night in a place that is no longer just a participant in my daydreams.

CHAPTER 38

EREN

"Thanks for the ride." I climb out of the back seat of Adem's car, dragging my backpack—which I've stuffed full of clothes and necessities for the next four days— with me. I sling it onto my shoulder and bend to peer at Tanner and Adem through the passenger window.

"Safe travels," Adem says. "Enjoy Christmas in Prague."

"Go get your girl." Tanner fist bumps me.

"Have a good Christmas." Standing, I back towards the airport entrance. Once inside, I break into a run, heading for the security line. I'm not late for my flight, but I'm full of so much nervous energy that walking doesn't seem like enough. Besides, this is the beginning of my first grand romantic gesture. Don't those always involve running in some way?

I reach back to pat the front pocket of my backpack, double checking my passport and phone are in check. On the other side of the security line, I find the closest bar and order a glass of red wine. I drink it slowly, my nerves calming with every sip. Out of habit, I check for texts from Ellie. It's 1:00 a.m. in London, so of course there aren't any.

The time difference is actually a blessing in this scenario.

When she wakes up, it will still be the middle of the night in Florida, which is the perfect excuse for me to be unreachable for a while. She'll think I'm snoozing away, when really, I'll be in a plane getting closer and closer to her.

"Another?" the bartender asks, collecting my empty glass.

"Yes, please," I tell him. "Make it a double pour."

"Anxious flyer?"

"No, not at all." I laugh. "I'm...going to surprise someone, and I'm kind of nervous about it."

"Ahhhhh." Interested, he crosses his arms and leans into the bar. "A woman?"

"How'd you know?"

"Well, I serve a lot of nervous travelers every day," he explains. "And from my experience, if the stress isn't a result of flying, it's a result of love."

"Wow!" I lean into the back of my stool. "Do people really open up to you like that?"

"You'd be surprised." He grins at me. "Good luck with everything."

"Thank you." I raise my glass to him. "I'll take my check when you have a second."

He shakes his head. "It's on me. Have a good flight!"

I've always viewed kindness from strangers as a good omen, and the interaction is enough to help me relax. By the time I land in Atlanta for my connecting flight, my anxiety has been replaced with excitement. Ellie's plane lands a couple of hours before mine. If my timeline coincides with her itinerary like I think it will, I should be able to catch her on Charles Bridge, or at least somewhere in the Old Town, which is where she plans to spend her first day.

I manage to fall into a restless sleep for a few hours, startling awake when we touch down in Prague. My phone screen fills with all of the notifications I missed while in airplane mode. I open Ellie's first, grinning when I remember how little distance there currently is between us.

ELLIE

Made it.

It's followed by a photo of the inside of the airport. The airport she has no idea I'm also about to set foot in.

ELLIE

In the taxi. I'm so excited!

After a painfully slow deplaning process, I finally make it to customs.

"Veselé Vánoce," the customs officer says as she passes my stamped passport back to me. And then again in English, "Merry Christmas!"

"Veselé Vánoce!" I repeat, smiling at her.

Then I make a beeline for the exit to find the first available taxi.

CHAPTER 39
ELLIE

I t's Christmas Day, and I'm in a different country.

    It's *Christmas Day*, and I'm in a *different country*.

The thought is so crazy, I have to let it filter through my mind twice before I believe it.

I stare out the window of the cab. The driver bumps us along cobblestone streets, passing gothic cathedrals, droves of tourists, and packed trams. Street artists line the sidewalks, offering caricatures and paintings of all the local sites. My driver doesn't speak much English, but he attempts to offer a tour as we drive. "Ah, the castle!" he proclaims when it comes into view. Goosebumps pop up all over my arms.

Prague Castle sits on a hill across the Vltava River, overlooking a sea of red roofs. Its gothic towers shoot spectacularly into the sky, claiming ownership of the city stretching below. I have plans to visit tomorrow, but I find it impossible to believe that the view from up there could be any better than it is down here.

We turn onto a bridge to cross the river. "Is this Charles Bridge?" I ask.

"No, Charles Bridge is there." He points further down,

and I spot the familiar statue-lined walkway that I've been staring at in photos for the past few weeks.

On the other side of the Vltava, we drive past rows of old, colorful buildings and into the center of the Old Town, eventually coming to a stop in front of my hotel. My driver hops out and helps me get my suitcase from the trunk. Thanking him, I pay him and wheel it inside to leave behind the desk until I can check in later. "Dobrý den!" the girl behind the desk tells me. "Hello, and welcome!"

Back outside, I walk through the Old Town, searching for lunch and deciding on a place that serves traditional goulash. I sit outside next to the river, watching boats and people pass, and listening to the unfamiliar language. It's cold but the sky is a vivid blue; not a cloud in sight. The server brings my food and I tear into the delicious beef and dumplings, savoring every bite.

After lunch, I finally head to Charles Bridge. For some reason I've been drawn to it since I started researching Prague. Tourists stand in clumps all along it, taking photos and pointing out the various sights along the river. Kids run through giant bubbles being blown by street vendors. Couples stroll hand in hand, stopping to kiss and look out over the water.

I wish Eren were here, I think.

I pull my phone out of my pocket to check for texts from him, already knowing there won't be any. It's too early. He's still wrapped in his sheets, sprawled out on his back, snoring with his mouth open. I smile at the thought.

I walk slowly, passing the famous statues of different saints, looking up into the faces of each one as I go by. In the middle of the bridge, I stop to turn in a slow circle, taking in the view from every angle. The bridge. The river. The Old Town on one side of the water, and Malá Strana, or Lesser Town, on the other. People continue to flow around me, but I don't mind. Just like Eren would, I'm trying to live in the moment.

I'm here. I'm happy. And no one can take that from me.

The crowd shifts, and I catch a brief glimpse of a tall man with a ponytail. My heart flips in my chest, then falls into my stomach. Of course I'm only imagining him. He's been on my mind nonstop, so how could I *not* imagine him here with me.

Then the crowd parts again, and this time I'm no longer sure it's my imagination.

The man walks quickly, disappearing and reappearing amongst the throngs, getting closer. "Ellie!" he calls.

"Eren?"

My legs move me forward. I push through a sea of arms, shoulders, and chests, fighting to keep him in my line of vision. He continues to disappear, briefly a few times, and then altogether. Frantic, I walk to the edge of the bridge, stepping up onto the lower ledge to get a better view.

"Ellie!"

Hearing my name again, I hop down from the ledge. I turn to my right, and there he is.

Tangible. Real. Eren.

I fly to him, jumping up to wrap my legs around his waist. "I love you," he says, spinning me around and kissing me. "I couldn't wait. I had to see you."

People stop to stare. Some even pull out their phones to take pictures of us, but I don't care and neither does he. I fold my arms around his neck, afraid he'll disappear if every part of me isn't touching him. He kisses me again before pulling away, and the tears start to flow when I look into the chocolate pools of eyes.

"Don't cry," he says, sitting me back on the ground, clasping my hands in his.

"These aren't sad tears," I say. "This feels too good to be true."

He takes my face in his palms, wiping the tears away with his thumbs. "But it is true."

"I've been thinking about you all week," I tell him. "I was just watching all these couples on the bridge, wishing you were here. And now you are."

He wraps his arm around my shoulders, pulling me to a less crowded area by one of the statues. "I'm here for the rest of the week, if you want me."

"Of course I do," I say, still sniffling. "I want you for the rest of my life."

He looks down at me, so much love in his eyes I could burst. "Me too," he says, pressing his lips to my forehead.

He pulls me into his chest, rocking us back and forth, creating our own little bubble amongst the tourists. I hold him there for a couple of minutes, reassuring myself that I'm not hallucinating.

"So what's next on the agenda?" he asks, pulling back to look me in the face. "The John Lennon wall?"

"Sounds like you already know." I smirk, grabbing his arm and holding tightly. "And if you found me here, you must have my itinerary memorized."

"Guilty," he says with a grin. "So let's go. To the Lennon Wall!"

I laugh, and we fall into step next to each other, walking hand in hand to another place we've never been.

EPILOGUE
EREN

One Year Later

"Everything is ready!" Ellie places the final wrapped gift beneath our Christmas tree.

Stepping behind her, I wrap my arms around her shoulders. She rests her head against my chest and I lean down to kiss her neck. "It all looks wonderful."

"Our first Christmas in our own place," she says. "I can't believe it."

I spin her to face me, pushing her hair behind her shoulders. She's been growing it out over the past year and complains about it constantly. I tell her every day to cut it if she wants to. I love her no matter the length of her hair, just like she loves me no matter the length of mine.

"It's perfect." I look around at the Craftsman-style home we've been renovating to make our own. It's just a few blocks from TST, and from her uncle's house, so we were lucky to find it. We were so excited to decorate for the holidays that it looks like Christmas threw up in every room. Garland, lights, paper snowflakes...you name it, we have it.

"They should be here any second!" Ellie says, walking over to peek out the window, looking for Rob's car.

What she doesn't know is I know exactly where they are, along with my parents, my brothers, and Scrabble. Rob and I have been coordinating for weeks, planning the ultimate surprise for Ellie. They're currently parked down the street, waiting for me to confirm Ellie is momentarily distracted. I text Rob.

EREN

I'm keeping her away from the door.
Release the hound.

"Help me decide what shirt to wear." I take Ellie's hand and lead her to our bedroom.

She rummages through our closet, pulling out a navy button-up with a tiny snowflake print. "Definitely this one."

"What else would I wear on an 80 °F Christmas?" I laugh. "Good choice."

I pull it on and she buttons me up. The doorbell rings just as she's securing the final button. "They're here!"

Her red dress billows behind her as she rushes to the door. I follow, lingering in the living room, my anticipation growing by the second. I put my hand in my pocket, double checking the velvet box is there, even though I've checked for it a million times already.

"Merry Christmas," she says, flinging the door open. Her smile falls, her face taken over by confusion. "Brat?"

She steps out onto the porch, looking right and left. "Uncle Rob? Uncle Sai?"

"What's wrong?" I ask, walking to the door and catching a sight of Brat sitting and grinning up at Ellie. Behind Ellie's back, I give him a thumbs up.

"Good boy," I mouth silently.

Her brows furrow as she grabs Brat by the collar to lead

him inside. "He was just out there by himself," she said. "Is this some kind of joke?"

I shut the door behind her. "Maybe they forgot something in the car?"

"If they're not here in two minutes," She sits on the edge of the sofa, leaning over to pet Brat. "I'm panicking."

"You would last two whole minutes before panicking?" I joke.

She scratches along Brat's neck and ears. "Seriously, where the fu—"

Stopping mid-sentence, she pulls something from Brat's collar. "What's that?" I ask innocently.

"I don't know..." She stands to move closer to me, unrolling the scroll of paper in her hands. "What the—?"

In her hands, is a small map of Italy. She studies it, looking up at me. "There's a heart around Florence."

Unable to keep up my clueless charade, I grin.

"Eren, what is this? What's going on?" She looks around like a guy with a hidden camera is going to pop out of some hidden corner.

"It's Florence," I tell her. "Where we're going to celebrate our engagement."

Her hands fall to her sides and the map flutters to the floor. "Our what?"

It's time.

Pulling the box from my pocket, I get down on one knee and reach for her hand. She claps a palm over her mouth and makes the same noise she makes when I kiss her neck.

"Eren, are you serious?" she says, her voice muffled beneath her hand.

"Ellie Amos..." I begin.

Happy to see a friend on the floor, Brat trots over and sits directly beside me. We both burst into laughter. Recomposing myself, I clear my throat and continue. "My former TST best friend, and current love of my life. You have completely changed my world over the past year. I'm inspired everyday by your resilience, and your ability to always find your way through the dark."

She drops to her knees in front of me and grabs my other hand.

"You're supposed to stay standing," I whisper.

"Oh, hush and keep going," she says.

"You've broken my forsaken curse, and you've helped me to see the best in myself when I sometimes didn't think it was possible. I'll follow you, anywhere. Will you marry me?" I hold the ring up, but she doesn't even look at it. Instead she flings her arms around me and smashes her face to mine. "Yes!" she says against my lips.

We separate and I pull the opal engagement ring out of its box. Taking Ellie's left hand, I slide it up her ring finger, then pull her hand to me and kiss it.

"I love it," she tells me, running a finger across the top of the stone. "And I love you more."

I go in for a hug and Brat barks, wedging his way between us. Ellie sits back on her heels, giggling. "Brat, you did such a good job!"

The doorbell rings and we help each other to our feet. She gives me one more kiss before going to answer it, looking back over her shoulder at me.

"Were they hiding in the bushes or something?" she asks as she opens the door.

"CONGRATULATIONS!" She jumps in surprise and I run to stand beside her. Our families stand on the front porch, arms open, faces glowing with excitement. They rush toward us and we take turns hugging everyone and thanking them.

"I didn't know y'all were here," Ellie says, squeezing my mom's shoulders.

"How could we miss it?" Mom says, then kisses Ellie's cheek.

"Welcome to the family, Ellie," Dad says, bending to hug her with the arm that isn't holding Scrabble, who hangs like he has no bones in his body, looking around at everyone with a blank expression.

"No need to get too excited, Scrabble," I say, scrubbing him on the head.

"Also, Florence!" Rob comes over to wrap us both in a hug. "That's one heck of an engagement trip."

"Right? Can we come?" Sai jokes.

"I forgot about the Florence part already!" Ellie runs over to pick the map up from the floor. "When are we going? Hopefully Sherry will approve the time off!"

"It's already approved," I tell her. "I talked to Sherry. We're going in April."

"Thank you." She stands on her toes and presses her forehead to mine. "I love you so much."

I wrap my arms around her lower back, picking her up off the floor and kissing her, not caring that our families are watching.

"Get a room," Tanner yells.

"So original," I tell him, setting Ellie back down. She walks away to show Mom the ring.

"Really though, congrats dude," Tanner says, giving me a fist bump.

"You're a lucky man." Adem claps me on the back. "I guess number thirteen isn't so unlucky after all."

"It certainly isn't."

Across the room, Ellie looks up to meet my eyes. I feel the way I always feel when she looks at me—like I could move mountains.

ACKNOWLEDGMENTS

Wow. Here we are! I have a second book in the world. How did this happen?

After publishing *Pulled to You*, I thought the hardest part was over. I had navigated the waters of self-publishing once, so it was going to be easy to do it again. Right?

In some ways, yes. In others, absolutely not.

But, we've made it. And the most important thing is, it's still just as exciting as it was the first time. Here's another giant piece of my soul, carefully slapped onto paper and just waiting to fall into the hands of the readers it's meant to find.

With that being said, it's only right that my first thank you go out to my readers. I've been so fortunate to connect with people over the past few years who enjoyed my first book, and who have been excited for this one. So, regardless of whether you've read one, or both, THANK YOU. I'm still just a wee baby author in the vast world of books, but you are all constant reminders of why I love to write. You're all the reason that I want to keep sharing the characters I create and building upon the random ideas that pop into my head. You're all the absolute best.

To everyone who has laid eyes on this story during any part of the publishing process, thank you for your critique, advice, and guidance. It never gets any easier to share something you have created, so to have people I trust so much makes it all easier.

Kelsey, thank you for another amazing cover refresh. Not only are you helping me beautifully represent my stories, you have also given me so much insight as to how I want my books and my author brand to be portrayed. You're the best!

Kristen, thank you for your expert-level proofreading and interior formatting. You caught every single one of my obnoxious typos and bad grammar habits. Your little notes about the story made my day, and also helped me to implement some last-minute improvements. I appreciate your thoroughness and obvious love for books and stories. (To any writers reading this, make sure you check Kristen out at Kristen's Red Pen. She's a great go-to for proofreading and editing services!)

To my friends and family who continue to cheer me on—I hope you know what a pivotal part of this process you are. I appreciate everyone who takes the time to check in on me, or give me a kick in the butt when I need it. I'm afraid I would miss someone if I tried to name names, but please know, if you're reading this, I probably mean you.

Last but not least, I absolutely cannot wrap up these acknowledgments without giving a shoutout to some of my fellow authors and bookstagram friends. Finding a community of people to relate to has been one of my favorite things about deciding to publish. The world is full of talented people, and I feel very fortunate that I've had the opportunity to cross paths with so many of them. Jessica Costello, Celia Ochoa, Holly Whitworth, K.H. Anastasia, Anna P., Bonnie Callahan, Stacy T., Alaina Rose, Millie Perez, Hannah Bonam-Young, Maria Patrick, Jessica Loveless, Kelsey Schulz, Blair Harton, Aly Lee, Stefanie Steck, and so many more—you all inspire me every single day. I'm always here to root for you, and can't wait to see what you all do next.

ABOUT THE AUTHOR

Miranda's earliest memory of writing goes back to a third-grade story competition, where she wrote about a cat and a horse who became best friends. Spoiler alert: it was bad and she didn't win. She's almost over it now.

These days, Miranda writes cozy contemporary romance novels. She lives in Florida, where she works in the travel industry and dreams about living somewhere with seasons. She hates raisins, and would put her life on the line for a good chocolate chip cookie.